Praise for Joan Hess
and her Maggody series
MARTIANS IN MAGGODY

"Joan Hess has written a mystery that is out of this world—wonderful, witty, and entirely credible."   —Dorothy Cannell, author of *How to Murder Your Mother-in-Law*

"Zany ... strikes a rich lode of lunacy, uninterrupted comic relief, and certified merriment."
—*Kirkus Reviews*

"Wildly funny adventures ... quite simply the most fun you can have with your clothes on."
—*Mystery Lovers Newsletter*

"Taut and funny.... Hess aims her barbed (and good-natured) sense of humor at tabloid journalism as well as at the foibles of her rural cast in this spirited mystery."
—*Publishers Weekly* (starred)

"Joan Hess deftly mixes humor and homicide in this backwoods cozy."   —*Naperville Sun*

"One of the funniest and most inventive mystery authors today."   —*Mystery News*

"A mix of murder, mayhem, and just plain ludicrousness. Don't miss it."   —*Booklist*

"Hilarious."   —*Murder Ad Lib*

O LITTLE TOWN OF MAGGODY

"All the ingredients of a good yuletide murder mystery."
—*Denver Post*

"A sturdy plot and keen satirical point. . . . In the spirit of the season, Hess is as generous with her affection as she is with her wit."
—*New York Times Book Review*

"The scales tip heavily toward jollity in *O Little Town of Maggody* . . . its tenacious characters will grow on you." —*Wall Street Journal*

"A gift in itself . . . will please fans of humor as well as those of whodunits."
—*Arkansas Democrat Gazette*

"Another uproarious visit to the backwoods."
—*Mystery & Detective Monthly*

"One of Hess's funniest mysteries."
—*Tower Books Mystery Newsletter*

"Hysterical . . . a perfect holiday story, filled with rollicking jokes and a lot of laughter. Just the tonic against the hum-drum of the season."
—*Ocala Star-Banner*

"Joan Hess is a wonderful writer."
—Charlotte MacLeod

"Another delightful installment in a superbly comic series." —*Booklist* (starred)

"A marvelous treat for Maggody fans."
—*Kirkus* (starred)

MAGGODY IN MANHATTAN

MARTIANS IN MAGGODY

◆

AN ARLY HANKS MYSTERY

JOAN HESS

To Mary Gene
All the best,
Joan Hess

AN ONYX BOOK

ONYX
Published by the Penguin Group
Penguin Books USA Inc., 375 Hudson Street,
New York, New York 10014, U.S.A.
Penguin Books Ltd, 27 Wrights Lane,
London W8 5TZ, England
Penguin Books Australia Ltd, Ringwood,
Victoria, Australia
Penguin Books Canada Ltd, 10 Alcorn Avenue,
Toronto, Ontario, Canada M4V 3B2
Penguin Books (N.Z.) Ltd, 182–190 Wairau Road,
Auckland 10, New Zealand

Penguin Books Ltd, Registered Offices:
Harmondsworth, Middlesex, England

Published by Onyx, an imprint of Dutton Signet,
a division of Penguin Books USA Inc.
Previously published in a Dutton edition.

First Onyx Printing, November, 1995
10 9 8 7 6 5 4 3 2 1

Cover art by Robert Giusti

 REGISTERED TRADEMARK—MARCA REGISTRADA

Printed in the United States of America

PUBLISHER'S NOTE
This is a work of fiction. Names, characters, places, and incidents either are the
product of the author's imagination or are used fictitiously, and any resemblance
to actual persons, living or dead, events, or locales is entirely coincidental.

To my son, Josh,
who remained steadfast
even when I bought tabloids
at the grocery store

ONE

◆

"It seems downright peculiar that all the alien babies are born in South America," Estelle was grumbling as I came across the tiny dance floor of Ruby Bee's Bar & Grill. She wasn't grumbling at me, or even at the comatose truck drivers in the back booth, but at the proprietress herself, who was wiping down the surface of the bar and visibly simmering over some unknown indignity. "This one here," she continued, jabbing her finger at a fuzzy photograph inside the tabloid spread in front of her, "was born in Brazil last year and already speaks seven languages and is learning calculus."

"Sez who?" countered Ruby Bee.

"Sez Dr. Raul Sancrispo, who's a child psychologist at a university in Rio de Janeiro. He took the baby to his clinic and has been observing it ever since it was born. According to him, the baby has all kinds of strange sexual organs. Poor little critter . . ."

"How 'bout a beer?" I asked as I slid onto a stool at a circumspect distance down the bar and smiled politely at Ruby Bee, who happens to be, among other exasperating things, my mother. Her round face looks innocent enough, except for a few too many streaks of undulating pink eye shadow and unnaturally blond hair (courtesy of Estelle's Hair Fantasies). She always wears a crisp apron with her name embroidered on the pocket, and she can sound real sympathetic when someone's crying in his or her beer (and unwittingly making a substantive contribution to the grapevine). Then again, there are plenty of good ol' boys who've smarted off once too often and found themselves in the gravel lot, their legs crossed and their ears stinging.

She raised her carefully drawn eyebrows. "Ain't you still on duty, Ariel Hanks?"

"I'm always on duty," I pointed out mildly. "I am the entirety of the police force, which means there is no one else to come on duty should I go off duty. Hizzonor the Moron explained this to me only last week at the town council meeting, right after they voted to cut the budget so deeply you could look through the hole and see China." I glanced at Estelle. "Anything in there about alien rice forms in China?"

"Don't go smirking at me, Miss Priss. I only buy these fool things out of idle curiosity. I know darn well they're made up."

Ruby Bee banged down a beer in front of me, at the same time slyly scooting the basket of pretzels out of reach so I'd know she didn't approve of this blatant dereliction of duty. "I just hope there ain't an accident or something that requires sober judgment," she said.

"Or a holdup at the bank," Estelle added sternly.

"We don't have a bank," I said, wondering why they were both so cantankerous. Outside on the streets (the street, anyway) of Maggody, Arkansas, the sun was shining and the weeds were swaying in a warm breeze. Across the way a goodly number of the 755 residents were going in and out of Jim Bob's

SuperSaver Buy 4 Less, and the Suds of Fun Launderette was doing a steady business as spring cleaning got under way. The bench in front of the barbershop was lined with grizzly old coots chawin' tobacco and gossiping worse than the Missionary Society. Ruby Bee's Bar & Grill was peaceful in midafternoon, but there were hungry crowds at noon and downright boisterous ones at happy hour, when draws were a dollar and the jukebox never cooled off. Rumor had it that rooms had been rented recently at the Flamingo Motel out back, but the molting neon sign still read: v CAN Y, and Ruby Bee was too diplomatic to confirm anything.

This isn't to say that three-quarters of the buildings weren't boarded up or that the merchants were getting rich, but it was a pleasant change after a cold, hard winter that dragged on until cabin fever was epidemic, if not worthy of investigation by the Centers for Disease Control in Atlanta.

They'd have a tough time finding us in the backwoods of the Ozark Mountains. Maggody's all of a mile long, with a single traffic light and a singular lack of charm. Tourists might gape at the odd shape of the Voice of the Almighty Lord Assembly Hall, the charred timbers of the bank branch, the occasional drunk sprawled in the mud outside the pool hall, the blinding pinkness of the bar and grill, and ultimately the skeletal remains of Purtle's Esso station, but that's about it until the Missouri line. Unless they're enamored of cows, scrub pines, and litter, of course. There's an abundance of all three.

Estelle tucked an errant whisp of bright red hair back into her beehive, took a delicate sip of sherry, and turned the page. "Listen to this, Ruby Bee. Down in Louisiana the police chased a 1990 Grand

Am until it smacked into a tree. It turned out there was twenty buck-naked Pentecostals inside it, none of them hurt on account of being jammed in thicker than fleas on a wisp. They said their clothes were possessed by the devil."

Ruby Bee snorted. "Sounds like something Brother Verber might find of interest. He's all the time worried that folks are getting naked without his knowing—or without his being there to sputter about eternal damnation and Satan's handiwork."

"He ain't said much about that since he and Mrs. Jim Bob were caught up on Cotter's Ridge dressed in lacy lingerie." She turned another page. "Did you know that a family in France has been living in a hollow log since the end of World War Two? They have it fixed up real nice, although they sometimes have a problem with termites."

I finished my beer. "I guess I'll go patrol for Bigfoot, ladies. He was last seen at the Pot o' Gold, knocking on Eula Lemoy's trailer door."

"She probably invited him in," Ruby Bee said as she took my glass and swished it in the sink. "If you're in the mood to patrol, you ought to look for a black limousine that was all over town this morning. It was longer than two regular cars, and the windows were so dark nobody could see who was driving it. Dahlia said it went real slow by her house twice, and Joyce Lambertino said it was up their way. Slinky Buchanon said he saw it going across the low-water bridge, but of course, he claims he sits with his grandmother in the front pew every Sunday and she's been dead for nineteen years. Still, I can't imagine why this limousine would be creeping around town."

"I'll bet that's how Bigfoot came to Maggody," I

said as I headed for the relative sanity of the street. "He's starred in enough movies to be able to afford a limo."

"It went by my house, too," Estelle said, although dismissively. "Here's where a man took his wife camping in Canada and she exploded from spontaneous combustion right there in the tent. There's an actual artist's depiction."

"Lemme see," said someone's mother.

I walked to the PD, which consists of a brick building with two rooms, one desk, three chairs (one of them the repository for junk mail), yellow and white gingham curtains, and a telephone attached to an answering machine. The red light wasn't blinking, but it rarely did. I picked up my radar gun and went back outside to run a speed trap by the school zone. With any luck at all, I could bust Bigfoot, sell my story to the *Probe,* and make enough money to escape a humdrum existence in a ho-hum town where nothing much ever happens.

"Did you see that limousine this morning?" Mrs. Jim Bob asked Brother Verber. They were standing outside the Voice of the Almighty Lord Assembly Hall, enjoying the sunshine and pondering what to do about the threatened rift in the Missionary Society. Out of deference to the weather, she wore a pale blue linen suit and was holding her white gloves in one hand. As always, her face was devoid of the devil's paint and her underwear was starched. Her lips were pinched, but that was on account of Elsie McMay's mulishness rather than her own mood, which was more mellow than usual. That very morning she'd managed a smile when Jim Bob announced he was staying late at the SuperSaver to inventory, even though she knew perfectly well that he'd stagger home stinking of whiskey and cheap perfume. He'd pay for it when the time came.

Brother Verber, who'd been lost in thought (or something closely resembling it), clasped his hands and beamed at her. She was nothing short of a source of inspiration and an obvious candidate for sainthood when her time came. She was looking particularly fetching in the Good Lord's golden glow. "See what, Sister Barbara?" he asked.

"A big black limousine went down Finger Lane this morning. I happened to notice it while I was straightening Jim Bob's dresser drawers."

"I'm afraid I didn't. I was down on my knees all morning, praying for guidance in the upcoming battle with Satan." He gave her a chance to nod approvingly, but she merely looked back at him. "Everybody knows that in the spring a young man's fancy turns to love," he went on, obliged to pull out a handkerchief to mop his neck. "I wish I could feel confident that our young will express their love by picking posies and sipping lemonade on their front porches, but they're more likely to go sneaking down to the banks of Boone Creek to engage in lustful depravity right there in the moonlight. I shudder to think how many innocent young souls will be lost to Satan in the next few months."

"What do you aim to do about it?" Mrs. Jim Bob asked curiously. Boone Creek ambled through the middle of a national forest crisscrossed by logging trails. It was likely that moonlight shone on a whole passel of idyllic clearings, and those who frequented them weren't apt to be passing out maps.

He closed his eyes as he imagined all that lustful depravity. Why, he could almost hear Satan rubbing his hands together and chuckling over ripe young bodies writhing and groaning on the very banks of the river Styx. "I've been thinking about patrolling the creek, armed with a flashlight and a Bible. If I was to chance upon a couple of young lovers fornicating on a blanket, I could fall to my knees beside them and counsel them to avoid eternal damnation by joining me in prayer. If they resist, I'll denounce them from the pulpit the very next Sunday."

Mrs. Jim Bob debated mentioning that he was more likely to end up with a load of buckshot in his backside, since most of the males in Maggody had shotguns before they had primers. However, he clearly was smitten with his idea, and she had more important things to do. "You might pray a little harder before you go tromping along the creek. I'm going to run over to Millicent McIlhaney's to find out where she stands on this problem with Elsie."

She drove away in her pink Cadillac. After a moment of thought Brother Verber went back into the trailer that served as a rectory and started hunting through his kitchen drawers for flashlight batteries.

"It drove by your house twice?" Eilene Buchanon asked her daughter-in-law, who was on her third piece of pecan pie and showing no signs of losing enthusiasm. "It came by here, too. I yelled at Earl to come see if he could tell who was in it, but by the time he came out of the bathroom, it was long gone."

"This sure is tasty," Dahlia (née O'Neill) Buchanon said as she licked her fingers. She paused in case another piece was forthcoming, then reluctantly set down her fork. "Kevin dint see it, either, on account of he was at work. I sure am glad Jim Bob gave him back his old job at the SuperSaver. He ain't nearly as tuckered out as when he was selling vacuum cleaners in Farberville. Kevin, I mean."

Eilene tried not to grimace as she recalled the bizarre string of incidents during Kevin's tenure at Vacu-Pro. None of them had been his fault. All of Maggody had gone flat out crazy for a month when a country music star named Matt Montana came to town, and only now were certain people able to make polite conversation when they couldn't avoid each other. "So you're adjusting to married life?" she said encouragingly.

"I reckon so, but some days I just don't know what to do with myself. Ruby Bee sez she might hire me back this summer when business picks up. Even though Brother Verber says it's a sin for a wife to work, I miss the jukebox and the laughter and the rednecks howling at me to fetch another pitcher and a basket of pretzels." She sighed so ponderously that all three hundred pounds of her quivered and flatware clinked in the drawer. "I guess I just miss the bright lights, Ma, despite bein' a respectable married woman. Sure, I got my own little home, a loving husband, a vacuum cleaner with thirty-five attachments, and a subscription to TV *Guide*. I fix Kevin tasty suppers every evening and biscuits and gravy every morning. All the same, something's missing from my life." She sighed again, at length and with wheezy, heartfelt misery. "When I saw that limousine, I started wondering what I'd do if it stopped out front and the back door opened and someone beckoned for me to climb inside it."

Eilene resolved to have a word with Ruby Bee.

Jim Bob scratched his bristly head as he read the article concerning the twenty Pentecostals. Why were there two pictures of a squinty-eyed little alien baby and not one of the buck-naked pilgrims, some of whom were women? He moved on to the horoscope page, where he knew he'd find a clear shot of Madam Kristen's cleavage. After he'd studied it for a long while, licking his lips and savoring a warm flush to his privates, he found his sign. It turned out to be right inspirational, if you interpreted the promise of meeting new people to mean meeting new people with cleavage like Madam Kristen's. For the first time in years Mrs. Jim Bob's suspicions were unfounded. Jim Bob hadn't screwed anybody (including her) for the best part of a month, and he was painfully aware of what was missing in his life. Just the other day he'd found himself appraising a heifer in a remote pasture beyond the low-water bridge.

The office door opened, and the newest employee shuffled in, his throat bobbling and his hands flapping like dying fish. His eyes had the same yellowish tinge as Jim Bob's, but they were noticeably blanker, and his beetlish forehead was a great deal more pronounced. Buchanons were scattered across the county like ragweed, but incest and inbreeding had taken its toll. Some of them could out-wit a possum (on a good day, anyway), but Kevin Fitzgerald Buchanon wasn't among the lucky few.

"What?" Jim Bob barked, annoyed at being interrupted while he was working.

Kevin tugged at his collar. "Kin I ask you something, Jim Bob?"

"You just did."

This resulted in a momentary silence while Kevin tried to sort this out. He finally gave up and said, "About the new schedule, I mean. It says I'm supposed to work every day from four till midnight."

"Where'd you learn to read, boy? On weekends you're working from three till midnight."

"Oh, I dint see that. Anyways, now that I have a wife, I was hoping I could have some nights off so we could go to the picture show in Starley City or even just stay home and watch television together."

"Are you implying your television set doesn't work during the day? Mrs. Jim Bob turns on those gabby morning shows the minute she gets up, and her soaps are on when I go home for lunch. Maybe you'd better get yourself a new television set."

"That ain't what I mean, Jim Bob. Dahlia's kinda moping around these days on account of not having anything much to do except things like laundry and washing dishes and—"

"Spare me the details. I got a whole pile of paperwork to do by the end of the day. If I don't get it done, I can't start figuring the paychecks. Do you want to explain this delay to all the dumbshits out there who are counting on getting paid on Friday?"

Kevin shook his head and went back to the bucket and mop in the produce aisle. He thought mebbe later he'd sneak out to the pay phone in front of the store and call his beloved in hopes of brightening up her dreary day. He knew it was dreary because she told him so every evening when he got home, sometimes explaining for the better part of an hour before she gave him his supper. He had a feeling she wasn't gonna clap her hands when he told her about the night shift.

"Get this," Darla Jean McIlhaney said to Heather Riley, both of them flopped across the bed and so bored they'd painted their toenails three times. Now they were reduced to hunting for stories in the

Weekly Examiner about grotesque sexual practices. "This scientist in Germany has discovered a new diet that's guaranteed to make you lose ten pounds in one week."

Heather reached for the fingernail polish remover and a tissue. "Does it involve self-cannibalism?"

Darla Jean squinted at the print. She knew she needed glasses, but she was damned if she was going to get 'em and be the laughingstock of Farberville High School. Not one cheerleader or member of the pom-pom squad wore glasses. Last year's homecoming queen wore contacts, but there wasn't any way her own pa would pay for 'em. "No, it says all you're allowed to eat are hot dogs and ice cream, but you can have as much of them as you want. There's some enzyme that goes to work and explodes fat cells like they were little firecrackers. Read it yourself."

Heather obeyed, but she wasn't nearly as impressed. "What about that unit on nutrition last fall? Miss Estes made it real clear that none of these crazy diets work."

"Then why does this German scientist swear it does? Miss Estes is just a teacher. She can't keep up with every scientific breakthrough."

"Go ahead and try it," Heather muttered as she kept reading. "Now what kind of crazy woman would steal Elvis's body, have it cremated, and use the ashes for breast implants?"

Darla Jean was about to offer an opinion when the phone rang out in the hall. It turned out to be a sight more intriguing than breast implants.

"That was Reggie Pellitory," she said as she strolled back into her bedroom and pretended she was looking for something on her dressing table.

"He broke up with Gracie last night, and he wants me to go out with him after supper. He's gonna borrow his cousin's four-wheel so we can go riding around."

Heather wrinkled her nose. "You better be careful, Darla Jean. When Gracie let him do it, Reggie did everything but announce it over the PA system at school. She liked to have died."

"Who says I'm gonna let him do it?"

"Well, everybody in town knows it wouldn't be the first time," Heather pointed out tartly. "Last Saturday night Beau saw you and Dwayne heading toward the creek with a six-pack and a blanket. Did y'all go out there to count lightning bugs?"

Darla Jean decided she needed to wash her hair again.

Raz Buchanon was mulling over something real important. He was also scratching and spitting and doing other less fascinating things that involved bodily functions and infestations, but they can be left unspecified. He was doing all this in the cab of his truck, which was parked outside a café in Hasty. Inside the café the waitress and the owner were discussing whether they should disinfect the booth or have it replaced altogether.

"I'll tell ya, Marjorie," Raz said, "it might jest work. Bizness was mighty slow last winter, and that's my best time of year. Come hot weather, folks prefer cold beer over my 'shine, and I don't rightly blame 'em." He glanced timidly at his companion. "Now, Marjorie, don't git all fractious jest because you had to wait out here while I talked with that feller what's slicker than a preacher's ass. There weren't no way they were gonna let you inside."

Marjorie stared out the window.

Raz sighed. "Iffen I pull this off, I was thinkin' we might look into one of those fancy satellite dishes that sucks in channels from all over the world. I hear tell ye can git movies all night long, and they don't cost you nuthin'. You'd like that, wouldn't ye?"

Marjorie's beady pink eyes blinked.

"What's more, we kin have our picture in the *Probe,* jest like that woman what had ever' last drop of blood sucked out of her body by vampire mosquitoes."

Marjorie relented, but only after he went back inside and bought her a candy bar.

Way down in Little Rock, which was only two hundred miles away but could have been on another planet, Cynthia Dodder checked in the bathroom mirror to make sure her gray hair was neat and her nose powdered. After further deliberation she removed her brooch and put it away in her jewelry box. As the featured speaker at the UFORIA meeting she knew it was important to present herself as a detached professional investigator.

She went to the kitchen table, currently covered with newspaper clippings and magazine articles, each marked with a date and ready to be filed. There were also journals and newsletters, letters begging her attention, and a list of telephone calls to be made when she had time.

Cynthia Dodder felt strongly about keeping her priorities straight, however, and her speech was in the forefront of her mind as she made sure the back door of the apartment was bolted and the porch light shining to ward off burglars. The neighborhood had deteriorated over the last twenty years to the point she hardly recognized anyone and spoke to no one. Had her budget allowed it, she would have moved to a nicer area, one inhabited by respectable folks like herself rather than whiny welfare mothers and impertinent young men of a different racial persuasion.

She watched them now as they gathered out in the parking lot, laughing and passing around a bottle in a brown paper bag. If any of them had dared set foot in the exclusive dress shop where she'd been a clerk for forty years, he or she would have been escorted out the door by a security guard.

It was nearly seven o'clock, and surely Rosemary was aware that it took more than half an hour to drive to the library. She needed time to review her notes before she called the meeting to order promptly at eight. Tonight's agenda would be brief because of the portentous content of her speech, during which she would prove conclusively that NASA officials had destroyed the Mars Observer spacecraft rather than allow it to transmit pictures of an ancient alien citadel. The real question was why NASA had sent the probe in the first place, since it and other government agencies (the CIA, FBI, USAF, and the top secret Majestic Twelve commission, just for starters) possessed physical evidence of an alien presence and had covered it up for forty-five years.

Cynthia was on the verge of calling Rosemary when a familiar white compact chugged into the lot. She picked up her purse, manila folders, clipboard, and packet of blurry photographs and let herself out, making sure the door was securely locked behind her. It was unfortunate that the hoodlums could watch her as she left, but there was nothing to be done about it.

"Sorry I'm late," Rosemary said as she maneuvered out of the parking lot. "I locked myself out of the car at the grocery store. The manager finally got it open with a coat hanger, but by then it was after six. I barely had time to eat a bite of supper and clean Stan's litter box before I came rushing here to pick you up."

"That stoplight was red, Rosemary," Cynthia said as the car lurched along the street like a three-legged dog. "Please pay attention to the traffic. I, too, am sorry you were late, but now it's more important that we arrive at the library in one piece. If you don't mind, I'd like to study my speech."

She took out a stack of index cards, but it was almost impossible to concentrate over Rosemary's atonal humming and occasional mumbles to herself about approaching intersections. Really, Cynthia thought with a sigh, it was so very challenging to imagine Rosemary Tant as one of ufology's most vital contributors. She was scatterbrained and forever late. She dressed with no attempt to downplay her thin shoulders and heavy hips. Her hair was a particularly drab shade of brown, her long face perpetually riddled with anxiety, her voice tremulous and uncertain even when discussing the weather.

But she was.

TWO

◆

"Okay," I said into the telephone receiver, "I'll write up the damn accident report by the end of the week and drop it by, but you owe me, you manipulative bastard."

Harve Dorfer chuckled, but he could afford to be amiable since he'd just won the skirmish. He's perfected the role of redneck southern sheriff, replete with straw hat, beer belly, splintery cigar butt, and mirrored sunglasses, but he's a pretty sharp guy. He's a really sharp guy in election years, when he and his deputies manage to discover marijuana fields and caches of illegal arms every week. On the basis of the number of press conferences he conducts, criminal activity appears to peak right before a primary. And you probably thought there was a correlation with the full moon.

"It ain't that I don't want to do it myself," he said, "but your prose is a sight prettier than mine. You ever wonder if you should have been an author rather than a cop? You'd be rolling in dough, riding around in a limousine, appearing on morning talk shows, being wined and dined in New York City."

"No, Harve, I have way too much fun trying to run a hick town in the hinterlands," I said, not bothering to mention the limousine with the tinted windows that had been spotted several weeks ago. It hadn't seemed significant then, and even the grapevine had quit speculating and moved on to other perennial favorites—like my lack of a potential husband. "As for New York, there's more whining than anything else. I lived there, remember?"

"Hey, did ya hear what we were called in on a couple of days ago? One of the deputies liked to heave up his guts, and I felt a little queasy myself."

If I could have stopped him from telling me, I would have. However, the most expedient way to get him off the phone was to let him have his say. "What?" I said without enthusiasm, hoping I wasn't going to be regaled with the olfactory impact of the latest floater in the reservoir or the details of some gawd-awful sex abuse case.

"You ever heard talk of cattle mutilations?"

"Awhile back I saw some stories in the newspaper. Everything was taking place over in Stonecrop County, so I didn't pay much attention."

"This one woulda caught your attention," Harve muttered. I heard a scritching sound as he paused to light one of his notoriously cheap cigars; I was thankful I was twenty miles upwind. "According to some material that showed up on my desk the next morning, we were treated to what's called a classic case. One eye plucked out like it was a marble in a leather pouch; the tongue, lips, and sexual organs removed; a triangular patch of hide cut off the belly. The cow'd been dead for the better part of a week, but for some reason the scavengers hadn't found it— despite the stench and the flies." He puffed on the cigar for a moment, perhaps to give me time to assimilate the significance of his remark. When my only response was a yawn, he continued. "There were a couple of other odd things about the carcass. The cuts were all real clean, like they'd been done with a scalpel, and there was no blood on 'em or on the ground."

"Maybe they'd been done with a scalpel or a more prosaic pocketknife. I haven't heard anything about a new satanic group, but you know how the kids are when the weather turns nice. They'll jump on any excuse to make themselves feel like beleaguered social mavericks, piss off their parents, and go sneaking around after dark. You can bet the farm their rituals involve a lot of beer, pot, and pairing off. Then again, you could be dealing with a pack of wild dogs with exceptionally keen canines."

"What about the lack of blood?"

I gazed longingly out the window in the direction of Ruby Bee's, where a blue plate special had my name written on it. "Have you talked to the county extension office, Harve? I seem to recall they investigated the incidents in Stonecrop County and concluded they were all caused by common predators and predictable physiological responses. Maybe all the bleeding occurred internally."

"I don't know," he said uncomfortably. "This literature is kinda spooky. There's a group that's been investigating these mutilations for years, and they—"

"Write and sell books about it. They also charge money to lecture about it to vast audiences of very gullible people who would much rather hear about little green vivisectionists than mangy, malnourished dogs."

"I'll look for that accident report by Friday," Harve said, then hung up without so much as an admonishment to have a nice day. Darn.

The report was of minor significance (except to the participants and their grieving families) and could wait for a day or two. I walked down the side of the road, pausing to wave at my landlord as he arranged vases and lamps on a table in front of his antiques store, formally known as Roy Stiver's Antiques and Collectibles: Buy, Trade, or Sell. I resided upstairs in what was euphemistically called an efficiency apartment. It was quite a contrast with a certain condo on the Upper East Side, but I was the one who'd filed for divorce and skulked home to lick my wounds. I'd be hard pressed to explain why I was still moping around Maggody a couple of years later, especially when I was at the mercy of Ruby Bee and all the other local loonies. Roy is one of damn few exceptions. Every once in a while I go downstairs to the shop to share my discontentment and a bottle of wine.

"How's business?" I called.

"Fair to middling," he said distractedly, his expression akin to that of a turkey vulture as he watched an approaching RV.

I left him to play the ignorant hayseed for the benefit of the wily city slickers, who would be grinning smugly as they drove away with "a real steal" in the backseat. I wondered how they'd feel if they ran into Roy in Palm Springs, where he sometimes spends the winter. His income is not derived from his occasional sales to poetry magazines.

Pickup trucks were lined up in the parking lot of the bar and grill, but their drivers were standing outside, gesturing and scratching their heads while gunky-eyed hound dawgs growled at one another from the beds. I may have growled myself when I caught sight of the Closed sign on the door.

"Where's Ruby Bee?" I asked one of the regulars.

"Dunno. It being Wednesday and all, I was looking forward to chicken-fried steak and mashed potatoes. She say anything to you about closing?"

I shook my head, having entertained some decidedly lyrical thoughts about the chicken-fried steak myself. None of us would starve, of course. The SuperSaver across the road had a deli, and the Dairee Dee-Lishus was only a couple of blocks away. However, there was an increasingly unhappy rumble from the collective belly of the crowd, and I was backing away when Mizzoner (aka Mrs. Jim Bob) drove up.

"There you are!" she snapped at me. "I should have known you'd be avoiding your official responsibilities at a time like this. Bear in mind you're a salaried employee of the town council, Arly Hanks. I told Jim Bob when he hired you that a woman has no business being chief of police. It violates the Almighty Lord's standards of decency and smacks of lesbianism."

Mrs. Jim Bob and I lack rapport.

I slapped my forehead. "And you were right! Last week when there was a holdup at the bank, I was too busy giving myself a home perm to investigate."

"What bank?"

"Just how am I avoiding my official responsibilities today, Mrs. Jim Bob? Has Ruby Bee been kidnapped by Bigfoot and dragged away to a certain cave up on Cotter's Ridge? Shall I round up a posse?" I may have added a bit of emphasis when I mentioned the cave, which had caused her a great deal of well-deserved embarrassment. I can swallow only so much self-righteousness on an empty stomach, and she was dishing it up with a particularly generous hand.

"I have no idea what you're talking about," she said tightly. "I'm talking about Raz Buchanon's cornfield."

I stared at her, as did everybody else in the parking lot. As dumbstruck as your basic Buchanon, I mentally replayed our conversation, then said, "You are?"

Satisfied that she'd done her duty, which may well have been to render me momentarily inarticulate, she rolled up her window and drove away. Rather than go back to the PD to get my car, I asked one of the guys for a lift, and he agreed. We were heading an impressive caravan as we turned onto a dirt road and rolled up the hill toward Raz's place.

We didn't roll up to the shack, however, because the road was blocked by a variety of parked vehicles, one of which belonged to Ruby Bee and another to Estelle. I thanked my driver and walked the rest of the way. Raz stood at the gate, his thumbs hooked on the straps of his filthy overalls and a shit-eatin' grin on his face. His stringy gray hair and crumb-infested whiskers were marginally tidier than usual, but there was no indication he'd bathed in the recent past. Or brushed his sparse, mossy teeth.

"Howdy," he said, then sent a stream of amber tobacco juice into the weeds. "Purty day, ain't it?"

"What's going on?" I asked. Raz and I are not sworn enemies, even though he operates a moonshine still up on Cotter's Ridge. Every now and then I go out to look for it. It's an exercise in futility, but the solitude and picnic lunches are equally satisfying. On the other hand, he's a royal pain in the butt, and that's being magnanimous. "Did Marjorie chew off somebody's leg?"

"You ain't got no call to say that, Arly," he said, his face puckering like a dried apple. "Marjorie mighta had a spell last winter when she was madder'n a coon in a poke, but she's settled down right nicely. She came with a pedigree, ya know. She's got a more delicate nature than your ordinary sows."

"What's going on?" I repeated.

He tugged at his whiskers and gave me the same shrewd look as when he tells me he "don't know nuthin' 'bout no still." "I can't rightly say. I first saw 'em this morning when I went out to git some wood for the stove."

"Saw what, Raz?"

"Circles out in the cornfield."

For the second time in less than an hour I was speechless. I was frowning at him and trying to formulate a question when a smartly dressed woman and a pudgy young man with a camera came up the road.

"Raz Buchanon?" she asked him purposefully. He nodded. "I'm from the television station in Farberville. We'd like to do a segment for the evening news about these mysterious crop circles behind your house."

"I'm chargin' a dollar to folks what want to take a gander at it. I ain't sure how much I ought to git for taking pictures of it. Whatta ya think, Arly?"

I shrugged, even more bemused. They settled on five dollars; then Raz opened the gate and sent them around the corner of the shack. As I stood there, more gawkers arrived, forked over the admission fee, and took off down what was now a visible path through the overgrown yard.

Eventually I came to my senses (although there

were damn few of them), and after a brief yet spirited discussion with Raz regarding my lack of a dollar and my willingness to rip his whiskers off his chin, I was ushered through the gate.

There were twenty or so people beside a barbed wire fence. The television reporter stood in front of the camera, her eyes wide and her voice oozing wonder as she described the inexplicable appearance of crop circles in Maggody. The crowd watched her with gaping mouths, in that she was on television every day at five o'clock and therefore qualified as a celebrity.

Wishing I were in disguise, I stepped on a foot or two and threw a couple of elbows as I made my way to the fence. The field sloped downward to a distant line of brush. The corn was green and waist-high and rustled in the light breeze. The sky was dotted with puffy clouds. Unseen birds twittered in the distance. Grasshoppers whirred like tiny helicopters *(Orthoptera rotorus?)*.

"Ain't that the darndest thing?" whispered Ruby Bee, who'd wormed her way to my side. "I don't recollect seeing anything like that in all my born days."

I finally spotted the object of her avowed astonishment. Toward the far edge of the field was a rounded expanse of flattened corn with a diameter of perhaps fifteen feet. A trail led to a somewhat smaller circle, and another trail to the smallest of the three. From my perspective, the circles looked almost perfect, and the trails of uniform width. I'd seen a textbook drawing of such a syzygial pattern, although it had illustrated a lunar eclipse rather than a cornfield. I rubbed my face, trying to remember stories and photographs from a few years back.

The television reporter politely, if inadvertently, produced the details for the enlightenment of her viewers. "This phenomenon was first reported nearly fifteen years ago in the English county of Wiltshire, and since then as many as five hundred such circles have been documented each year, primarily in Wiltshire and adjoining Hampshire. Over the decade the patterns became increasingly intricate, with designs often compared to ancient symbols. Various theories have been offered, including whirlwinds, fungus, plasma vortices, extraterrestrials, and even pranksters. No explanation has been fully accepted by the scientific community. As far as KARP can determine, this is the first such mysterious circle to be found in Arkansas. We'll have further developments at ten o'clock."

She nodded regally to the crowd, then pulled the cameraman aside for a hushed conference that included surreptitious glances in my direction. I would have swapped my uniform for one of Dahlia's tent dresses, but it was too late to go under cover, so to speak. I went over to them and said, "I have no comment. I just laid eyes on those circles a few minutes ago, and I have absolutely no information or theories. If I were you, I'd take into consideration the identity and reputation of the field's owner before I went too far with the story."

"Are you implying he made the circles himself?" the reporter asked.

"I'm implying he's as trustworthy as a rabid polecat. How did you find out about this?"

"An anonymous call to the station. I had a choice between this story or a junior high science fair." She gestured for her companion to shoulder his burden. "Let's get an interview with the owner, then head back to the van to run the footage. The wind was mussing my hair the entire time. We may have to reshoot it."

I winced. "You're actually going to put this on the news tonight?"

They didn't bother to answer such an absurd question and started around the corner of the shack. I was glaring at their backs as Estelle and Ruby Bee joined me.

"You gonna investigate this?" asked Estelle, her eyes unnaturally bright with excitement.

"I don't know how to investigate this. There they are, and I doubt Raz or anyone else is going to claim to be the architect. Within a few days the cornstalks will perk up, and that'll be the end of it. I'm not real pleased this is going to be on the news tonight. Half the audience will think we're idiots, and the other half will show up with picnic baskets, coolers, and aluminum chairs to wait for the flying saucers to appear."

Ruby Bee put her finger to her lips. "Don't start talking about flying saucers," she said in a steely whisper. "There was an episode about these crop circles on *Strange Stories* not three months ago. The investigators concluded that the circles were made by aliens, although they couldn't exactly say why the aliens would want to make complicated designs in folks' fields."

I bit back a sarcastic comment since I hadn't had lunch yet and a chili dog could never compete with a crisp chicken-fried steak. "How did they arrive at this conclusion?" I forced myself to ask humbly.

"I disremember, but they did all kinds of measurements and searched every square inch of ground to make sure there weren't any ordinary footprints."

Estelle nudged her aside. "But the first thing they did was measure the circles. I brought you a tape measure and a little notebook so you can keep track of the figures." She stuffed both in my shirt pocket.

I'm not ashamed to admit I was curious about the circles. It was also apparent that Ruby Bee wasn't going to return to her skillet until I'd done something, no matter how foolish. To the crowd's murmured delight, I slipped between the strands of barbed wire and walked down a row that led in the general direction of our Martian manifestation. I wasn't especially surprised when Ruby Bee and Estelle came panting up behind me. They have a real bad habit of deputizing themselves whenever I turn my back on them. There are inmates in rehab clinics with lesser habits.

Ruby Bee grabbed my arm. "There's a footstep right there in the dirt!"

"Made by Raz," I said, "with Marjorie hot on his heels. I forgot to ask him if he came down here this morning for a closer look."

Estelle was in no mood to be regarded as a less diligent sleuth. "They stopped right here," she said, bending over to stare at a collection of marks. She stood up and waved at the crowd. "We found footprints!"

"And hoofprints!" Ruby Bee added for their benefit.

I ignored the patter of applause as I studied the marks. They seemed to indicate Raz and his sow had stopped some ten feet away from the nearest circle. If Raz had made the circles at an earlier time, he'd approached from a different direction.

"Stay here," I said, then began to move carefully along the perimeter. The smallest of the circles was near the undergrowth, but I could find no footprints leading toward or away from it. I completed the circumnavigation and rejoined Ruby Bee and Estelle. "I didn't find anything," I confessed.

"Then let's get busy with the tape measure," Estelle said with the briskness of a trained investigator who'd examined such phenomena innumerable times and reported her findings on *Strange Stories*. "You take the tape and go right over there. I'll call out the numbers for Ruby Bee to write down."

"Not yet," I said grimly. "I want to check the circles themselves for footprints before you go stomping around in them."

They muttered rebelliously but waited as I approached the edge of the largest circle. The corn had been flattened in a uniform clockwise swirl. Uncomfortably aware of my audience and the terrifying specter that the cameraman might immortalize the moment for the ten o'clock news, I squatted down and searched for so much as a heel print in the crusty soil. Beneath the stalks were some flat marks, but I didn't know what to make of them. The corn itself looked healthy, although it was possible it had been stricken by some invisible disease that would show up under a microscope. I crawled out to the middle of the circle, where I found a small area of disturbed soil. To my regret, I did not find a single footprint.

"Well?" Ruby Bee yelled at me.

"Well, come on," I said as I stood up. "Let's measure the damn things for posterity."

We eventually determined that papa circle had a diameter of eighteen feet; mama of twelve, and baby of six. The paths linking them were twelve and six feet long respectively. After all this had been carefully recorded and presented to me with great solemnity, we hiked back up the hill to Raz's shack.

More folks had shown up as the story raced through town like a snake going through a hollow log. Some of the high school kids had slipped away from classes to point and goggle. Mrs. Jim Bob and Brother Verber were having a whispered conference in the shade of the ramshackle barn. Dahlia and Kevin looked deeply bewildered, but they usually did when confronted with anything more complex than a comic strip. Other recent arrivals included Elsie McMay, Lottie Estes, Eula Lemoy, Millicent McIlhaney, Kevin's parents, and even a few backwoods Buchanons who normally surface only after a hard rain.

"Raz must have made more than fifty dollars by now," I said as I held up a strand of wire to allow my deputies to crawl into the yard.

Ruby Bee gave me a hard look. "So he's taking advantage of the situation. That don't mean he created it. You didn't find any footprints, did you?"

"No, but I didn't find any traces of extraterrestrial involvement either. I'll run a cornstalk over to the county extension lab this afternoon and let them examine it with the proper equipment. In the meantime, don't start spreading any crazy stories, okay? Maggody's been the butt of a lot of jokes in the last few years, and I still hear about certain events every time I go by the state police barracks. Just this one time let's not go totally hog-wild."

"I do not gossip," she said with a prim frown, then hustled over to the nearest group to expound on the impeccable roundness of the circles and the very peculiar absence of footprints any closer than ten feet. Estelle was kind enough to contribute the statistics.

There wasn't anything more for me to do, I decided as I headed for the gate. If I was lucky, I'd get back results from the lab before we had a three-ring circus on the hillside. I had a bleak suspicion that the clowns were already on their way, crammed in their car like naked Pentecostals.

"Arly Hanks," called Mrs. Jim Bob with her customary charm, "Brother Verber and I need to have a word with you."

I reluctantly veered toward them. "Any word in particular or just a word?"

Brother Verber's ruddy face looked a little pale, and his forehead was beaded with sweat. He sucked on his lip for a moment, then said, "What's this I heard about cattle mutilations right here in Stump County? Is there a blossoming satanic cult in our midst?"

"Where'd you hear about it?" I asked him. "And what exactly did you hear, for that matter?"

"I cannot reveal my sources," he said piously. "As a minister I took vows to protect the identity of any wretch who comes to me to confess to sinful and lascivious behavior. You'll just have to respect the confidentiality of the pulpit and answer my questions."

I smiled sweetly. "Good heavens, has hell frozen over? I must run home and get my ice skates."

Mrs. Jim Bob failed to appreciate my wit. "Now listen here, Chief Hanks, I've had enough of your smart mouth to last me a lifetime. Something is going on around here, and whatever it is stinks worse than a buzzard's nest. It's your responsibility to get to the bottom of it."

I decided not to tickle her nose with the stalk of corn, although it might have been a pleasant diversion. "Okay, Brother Verber, you go right ahead and protect the confidentiality of the pulpit till the cows come home—the ones that aren't mutilated anyway. I've got some business at the county extension office."

I left them fuming and walked down the road to the highway. I looked wistfully in the direction of the Missouri line but went on back to the PD and made a call to be sure I'd be welcome at the county extension office. After a small detour by the Dairee Dee-Lishus, I and my cornstalk left for Farberville.

Being a dedicated law enforcement agent and all, I ate the chili dog in the car.

THREE

◆

Ruby Bee hurried back to the kitchen to see how the black-eyed peas were holding up, barely avoiding a collision with Dahlia in the doorway. "Take menus to the folks in the last two booths," she said, "and ask the men in the first booth if they want dessert. If they don't, hustle 'em out the door and seat that couple standing in the back."

Dahlia nodded and trudged away to do as much of that as she could keep straight. It was awful hard what with the jukebox blaring catchy tunes and folks jostling for stools at the bar. Her feet were already getting achy, and she hadn't been there but mebbe two hours. There was such a crowd waiting in the back that the noon rush might not let up till happy hour. It seemed like ever'body in Stump County that watched the news the night before had come to Maggody to take a look at the crop circles in Raz's cornfield.

She dint know what to make of them herself, but at least she had her old job back and was smack-dab in the middle of the excitement. "How're y'all?" she asked the five women crammed in the last booth, giving them menus and a right friendly smile. "You just take your time. I'll be back afore too long."

The folks in the next booth were expecting something, but Dahlia couldn't recollect what it was, so she went on to the first booth and started stacking up the dishes and utensils. The men acted like they wanted to say something, but she warned 'em off with a frown, slapped down their bill, and headed for the kitchen with her greasy load.

"I'm out of cherry pie, so there's no point in whining about it, Gilly Jacana," Ruby Bee was telling a customer as Dahlia went past the end of the bar. "I won't argue with you that I should've made twice as many pies. For that matter, I should've printed up maps to Raz's place and sold them for a quarter. Now you either have a piece of carrot cake or put three dollars and seventy-seven cents on the bar and be about your business."

Gilly Jacana opted to be about his business (which was conveying a truckload of doomed chickens to the poultry-processing plant in Starley City). Ruby Bee was wiping up the corn bread crumbs when a pretty girl of not more than twenty-five slid onto the stool. Her hair was short and dark; her features were perky, her eyes big and watery like a doe's, her puffy lips outlined in pink. Considering the rowdy crowd along the bar, it was remarkable that such a skinny little thing had grabbed an empty stool, Ruby Bee thought as she set aside the dishrag and handed the girl a menu. "We're out of chicken and dressing, but the pot roast is real good."

"I—uh, I was wondering about the Flamingo Motel out in back. Where can I find out if there are any rooms available for the next three or four nights?"

"You just did." Ruby Bee went to the drawer beneath the cash register, selected a key with a plastic tag, and took it back. "You can take number three. It's down at the end, where it's nice and quiet. Get yourself settled in, then come back later and sign the register. Things are mighty hectic at the moment. If they don't ease off before too long, I'll be staggerin' like a buckeyed calf."

The girl picked up the key and melted into the crowd. A fat, hairy fellow in overalls sat down and began to read the menu. Ruby Bee wasted a minute wondering who the girl was and why she wanted a room, then forgot about it and said, "How 'bout a thick slab of pot roast and some scalloped potatoes, Floyd?"

Jim Bob swung open the glass door and smiled broadly at the two women. "Welcome to Jim Bob's SuperSaver Buy 4 Less," he said. "Today in the deli we have a special box lunch for only three dollars and forty-nine cents, plus tax. In it you'll find a ham sandwich, a pickle, potato chips, and two freshly baked oatmeal cookies. Your drinks are extra."

The older woman had stiff gray hair and a face that reminded Jim Bob of a disgruntled bulldog. "We had lunch earlier," she said. "We stopped here to get directions to the farm with the crop circles. A member of our organization from Farberville called me this morning with the report."

"We're from Little Rock," the second woman contributed. She fluttered her hand in that general direction, as if Jim Bob could see the skyscrapers above the treetops.

He didn't care if they were from another country. He gestured for them to stand aside, gave the details of the box lunch special to a group of teenagers, and considered telling the woman to kiss his ass on account of he wasn't a fool travel agent. However, something she'd said finally clicked, so he went over to them and said to the bulldog, "What organization?"

"UFORIA. It's an acronym for Unidentified Flying Objects Reported in Arkansas. There are more than a hundred members across the state. I'm Cynthia Dodder, the president, and this is Rosemary Tant, our secretary."

"And you came to see the crop circles?" asked Jim Bob, wondering if he could figure out a way to get the whole fuckin' organization to buy box lunches. Hell, he'd knock off 10 percent or put in an extra pickle.

Cynthia nodded. "Many cereologists in England feel strongly that there is a link between the corn circle configurations and extraterrestrial activities. The numerous UFO sightings in Warminster in the mid-1960s evolved into crop circles by the end of the decade. And you must bear in mind that this area of England is home to Stonehenge, Avebury, and Silbury Hill."

"No kidding." Jim Bob whistled under his breath and tried to look impressed by whatever the hell she'd been saying. "So you think UFOs might be responsible for what happened in Raz's field?"

Cynthia gripped Rosemary's elbow and steered her toward the door. "We intend to prove it, my dear man. Arthur Sageman is flying in from California and should arrive sometime this afternoon. He is the foremost authority in ufology in the entire country. Come along, Rosemary. We need to arrange for motel rooms before Arthur and Brian get here."

The women climbed into a dusty white car and drove away. Jim Bob went out into the parking lot and counted the cars across the road at Ruby Bee's. There were three times as many of them as he'd ever seen on a Thursday afternoon. Come the weekend, all the folks who couldn't get away from work would come streaming to town like ants to a Sunday school picnic.

He decided he should rent one of those portable signs and park it down by the edge of the road. Surely he could get a dollar more for the box lunches, or two if he threw in a free soft drink.

I was working on the accident report when a man rapped on the screen door of the PD. "Come on in," I said with a sigh, wondering if real writers were besieged with visitors just as the plot was getting steamy or, in this case, gory. "It's not hooked."

I felt a tad more cordial as I got a better look at him. He had curly black hair, a dark tan, and white teeth. He was short, but everything was firm under a veneer of Italian silk and 100 percent cotton. I put his age at thirty, give or take a few years. Most important, he lacked the glint in his eyes that was symptomatic of a flying saucer fanatic. I'd seen a lot of glints in the last twenty-four hours.

"I'm Jules Channel," he said as he sat down across from me and leaned a briefcase against the wall. "I work for a magazine based in Florida, and we're planning to do a story about the crop circles."

"You came all the way from Florida?"

"I was on assignment in Louisiana when my editor called this morning. He was alerted to a story on your local news and thought it had potential."

I leaned back in my chair and propped my feet on the corner of the desk. "I hope you're not expecting a comment from me, Mr. Channel, because I'm fresh out of them. Do you need directions?"

"I was hoping for an interview with the chief of police." He glanced at the back room, which by no stretch of whimsy could pass for an office. "May I assume you're it?"

"Assume whatever you like, but I am not going to be interviewed about this nonsense. After I've heard from the county extension office, I may be in a position to make a brief statement. What's the name of your magazine?"

"The *Weekly Examiner*," he said evenly.

I rocked back so violently that I banged my head against the wall. "You're from a tabloid?"

"I used to work for the Washington *Post,* tracking down politicians and assiduously recording their perfidious bullshit. I finally realized I could make a lot more money tracking down weirdos and assiduously recording their sincere bullshit. It's much more entertaining to write about toilets possessed by demons than the trade deficit. It's more lucrative, too."

"I thought you all sat around your offices and made up the stories."

He gave me a wry smile. "And breach our professional ethics? Believe it or not, there is a tiny thread of truth in most of the stories we report. Well, some of them anyway. We merely take what might be called a fresh approach to the subject and expand on the elements our readers find most intriguing. Eyewitnesses may be encouraged to use their imaginations to fill in some gaps. But there are some pretty amazing stories out there in the real world."

"Like the alien offspring in Brazil?"

"The mother had the baby during a two-year period when her husband was working on a freighter. When he returned home, all her relatives agreed that she'd been raped by small purple men from a flying saucer. No one can understand the baby's babbles. It could be a foreign language."

"And I could sprout wings and fly out the door," I said, unimpressed.

"That might get your picture on the cover."

Struggling not to giggle at the images that came to mind, I stood up in hopes of ending the conversation. He was attractive, but I needed to finish my diagram of where the body parts had landed. "You'll be the first to know, Mr. Channel. Would you like directions to the cornfield?"

"I need to find a motel first," he said. "Are you sure you won't make a statement? Otherwise, I'll be obliged to report that the local authorities refused to rule out the possibility that the circles were created by alien spacecraft."

"Who said anything about alien spacecraft? These are circles of flattened cornstalks, for pity's sake! The director of the county extension office must have rattled off two dozen possibilities, including the corn borer, corn ear-worm, corn weevil, corn beetle, corn-root aphid, and a very common parasitic fungus called corn smut. You'd be better off interviewing the naked Pentecostals about their brand of clothing."

"That's why I was in Louisiana," he said as he started for the door. "It seems that only the driver was jailed. His companions slipped away from some minimum security facility and fled into the woods. There'll be a story in the next issue about their exorcism ritual, which they no doubt performed on the banks of a bayou."

"No doubt," I said, then waited until he was gone before collapsing in my chair and cradling my head in my hands. When the high school basketball team won the conference title, there was nary a word in the area newspaper. When the FHA club won a blue ribbon for its booth at the county fair, there was a single sentence buried in a long paragraph.

But now we were going to be featured in the *Weekly Examiner,* right next to demonic toilets and errant Pentecostals. What I needed was a bulldozer and a moonlit night, I decided. The resultant destruction wouldn't merit a mention in a church bulletin.

Arthur Sageman shook his head as he looked out the car window at the dismal little town. "I hope this is worth the trip," he said. "The manuscript is late, and I really need to spend more time polishing my keynote address for the conference in Houston next month. Book sales have been slacking off, and the conference may be my last chance to regain international prominence. If only I hadn't fallen for that woman's story and featured her in *The Roswell Incident Revisited,* but I had no idea she would turn out to have been institutionalized more than a dozen times. Once the reviewers got wind of it, they were merciless."

His secretary, an exceptionally pale young man named Brian Quint, didn't bother to reply. Arthur had been complaining steadily since they'd left LAX five hours earlier. Brian was aware of the unfinished manuscript (since he was word-processing it) and of the approaching conference (since he'd negotiated the fee and made the necessary reservations). He was also aware of the substantial salary he received in exchange for such duties and therefore managed a sympathetic murmur.

"Surely Cynthia has her facts straight," Arthur

continued in his vaguely British accent, which he'd adopted after deciding a Texas twang diminished the impact of his lectures. He'd adopted a new name, too; Leroy Longspur did not inspire reverence. "If so, I can use this in Houston and literally bring down the house. Very little has been done with corn circle configurations in the United States, I suppose because of the crude forgeries in Kennewick several years ago. This will be quite a coup."

"And Rosemary will be here," Brian said as he braked at what appeared to be the only stoplight. "Oh, shit," he added, then pointed at a figure walking alongside the road. "Look who's here—your favorite tabloid reporter, Jules Channel."

Arthur was distressed enough to ruffle his sculpted silver hair and allow a deep crease to cut across his wide forehead. He pulled off his wire-rimmed glasses, polished them on a silk handkerchief, and resettled them on his undeniably patrician nose. Keeping all but the faintest hint of vinegar from his voice, he said, "We could have done without the chap. His edge of sarcasm makes legitimate sightings sound like a quaint elementary school theater production."

"He turned into the parking lot with a motel sign. It's likely to be the only one around, so it's probable Cynthia booked us rooms there. Talk about your strange bed-fellows . . ."

They found the motel behind a pink building, but there was neither office nor any hint of the registration procedure. There were three cars, however. Two had stickers indicating they were rented, but the third had a metal plate from a Little Rock Honda agency.

"That could be Cynthia's or Rosemary's," Arthur

said. "I have no desire to encounter Mr. Channel, but I would like to get settled in so we can start taking slides this afternoon. Knock on the door, Brian."

As Brian climbed out of the car, a door at the end of the building opened and a young woman emerged. She was burdened with a briefcase, several camera bags, and an enormous leather purse. He watched as she staggered to one of the rental cars, made a futile attempt to open the door, looked around with a fetchingly helpless expression, and then dumped her load on the hood of the car. Only then did she realize she was being observed.

"Hello," she said with a strained smile.

Brian wiggled his fingers. "Hello. You've obviously found the office and managed to register. Could you be so kind as to point me in the right direction?"

"Talk to the woman inside the bar." She turned away and began to dig through her purse, but her cheeks were noticeably pink. Somehow or other, she managed to knock the briefcase off the hood while spilling most of the purse's contents at her feet. "Darn!"

Brian thought she was adorable. "Are you here to see the crop circles?"

"Yes." She cleared her throat. "I'm a reporter."

Arthur stuck his head out the car window. "Brian, my boy, we cannot sit here all afternoon and natter with other guests. If this car is not Cynthia's, then we must track her down and determine where we are to stay tonight. It's imperative that our cameras are placed before dark."

Brian obediently knocked on the door of No. 2. When Rosemary peered timidly out the window, he beckoned to Arthur. The girl from No. 3 drove away as Cynthia opened the door and stepped outside.

"Welcome back to Arkansas, Arthur!" she boomed. "You haven't been here since the MUFON conference in Eureka Springs four years ago, have you? I was so hoping you might speak at our UFORIA conference last month. We had a decent turnout, but we would have drawn attendees from across the country if you had come."

He shrugged modestly. "I am dreadfully busy these days. My fourteenth book just came out, although you must have heard that from Rosemary. I insisted her photograph be included on the interior of the dust jacket this time."

Cynthia was properly impressed with his magnanimity, as well as his prolificacy. "She loaned me her copy, although I haven't had time to read it yet. This business with the Mars Observer conspiracy has taken all my energy."

Rosemary wiggled past Cynthia. "Arthur, how are you? Did you have a nice flight? I've never flown, you know, except for my trips in Pleiadian spaceships, and those were absolutely terrifying—"

"Brian, you and Arthur are directly across from us in number five," Cynthia called as the former opened the trunk. "I tried to get you separate rooms, but these were the last two. I'm sorry about that, Arthur. I hope it's not inconvenient."

It was, but he was busy congratulating himself on the publication of fourteen books. It was even more amazing if you took into account his numerous scholarly contributions to the *Journal of the ETH Research Foundation*. He was also in the midst of a caustic exchange that took place in the letters to the editor page of the *Chronicle of Cosmic Inquiry*. All that, he mused, and conferences at least every other month, some as far away as Australia and England. One of these days he'd have enough frequent flyer miles for a free trip to Alpha Centauri.

"Do you have the key, Cynthia?" Brian asked as he balanced the laptop, boxes of disks, and a stack of manila folders.

She did, and while Rosemary continued to describe her ordeal aboard the alien craft, Arthur to muse over his accomplishments, and Brian to glance wistfully at the door of No. 3, luggage was stored inside the room (cramped and cheaply furnished, but very clean). At some point Cynthia confirmed that Jules Channel was in the very next room and that the girl in No. 3 was indeed a reporter from the *Probe*. This cast a gloom on the group that was lifted only when Arthur said, "Well, then, shall we begin?"

Brother Verber inspected his gear to make sure he was ready to begin that very night. On the couch were an industrial-size flashlight, an extra package of new batteries, a can of bug spray, a plastic pith helmet, and a worn, well-thumbed Bible. On the floor were two rubber boots, each big enough to drown a cat. He'd driven to the army surplus store in Farberville that morning and, to his chagrin, had been informed that they were the only ones in stock. Even though they were size sixteen, the salesman seemed to believe that they'd do just fine with socks stuffed in the toes. Brother Verber believed it, too, once ten dollars was knocked off the price and the pith helmet thrown in for free.

He'd already decided which biblical verse to use (I Peter 2:11) and had been rehearsing most of the afternoon. " 'Dearly beloved, I beseech you as strangers and pilgrims, abstain from fleshly lusts, which war against the soul,' " he said, punctuating it with a string of sorrowful sighs for the wickedness that already would be in progress when he arrived. As disgusted as he would be, he could not shirk his duty; the mail-order seminary in Las Vegas had stressed selflessness and dedication, even when it meant going one-on-one with Satan hisself.

Something about the quote didn't sit just right, he thought as he poured a glass of sacramental wine and sat down at the dinette. He rolled his eyes in a heavenly direction to find out if the Good Lord might object to a little fine-tuning. The Good Lord didn't comment. That meant He most likely was too busy with famines and wars even to notice. Brother Verber pondered the verse, trying to give it a little punch, and came up with a much more potent version. It was so promising that he went into the bathroom and struck a pose in front of the mirror.

"Dearly beloveds, I beseech you as local teenagers whose parents attend the Voice of the Almighty Lord Assembly Hall on Sunday mornings and hardly ever skip Wednesday evening prayer meetings, abstain from fleshly lusts, which war against thine virgin souls."

Satisfied that he'd covered all the bases, he went back to the dinette and reached for the wine bottle. All that was left to do was to determine if he was going to patrol upstream or downstream from the low-water bridge. If the Good Lord didn't drop any hints before dusk, Brother Verber figured he could flip a coin.

Ruby Bee had sent Dahlia home to rest up before the crowd came back for happy hour. She herself was tuckered out, but she'd shooed out the last few customers and managed to get a dozen pies and cobblers in the ovens, along with briskets and green bean casseroles and scalloped potatoes. A vat of chicken and dumplings bubbled on the stove. Corn bread and biscuit batters awaited their time. Estelle had come to lend a hand, since crop circles seemed to have no impact on the cosmetology industry. Now the two of them finally had a chance to sit down at the end of the bar.

"All the units are rented?" Estelle said incredulously. "That ain't happened since the folks from Nashville came last year."

Ruby Bee wasn't in the mood to reminisce about that particular disaster. "Two of 'em are tabloid reporters, although that little girl doesn't look old enough to be anything but a baby-sitter. Her name's Lucy Fernclift, and her address is somewhere in Florida. I don't think she would have admitted she works for the *Probe* if I hadn't upped and asked her. Jules Channel, the other reporter, is from the *Weekly Examiner*. He's older—and a mite smirky."

"Arly's type, huh?"

"I reckon so," said Ruby Bee, "but I don't aim to be the one that tells her. The women in number two are from Little Rock. One of them was gabbling about some club or something when I gave her the keys, but it was noisier than a room full of fiddlers, and I didn't catch much of it. She also had me keep a room for two men coming all the way from California."

Estelle's jaw dropped so far it liked to bump her chest. "California? Are you claiming folks are coming all the way from California and Florida and Little Rock on account of the circles in Raz's cornfield?"

"I'm not claiming anything, Estelle. I am repeating what they told me. They could be crazier than any of the Buchanons, including Diesel. I heard just the other day that he's taken to living in a cave on the back side of Cotter's Ridge and biting the heads off live squirrels and rabbits."

"I ain't surprised," Estelle said, trying to sound as if she'd known it all along and just hadn't bothered to repeat it. She did some calculating on her fingers. "That leaves one more unit, doesn't it?"

"Last night right after the news a man called me all the way from New Mexico to reserve a room. His name is Hayden McMasterson, and he's the director of some research place that investigates mysterious happenings. He told me the name of it, but I can't recall what it is. He should be arriving shortly."

"Folks sure are getting fired up over this. The next thing you know, we'll be hearing how Bigfoot moved in with Diesel and the Pentecostals are hiding out in the woods behind Joyce Lambertino's house. Arly may have had a point about everybody getting hysterical over three silly circles."

"I seem to remember someone bringing a tape measure."

"Well, I seem to remember someone talking about how flying saucers made the circles."

The exchange might have built up some momentum, but they were both too tired to bother. They munched pretzels in companionable silence for a long while, thinking their own thoughts.

Ruby Bee realized it was time to check the pies. "I don't know what made those circles," she said as she slid off the stool, "but I can't deny business has picked up. There was a traffic jam over in the parking lot at the SuperSaver this morning. You couldn't see the front of Roy's store for all the RVs and cars."

"I'm so thrilled that some of us are doing better," Estelle said with a snort. "Maybe I ought to offer to spray folks' hair green and purple."

"Maybe." Ruby Bee disappeared into the kitchen.

Estelle was considering some sort of innovative "Alien Coif" when the door opened and a man came in, then hesitated on the far side of the dance floor like he expected an invitation to two-step. She studied him critically. He wore a loose white shirt with lots of colorful embroidery on the yoke, a knotted cloth belt, khaki trousers, and sandals. A funny little beard clung to his chin; a slap on the back might send it flying in the air. The rest of his hair was frizzy, peppered with gray, and pulled back in a ponytail. He'd have fitted in well with the hippies that had run the New Age hardware store until the previous fall—except that he was likely to be thirty years older than any of 'em.

"The bar and grill's closed till four," she said in a friendly fashion, seeing as how he might feel the need for a trim one of these days.

"I have a reservation at the motel, but I can't seem to find the office."

"This is where you register." Estelle went to the kitchen door and opened it long enough to say, "You got a customer," then returned to her stool and patted the one next to it. "Why doncha sit right here by me, Mr. ah . . . ?"

"Dr. Hayden McMasterson," he said. "I truly am in a bit of a hurry to stow my luggage and get to the field before dark."

Ruby Bee was drying her hands on a dish towel as

she came out of the kitchen. Estelle graciously made the introductions, which appeared to annoy one of the parties, and then offered to draw a map. This seriously annoyed one of the parties. Dr. McMasterson managed to avoid noticing anything amiss and fled with his key.

Estelle eyed the door. "I wonder if he's a medical doctor or a college doctor."

"Why does it matter to you?"

"I was wondering out loud, so there's no reason to get all riled up." She caught a curl and twisted it around her finger. "I was just thinking—"

"I was just starting the corn bread."

"—that if there really were flying saucers out at Raz's last night, they might come back tonight. All these people from Little Rock and California and Florida and New Mexico seem to think something strange is going to happen. If these investigators are going to be there tonight, it must be because they believe they're gonna see something."

"Like Marjorie rolling in the corn?" said Ruby Bee as she turned around like she was going back to the kitchen. She wasn't, naturally, because she was curious about what Estelle was gonna say next.

"If you were to close up early—say, at ten—we could walk up there, cut around the opposite side of the cabin, and slip into the barn. Then we could keep watch out the knotholes in case—" Estelle stopped and shivered like a wet dog.

"What if Raz catches us?"

"What if flying saucers come floating across the cornfield?"

Ruby Bee had to admit Estelle had an interesting, if half-baked, point.

FOUR

Raz grinned as more folks came up the road. His pockets were already stuffed with dollar bills, and in the shack was a whole jarful. Marjorie weren't very happy about all the ruckus, but Raz figgered as long as he kept her locked inside, she wouldn't git riled enough to draw blood.

He held out a gnarled hand. "Two dollars from each of you iffen you want to come into the yard."

Cynthia Dodder glanced in horror at her companions, then stepped forward. "Don't be ridiculous. This is Arthur Sageman, director of the ETH Research Foundation in Los Angeles, and his secretary, Brian Quint. Ms. Tant and I represent UFORIA. We are here to conduct a thorough investigation into the configurations in order to—"

"Two dollars from each of you iffen you want to come into the yard." Raz spit into the dust, careful to miss her shoe. "And ten dollars fer takin' pictures. Otherwise, you kin hike your tails."

He collected the fee from the young feller and opened the gate. Before they was out of sight, a girl about as skinny as a poker appeared, her cheeks flushed from the walk and her voice all chirpy. She was a purty little thing, so he let her in for a dollar. The man that came on her heels forked over ten dollars like they was burning a hole in his pocket and asked if Raz would pose for a picture and tell about finding the circles. After some dickering, they settled on twenty-five dollars for what the man called "an exclusive" the next morning. He seemed right tickled when Raz insisted Marjorie be in the picture.

Raz didn't charge Dahlia on account of her bein' a neighbor and having her driveway blocked for two days running, and he let Earl and Eilene in cheap 'cause they were kinfolk. His goodwill dried up when Mrs. Jim Bob pranced up to the gate like she was something on a stick and started carryin' on about how aliens were heathens and bringing their depravities to Maggody in hopes of corrupting folks. He held his ground until she thrust two dollars at him and walked past him with her nose stuck up so high she was in danger of drownin' in a rainstorm.

It was beginning to get dark. Raz wasn't sure why folks were still coming, but they were. As soon as there was a break, he figgered he could go inside and see about changin' channels for Marjorie. She felt strongly about *LA Law*.

Over on the far side of the county Sheriff Harve Dorfer was working a cold cigar butt from one corner of his mouth to the other as he looked down at the carcass. "Seen any coyotes in these parts, Aldus?"

"Not in over a year. Besides, any fool can see she wasn't taken down by a damn coyote. She was cut, not gnawed. When did a coyote ever pull a flap of skin off a heifer's belly like it was a banana peel? There ain't a single drop of blood in sight." Aldus, who was not a Buchanon (and once had threatened a niece with bodily harm for dating one), walked over to his truck and took out a shovel. "Guess I better bury it before it gets dark. The rest of the herd's so damn spooked they won't come into this part of the pasture."

"Did you see any unfamiliar cars or trucks out on the road last night?"

"No, can't say I did. Then again, me and the missus went over to Maggody after supper to see the corn circles for ourselves. What do you make of 'em, Harve?"

"I'll tell you after Arly gets a report from the county extension office. Lemme take some pictures of the heifer before you bury it, Aldus. It won't do any good, but I suppose I'd better start a file. This is the third one in two weeks."

"That so? You think there's something funny going on in Stump County?"

Harve flipped the cigar butt into the tall grass. "Yeah, Aldus, I think there's something funny going on in Stump County. I just wish to hell I knew what it was."

Darla Jean McIlhaney wished she were home in her own room, or hanging out at the Dairee Dee-Lishus, or even baby-sitting for her bratty little cousins. Heck, she'd have preferred to be at a tent revival than parked on this shadowy back road with Reggie Pellitory. She and Reggie had been going together for more than two weeks, and she knew they were getting to the critical point when she either had to prove her love or risk losing him to Bethany Pickerell, who salivated every time she waylaid Reggie in the hall.

Reggie slammed the trunk and came around to her

door, holding a cooler in one hand and a rolled-up blanket in the other. "Why're you still sitting there?"

"I told you what Mrs. Jim Bob said to my ma about how Brother Verber is gonna start trying to catch kids down by the creek. They thought it was real funny, but they were in the kitchen having coffee and cookies. I don't reckon my ma will laugh if she hears my name said in church come Sunday morning."

"Fer chrissake," Reggie said as he put down the cooler so he could open her door, "the only thing he's gonna catch is a cold. How's he gonna know to come to this exact spot? I told you when you got in the car that I was coming here to drink beer. You're the one that said you wanted to come with me. Quit your whining, and let's go."

Darla Jean got out of the car and followed him down an overgrown path. "You better be right about this, Reggie," she began, then stopped when a branch caught her square in the face. She was still picking fuzzy things out of her hair when Reggie put down the cooler, unrolled and spread out the blanket, and sat down right in the middle.

"How 'bout opening me a beer?" he said.

"Hush, Reggie! I hear voices."

"Yeah, you do, seeing as how we're directly across Boone Creek from Raz Buchanon's place. I'll bet half the town's standing around his yard gawking at those circles. You wouldn't believe the number of people that came by the SuperSaver today to git directions." He patted the blanket. "Just fetch me a beer and sit down, honey. This way we can watch for flying saucers without paying any money to that asshole. Did you see the new issue of the *Weekly Examiner*? There's a story about how aliens

kidnapped this housewife in Kansas and took her up
to their ship to perform sexual experiments on her.
Whatta ya say we try some ourselves?"

The only experiment Darla Jean was interested in
was finding out if she could wish hard enough to
make herself disappear right then and there. She
didn't care where she reappeared, as long as she
went someplace that wasn't across the creek from all
sorts of folks—including her ma and pa, who'd
mentioned going there after supper.

"I don't know, Reggie," she said, frowning at the
flickery lights behind the undergrowth. "I'm still
afraid of gettin' caught by Brother Verber."

He got to his feet and went over to pull her
against him so she could feel the telltale bulge in his
britches and realize he wasn't just whistlin' "Dixie."
Nibbling her neck for good measure, he said,
"There's another reason why we don't have to worry
about. Me and some of the boys went up to the Missouri line one night last week after work. There's a
place that sells fireworks all year round, even the illegal ones. We bought us a whole box of cherry
bombs and divvied them up when we got back."

"But you didn't know about Brother Verber until
tonight, did you?"

"Are you gonna ask questions all night?"

Darla Jean's resistance was eroding, but she
wasn't quite ready to fling herself onto the blanket.
"What are the cherry bombs for?"

"Brother Verber's not exactly a commando. If we
hear him stumbling and thrashing through the brush,
this little ol' cherry bomb'll scare the holy shit out of
him. You and me will be at the Dairee Dee-Lishus before he can twitch a toe." Reggie took an innocuous-

looking round object from his pocket. "See? I'll put it right next to the cooler."

Pretty soon Darla Jean found herself in a good-natured tussling match, trying to keep Reggie's hands away from her zipper and buttons without making him mad. He didn't seem to pay much mind to her whispered protests, and to be honest, she would have been a sight more resolute if he hadn't kept swearing that he loved her, and to prove it, he'd bought the most expensive condom at the SuperSaver. Darla Jean thought that was real sweet. After a few more perfunctory protests so he'd know she wasn't a slut like Bethany Pickerell, she helped him unhook her bra.

They'd rounded third base and were heading for home when he sat up and growled, "Fuck! Do you hear something?"

"Why, Hayden, I had no idea you were coming," Arthur Sageman said with a thin smile. "I hope you had a pleasant flight from wherever it is you live in the mountains. I've been told the high altitude can have a deleterious effect on one's neurological activity."

"The foundation for ITH Research is still in Taos," said Hayden McMasterson, his smile no warmer and his voice a degree or two icier. He rubbed the crystal that hung around his neck from a leather thong until he felt a subtle sense of potency throughout his inner being. "I see you have your cameras positioned to capture the arrival of alien spacecraft. Won't you ever give up and admit you're wrong, Arthur? Surely *The Roswell Incident Revisited* debacle taught you something."

"Only," Arthur responded with a chuckle, "to be

wary of pathological liars, but you're much more familiar with them than I."

"Five hundred and eleven crop circles were recorded last year alone. In not one instance were unidentified lights seen in the vicinity, much less malnourished gray chaps with bug eyes. These crop circles are clearly the product of intraterrestrial activity, as I proved conclusively in last month's *Chronicle.*"

Arthur's nostrils quivered. "I examined that aspect at great length in the *Journal* six months ago. It's your ilk who keep insisting aliens must arrive in craft with pulsating lights. Any civilization capable of intergalactic travel does not require front-wheel drive and headlights to locate a cornfield. Furthermore, at the conference in Biloxi, I presented the supposition that mass hypnosis may well have been utilized in the rare instances in which witnesses were present."

"Ah, yes, Biloxi. I had to decline to give the keynote address because I was taping a segment for *Strange Stories* in Puerto Rico. It's good to know they found a substitute at the last minute, and I'm sure your hypothesis was presented with great sincerity, if not logic. Did you hypnotize the audience into buying it?"

Cynthia intervened before Arthur could reply. "Dr. Sageman uses hypnosis only in carefully controlled situations, Dr. McMasterson. He would never engage in cheap parlor tricks. You have read *Rosemary T. and the Extrinsic Paradox,* haven't you?"

Hayden gave her a grave nod. "How nice to see you again, Ms. Dodder. Yes, I read Arthur's little book about Ms. Tant's abductions during her childhood. Isn't it fortunate she was able to recall them in a timely manner so the book would be available at the convention in Peoria?"

"Listen here," Arthur said, his fist drawn, "I will not stand here and listen to your—"

"Dr. Sageman! Dr. McMasterson! Could I get a shot of the two of you before it gets too dark?" Jules Channel stepped in front of them and held up a camera.

Animosity evaporated for the moment, and the two men arranged their expressions for maximum scholarly effect. After all, each was thinking, one has one's reputation to consider, and even though Jules Channel was a skeptic at best, his work often appeared on the cover of the *Weekly Examiner*. Media were media.

"Could I have a shot, too?" asked a young woman. "I'm Lucy Fernclift from the *Probe*." The two men swiveled obligingly. After much fumbling and squeaking, Lucy managed to take several pictures. She was about to ask them for a comment when Brian appeared at her side and gently led her away.

"You say you're from the *Probe*?" he asked. "I'm afraid I must examine your credentials before Dr. Sageman poses for any more photographs. There are so many crackpots that we've learned to be cautious."

Lucy noticed with some irritation that the man from the *Weekly Examiner* was immune from suspicion, but she set down her camera and hunted through her purse for her wallet. "I have my press card somewhere," she said. "I know I had it in the motel room before I left. Is it possible to show it to you later?"

"How long have you worked for the *Probe*?"

"Just a couple of weeks. After I graduated from journalism school three years ago, the only job I could find was on a little weekly paper that needed someone to sell ads. I realize the *Probe* isn't as highly regarded as *The New York Times*, but I needed a job, and the pay is—"

"Are you married?"

"I thought you wanted to examine my press credentials. My private affairs have nothing to do with—"

"So you're the competition," Jules said, sliding into the conversation with practiced ease. "We must get together and compare notes. I have several buddies who work for the *Probe*, and I've heard your new editor is something of a character."

"He's been very kind to me," said Lucy.

Jules smiled. "Is that so? Let me tell you what I heard," he said, putting his hand on her shoulder and lowering his voice to a conspiratorial whisper.

Brian stalked away to make sure Arthur and Hayden did not lapse into virulent exchanges that might lead to violence. They had come close on numerous occasions; some of the more heated incidents had become legendary. The panel in Pasadena was still discussed with a certain reverence. Not even Brian had been prepared when Arthur dashed the contents of the water pitcher into Hayden's face. The pitcher had been full. Arthur had been surprisingly nimble when Hayden recovered and charged like a slavering mastodon.

To his relief, Cynthia had lured Arthur away with questions about the camera position and Hayden was busy setting up his tripod. Rosemary was conversing with a woman of monstrous proportions and an expression not unlike Hayden's as the water dripped off his nose. Beyond the fence the corn rippled seductively as the moon rose over the ridge. Stars unseen in Los Angeles glittered, and the Milky Way was a gossamer swath across the sky. It was a fine night for a close encounter, Brian told himself with only the faintest sneer.

"Duck," whispered Ruby Bee over her shoulder, then tripped over the remains of a bushel basket and barely saved herself from a fall. "If Raz should look out the window, you might as well wave and holler howdy."

Estelle was having her own problems with a piece of wire that was curled around her ankle like a snake. "Then stop gabbling, Mrs. Livingston-I-Presume. I don't see why we didn't just give him a dollar like we did this morning and go stand by the fence. I may have been the one that said we could creep around to the barn, but I'd forgotten how ornery his yard is. Ouch!"

Ruby Bee grabbed Estelle's wrist and hauled her around the corner of the shack. They picked their way through more debris and finally slipped into the barn, where the rankness was enough to make them gag. Once their eyes had adjusted to the diminished light, they found convenient knotholes and assessed the scene.

"Who's that white-skinned man?" Estelle said softly. "He looks like one of those Albanians."

"The word is 'albino,' and he ain't one. He's a male secretary."

"I've never heard of such a thing."

Ruby Bee moved a ladder aside and tried a bigger knothole. "Well, now you have. He works for Dr. Sageman, who's written a bunch of books about flying saucers and how the aliens kidnap unsuspecting folks and perform unnatural acts on them. His name's Brian, and he said he'd get me an auto-graphed copy of one of the books." She allowed Estelle a little time to be impressed, then added, "See that woman talking to Dahlia? Dr. Sageman has written at least three books about her experi-ences being poked and probed by little gray men."

"She looks fine to me."

"Of course she does, Estelle. It happened a long time ago, and she'd forgotten all about it. Dr. Sageman had to hypnotize her so she could remem-ber."

"How did he know to hypnotize her?"

Ruby Bee was trying to come up with a caustic re-ply when the barn door opened with a faint squeak. She pulled Estelle behind a bale of hay, then peered over the top of it. She recognized Lucy Fernclift from her slight stature, but whoever else was there was shielded by the door.

After some murmuring back and forth, Lucy said, "All I can give you is a thousand dollars."

"We'll be here for several days," said a low male voice. "It's too risky to talk now. We can continue the negotiations back at that fleabag motel."

The barn door squeaked once more. Ruby Bee and Estelle looked at each other, then resumed their earlier positions. The phrase "fleabag motel" wasn't sitting real well with one of 'em.

" 'Yes, we'll gather at the river, the beautiful, the beautiful ri . . . ver,' " Brother Verber sang as he slithered and slid along the bank of Boone Creek. He was sorry he'd ever bought the boots, much less put them on and left his shoes in the rectory. They were so caked with mud that each step was requiring something of a minor miracle. He'd dropped his flashlight so many times he'd lost count. The pith helmet was about as useless as a one-horned cow, but it made him feel like he was on a safari in some foreign country where the jungle was filled with tigers and godless cannibals. If he hadn't been so sure that the Good Lord had blessed the mission, he'd have been a mite crumpy about what was turning into an exhausting ordeal.

The Good Lord hadn't been picky about which way to go, and upstream had seemed easier on account of the pastures alongside the creek. Brother Verber knew he wasn't gonna chance upon any fornication in those stretches, but he also knew he'd appreciate an occasional respite from the mud and mossy rocks and the alarmin' possibility that he might step on a water moccasin. He mouthed a prayer of gratitude to the Good Lord for throwing in some free moonlight.

After a time he sat down on a handy stump, blotted his face and neck, and took the flask of sacramental wine from his pocket. He was disappointed when the last mouthful trickled down his throat, and he spent awhile wondering if he should fill the flask with creek water and hope for something of a major miracle.

It didn't seem likely, he decided with a morose sigh. The thing to do was . . . why, it was to get back to business and follow the creek to the north end of town. He could scramble up to the road by the Esso station, secure in knowing he'd saved young souls from eternal damnation (for the night anyhow), and walk over to Raz Buchanon's shack to purchase a jar of sacramental moonshine. After all, some of the ol' boys called it kill-devil, and that was the exact reason Brother Verber had been put on this earth. It was an amazing coincidence.

He brushed off the seat of his pants, replaced the flask in his pocket, and turned on the flashlight. He couldn't quite recollect the second line of the hymn, so he hummed the tune as he set off with a renewed spirit.

"You had their baby?" gasped Dahlia, her chins quivering in astonishment. She had to grab the fence post to steady herself as the words slowly filtered into her head. "I read something jest this past week about an alien baby, but I don't recall the details. What did it look like? Was it all green and covered with scales?"

Rosemary Tant shook her head sorrowfully. "I never saw the little thing."

"You dint?"

"No, it was taken from me. I was so young, a mere girl of sixteen, but I felt an enormous emptiness that tormented me for more than forty years. Only with the help of Arthur—Dr. Sageman, that is—was I able to allow the memories to surface and come to grips with them."

Dahlia's eyes were getting wider than the moon, and her voice was hardly more than a croak. "When Malta May Buchanon had a baby, the social worker woman took it away on account of Malta May insisting it was Elvis's love child when ever'body knew it was her pa's. Did the social worker woman take away your baby, too?"

"At least I should have been allowed to see it. I never even knew I was pregnant."

"You dint?"

"It must have been the sixth or seventh time they'd abducted me that I was implanted with their sperm. It was horrible, lying there paralyzed on a cold metal table, watching them as they brandished their vile instruments. I wanted to scream, but they always did something that left me unable to speak. Oh, how they chirped among themselves as they forced apart my legs and—"

"Excuse me, Rosemary," said an unfamiliar man. "If you don't object, Arthur would like to put you in a light trance to determine if you have any unconscious premonitions of a manifestation."

"Of course, Brian." Rosemary gave Dahlia a watery smile as she went over to the group by the fence.

Dahlia was standing there, as confounded as she'd ever been, when another stranger, this time a woman, came up to her and said, "Are you an abductee?"

"A what?"

"An abductee," the woman repeated carefully. "I've read about Rosemary Tant's experiences, and when I saw her talking to you so intently, I wondered if you were also a patient of Dr. Sageman."

"Are you asking me if I was kidnapped by aliens and raped in their flying saucer?" Dahlia said, her face wrinkling up like a pitted prune as she tried to follow along. "Me?"

"I can understand if you prefer not to talk about it. I'm Lucy Fernclift, a reporter from the *Probe*. Should you change your mind, I'd like to interview you. My editor wants some human-interest stories to run in the same issue with the story about the crop circles."

"You're a reporter, and you want to write a story about me and put it in the *Probe*?"

Lucy was beginning to regret she'd approached this bovine creature, but she needed to conduct interviews or at least schedule them. "I'm staying at the Flamingo Motel for a few days. Think it over and give me a call if you're interested. We can pay two hundred dollars for the story and another fifty if you allow us to take photographs."

Dahlia was still working on the arithmetic when a boom rocked the valley. The next second the reporter was grabbing at her camera and the folks by the fence were going wild.

Most of what was babbled involved the proximity of the flying saucer and the possibility that they were all going to die right then and there in Raz Buchanon's yard. The McIlhaneys were hightailing it around the corner of the shack. Mrs. Jim Bob was hot on their heels, her navy raincoat flapping like a cape. Elsie McMay was hanging on to Eula Lemoy's arm, and both of them were shrieking about heart attacks and ambulances.

"Over there!" barked Arthur Sageman, pointing at the field as Brian snapped photographs. "Beyond the crop circles!"

Dahlia went over to the fence and squinted in the direction he was pointing. Way back in the brush was a beam of light that was bobbling every which way. She was about to say it looked like a flashlight when a bearded man shoved her aside and started clicking his camera like there was no tomorrow. About the time she got her balance, the woman from the *Probe* liked to knock her down from one side and the man with the curly hair from the other.

Deciding it might be wise to move away from the

fence, Dahlia began a retreat and bumped square into Ruby Bee and Estelle. She expected them to chew her out, but they went on around her and started pointing at the light and jabbering like jaybirds.

"I see a figure!" shouted somebody.

"With a saucer-shaped head!" shouted somebody else.

"Shimmering white skin!"

"Did anyone see the craft land?"

Suddenly the light vanished, although this hardly shut up all the folks lined up at the fence. The man with the silver hair ordered his assistant to climb through the fence and run down the hillside. Some of the others followed suit, stumbling into one another and sprawling out head-long into the corn.

"Well, I swear," said Ruby Bee, who'd opted to stay right where she was, thank you very much. "Look right up there, Estelle. There's a blinking light, and it's going real fast. You think—"

"It sure is zipping away," Estelle said thoughtfully. "It could be going a thousand miles an hour, maybe more."

Dahlia finally spotted what they were talking about. There was a light, all right, blinking and everything. She dint know how they could tell how fast it was going, but they seemed real certain. Then a most terrible realization liked to slap her silly: Sure as God made little green apples she'd seen this light before.

Her blood turned cold, and her mouth dried up like someone had stuffed cotton in it. She was what that reporter had said. It took her a minute to come up with the word, but when she did, there was something deep inside her that fluttered like a duck. She, Dahlia née O'Neill Buchanon, was an abductee.

Was she having their baby?

FIVE

◆

"Where were you last night?" Ruby Bee demanded as she burst into the PD. Her face was flushed, but I wasn't alarmed. Everything and everybody in town had turned downright weird these last two days. Only in Maggody can the abnormal so quickly become the norm. "I must have called here and over at your apartment two dozen times!" she continued shrilly, looming over my desk to jab her finger at the insidious red light. "Look at that infernal answering machine of yours! It's blinking so hard it's liable to explode."

"I went to a movie in Farberville last night. I haven't gotten around to listening to you complain about how much you dislike talking to my answering machine. Has it ever occurred to you that you can just hang up and—"

"Don't start mouthing off at me, missy. I came all the way over here to tell you about the alien that landed by Raz Buchanon's field last night, but I can see you're a sight too busy reading a tabloid to pay any attention to the very woman who walked the floor with you night and day for five months on account of colic and—"

"Okay!" I put the *Weekly Examiner* in the bottom drawer, rocked back in my chair, and arranged my feet on the corner of the desk. "Go ahead and tell me all about the alien. Maybe I'll write up a report and send it over to Harve Dorfer so he'll have fresh reading material for the john. It might come in handy if they run short of toilet paper."

Her jaw flapped for a while, but she finally got hold of herself and sat down in the chair across from me. "If you make one more wisecrack, you're gonna find yourself eating canned soup for a month of Sundays."

"So tell me," I said meekly. Five minutes later, after she'd run out of hyperbole, I said, "Let me get this straight: You and other witnesses heard a bang across the creek, then saw a light and something white and shiny. Afterward you saw another light receding in the sky. Does that sum it up?" There may have been a sarcastic tinge to my voice, but I was keeping a remarkably straight face, all things considered. Canned soup was one of them.

"Ain't you gonna go investigate before folks start trampling on the evidence?"

"Investigate what? You just said these mysterious lights vanished."

Ruby Bee stood up. "You just trot yourself down to Boone Creek and have a look. I suggest you do it before you show up at the bar and grill to beg for a free lunch. The special today is meat loaf and fried okra."

I was still gaping at her as she sailed out the door. "Manipulative" was much too mild a word for Ruby Bee, but I couldn't think of one that captured her talent. Besides, we're not real fond of five-syllable words in Maggody. I was still working on it ("dictatorial" had the same syllable count, but "bossy" had promise) when the telephone rang. Secure in the knowledge Ruby Bee was in transit, I picked up the receiver.

What I heard was not heartening. My cornstalk had been examined at the agri department lab at Farber College. Thus far nothing had been found, not even one wee little corn borer or hint of smut. Nobody was giving up yet, but it wasn't likely that I'd end up with a tidy explanation anytime soon.

In the meantime, Maggody had just entertained its very first extraterrestrial. I dutifully listened to the messages on the answering machine, all of which were from Ruby Bee and pretty much incoherent. I then grabbed a notebook and drove out to the north end of town. Both sides of the road were lined with cars and trucks, some familiar and some with out-of-state license plates and bumper stickers extolling exotic locales like Mount Rushmore and Six Flags over Texas. The van from the local television station had appropriated the prime parking place. I left my car behind the old Esso station, scrambled down the slope to the creek, and headed upstream, following the babbling of voices rather than that of the brook.

Damned if they hadn't started the investigation without me. The woman reporter was speaking into the camera, this time sounding like a Methodist minister at a funeral. Beyond her were a good-size number of gawkers constrained by a droopy strip of yellow tape. Ruby Bee was not among them, but Estelle was relating her version of the "dadburn most incredible thing" she'd ever seen in all her born days, even counting the time she went to Noow Yark City. Her audience, which included Jules Channel (whose most recent by-lines were "My Dog Was Sucked Through the Ozone Hole!" and "Ship-wrecked Missionary Ate His Own Liver to Survive!"), appeared to be impressed, although her story seemed pale in comparison to his.

I didn't recognize anyone inside the secured area, but I'd heard enough gossip to have an idea who they were. I brushed past Estelle and stepped over the tape.

"Please don't come any further!" snapped a young blond man. "We must protect the sanctity of the site."

"The scene of the crime, so to speak?" I said as I let him have a clear view of my badge. "It seems to me that'd be my job. I'm Chief of Police Arly Hanks."

"I'm Brian Quint. The gentleman over there is Arthur Sageman, director of the ETH Research Foundation in California. Dr. Sageman is the world's foremost authority on extraterrestrial encounters."

I spotted a silver-haired man on his knees near the edge of the water, measuring something with a ruler. His mouth was pursed with concentration, and his eyebrows were racing back and forth like copulating caterpillars. "Is that so?" I drawled. "How convenient that he happened to be in town in time for our very first visitor from outer space."

"We came yesterday because of the crop circle configurations. Dr. Sageman is convinced they're the result of alien interaction."

"Aliens are interacting with Maggody, Arkansas?" I said as I searched Brian Quint's eyes for that tattletale glint. His skin was very light and unblemished, his hair so blond it was almost white, his features indistinct. His pale blue eyes seemed innocent enough, but I wasn't ready to make a judgment concerning his lucidity or lack thereof. If nothing else, he was from California. That automatically made him suspect.

Before he could respond, a man with a much more pronounced glint joined us. "I'm Dr. Hayden McMasterson, the director of the Foundation for ITH Research in Taos. I too came to investigate the crop circle configurations. Rest assured that they are not caused by any visitors from outer space, Chief Hanks. The idea is preposterous. Self-proclaimed authorities like Arthur Sageman are so enamored of their pet theories that they are blind to simple physical evidence."

"Good morning, Hayden," Brian said with a sigh.

I blinked at McMasterson. "Exactly what physical evidence are we talking about?"

"Brian!" shouted Sageman. "Mix the plaster so that we can make a cast. This is an excellent footprint, by far the most highly defined."

McMasterson rumbled angrily. "See what I mean? He finds a footprint and assumes it's of extraterrestrial origin. He sees a flattened expanse and a charred circle and starts hypothesizing about the dimensions of the spacecraft. Last night he observed a light in the sky and announced it to be the departure of said craft. It was nothing more than an airplane, naturally. Arthur is overly enamored of his quaint little findings, as well as secretive. Had he shared the name of his witness when he reinvestigated the Roswell incident, I could have told him she was a nut. Arthur has even lied in order to conceal evidence from his fellow investigators."

I wondered if I'd been wrong about the glint, even though he had a ponytail and was wearing a turtle neck sweater and a gold earring in his left ear. "When I heard about all this," I said, "I presumed there'd be some logical explanations. My only witness is on the excitable side, and her credibility's not worth a plug nickel."

"Let me give you my card," he said with a warm smile, stopping short of patting me on the head but coming dangerously close to it. I do not care to be mistaken for a sheepdog. "I can see you're a sensible young woman. The others are prone to hysteria, and the level of suggestibility last night was higher than the maligned airplane. It's encouraging to know that we won't be having any premature statements from the authorities."

I tucked his card in my back pocket and went over to the edge of the creek, where a huddle had formed. Brian was stirring a batch of plaster in a plastic pail. Two women were hovering nearby. One gave me a frown; the other waggled her fingers and giggled. I surmised they were the women from Little Rock.

"It's eighteen and one-half inches in length," Sageman intoned as if he were measuring the Ark of the Covenant, "and almost five inches at the widest point. The treadmarks are bizarre and unlike anything I've ever seen."

I peered over his shoulder at the footprint. There was no doubt that it was large; I could have put both of my feet in it. The treadmarks looked ordinary, but I was hardly an expert in that field. "Dr. Sageman," I said, "I'm Arly Hanks, the—"

"Brian, is the plaster beginning to set? There are rain clouds approaching, and it is vital to preserve the evidence for further study. Cynthia, do you have an adequate number of photographs of all pertinent manifestations?"

"The chief of police, Dr. Sageman," I continued with only the faintest exasperation in my voice.

"The town council promised that all the evidence discovered within the city limits belongs to me. Most of the time it's dog poop or broken glass, but it's still mine and mine alone. Furthermore—"

He glanced up, clearly annoyed at my persistence. "Yes, but you have no experience in what well may become classified as a close encounter of the second kind. That's defined as detailed observation without actual contact. You're not equipped to deal with an extraterrestrial biological entity, are you?"

I wanted to tell him that all the years spent with the Buchanon clan had equipped me to deal with the whole gamut of biological entities, but the crowd was straining against the tape, and the television camera was aimed in our direction. Grumbling, I stepped aside and waited until Brian made a plaster cast of the footprint. "Okay, Dr, Sageman," I said, trying once again to be civil, "the evidence is preserved. If you don't mind, I'd like to—"

He stood up and spoke to the whirring camera. "I believe that we have categorical proof of alien interaction in this location. The list of witnesses to last night's encounter continues to grow as we conduct individual interviews. Within a matter of hours I shall be in a position to make a statement as to the validity of the incident."

"We'll have an update at six and again at ten," said the reporter. "And cut. Can we count on you to come to the studio tomorrow afternoon, Dr. Sageman? I'd like to do in-depth interviews with you and Dr. McMasterson, say, three minutes each, and then allow the two of you to exchange opinions regarding the possibility that an alien was at this spot last night."

Sageman pointed a trembling finger at McMasterson. "Under no circumstances will I participate in an exchange with this euhemeristic pseudo-intellectual who relies on psychosociological gibberish to discredit those of us—"

McMasterson bristled to the tip of his ponytail. "No more than I would deign to appear on any show with this pontificating, underhanded, dishonorable—"

"How dare you!" roared Sageman as he flung himself across the gravel bar and began to choke the living daylights out of McMasterson. The victim responded with kidney punches and a string of expletives unfamiliar to most of his audience. They careened around the gravel bar in a grotesque dance, annihilating the footprint as well as any reservations I had concerning their sanity.

It took awhile, but eventually Brian, the cameraman, and I pulled the combatants apart.

I stepped between them. "Listen up, I don't care if you two decide to meet at dawn with pistols, but you are not going to pull this shit while you're on my turf. You don't have to kiss and make up or even shake hands. However, I can run you into the county jail for disorderly conduct, and you'll find yourselves in a lot less cultivated company until the judge shows up Monday morning. Do we all understand?"

Sageman and McMasterson stalked away in opposite directions. The reporter and cameraman left, as did the majority of the crowd. Once I'd decided the two men were under control for the time being, I went over to Jules Channel, who was sitting on a log with his notebook on his knee and a distinctly amused expression on his face. If I hadn't been such a trusting soul, I might have wondered if he'd enjoyed the fracas.

I sat down beside him and rubbed my throbbing shin. "For a minute there, I thought I was going to be filing homicide charges."

"A close encounter of the worst kind, I'm afraid. There's long-standing animosity between them, and your threat of incarceration won't keep them apart indefinitely. Sageman's the leading proponent of the ETH movement, and McMasterson of the ITH. Both schools are locked in intergalactic combat to dominate conferences, sell books, and get slots on the talk shows. There's a lot of money at stake, a lot more than you imagine."

"There is?"

"Yes, indeed. One author who claims to have proof that aliens shared technology with the Mayans has more than thirty-six million books in print. Another made a fortune via Hollywood and now is the CEO of a heavily endowed research facility that collects data from so-called abductees. Sageman's a silverback with fourteen books. McMasterson's hot on his heels with a dozen. Royalties start to add up if you can command the public's fickle interest."

"But why are they here?" I asked in what may have been a rather pathetic bleat. "This town's not even a flyspeck on most maps—and for a good reason. Wouldn't they get better media coverage elsewhere?"

"There hasn't been a really hot incident since the uproar in Gulf Breeze, Florida, when some spoilsport examined the photographs more carefully and noticed the wires holding up what he described as pie pans. Without a moment's hesitation, Sageman claimed the photographs had been doctored by a top secret government agency in order to discredit the incident, while McMasterson chortled and made snide remarks to every reporter he could corner. The tabloids were ecstatic, of course, but the major networks and less imaginative publications failed to appreciate the drama."

I was shaking my head when the reporter from the *Probe* sat down on the other end of the log. "Hi," she breathed at me, then casually tried to take a peek at Jules's notebook. "Do they behave like that often?" she asked him.

He closed his notebook. "Every chance they get. I was just telling Chief Hanks—"

"Arly," I said.

"I was just telling Arly about the financial realities of the business. Whatever took place down here last night will be blown completely out of proportion, courtesy of the two of us, the local television station, and whatever other media McMasterson and Sageman can lure in. I wouldn't be surprised if both of them haven't started outlining their versions of 'Martians in Maggody' or whatever idiotic titles they come up with."

"Come on," I said with a shaky laugh, "the only thing that happened last night was that someone with large feet stomped around in the mud, waving a flashlight. The explosion was most likely a truck backfiring up there on the bridge. The light in the sky was an airplane."

Lucy Fernclift blinked at me. "Gosh, I hope there's more to it. First thing this morning I went into Farberville and faxed the story to my editor. It's the first very really big one I've sent."

"So did I," Jules said comfortingly. "What neither of us will do is ever repudiate our initial accounts of the event. Our readers don't want to hear about trucks backfiring and flashlights waving, and we love them too much to let them down—right?"

"I don't agree," she said. "If nothing really happened, we should say so. People who get carried away with accounts of aliens and abductions can end up dangerously unbalanced. We don't pass out crack to drug users. Isn't an obsession with UFOs as dangerous an addiction?"

Jules looked at her as though she'd developed a third eye. "Didn't I see your by-line on the story about the fisherman who sliced open a shark and found a live human baby in its belly?"

"That was different," she mumbled.

I left them to ponder the ethical perplexities and stepped back over the tape. There was a roughly rectangular area of weeds that had been squashed, but with none of the symmetry and finesse of Raz's crop circles in the field across the creek. After prowling around for a few minutes, I found a spot where a few weeds had been blackened.

And that was it for Sageman's "categorical proof." As I hiked back to the car, I debated whether or not to write up a report. I finally decided to concentrate my energies on meat loaf and let Harve find out the details on the nightly news.

Mrs. Jim Bob was getting fed up with Brother Verber's unresponsiveness, but she couldn't come out and say so without sounding hardhearted. He was as gray and limp as a dishrag, and he'd nodded off more than once since she'd arrived at the rectory. Each time she'd raised her voice to remind him of her presence, he'd acted like somebody poked him with a sharp stick. Having to repeat half of everything she said was annoying, too. She almost felt like she was talking to Adele Wockerman, who couldn't be trusted not to turn off her hearing aid when she felt cantankerous.

"There's something going on that smacks of evil," she said, smacking him on the knee with her Bible in case he was drifting off again. "In the past we've had to confront promiscuity, drunkenness, blasphemy, pornography, and feminists. We did it because it was our duty as virtuous Christians." She smacked him again. "We can't just sit back and allow this business to go on without making sure it's not Satan's handiwork."

Brother Verber thumped the side of his head. "Say what, Sister Barbara?"

"Satan's handiwork!" she shouted into his ear. "I already told you what I saw with my own eyes last night in Raz's cornfield. If aliens are gonna start showing up in town, we have to devise a plan to convert them to Christianity before they have a chance to perform their heathen rituals. We can't allow impressionable teenagers to be led astray."

"Bed away?"

"Led astray! I just don't understand what's wrong with you, Brother Verber. Here we are facing a crisis, and you can't be bothered to listen carefully." She pursed her lips briefly as a disloyal idea flashed across her mind. "I do hope you haven't been sampling any of Raz Buchanon's moonshine, especially after all the praying we did last time to cleanse your soul and get you back on the path of righteousness."

Brother Verber battled back a bout of nausea and tried to think. At some time last night he'd thought about stopping by Raz's place, but he didn't recall actually doing it—or what it was he'd gathered by the river. He wasn't all that sure what he'd been doing there in the first place. No one had been baptized in Boone Creek for years; the water moccasins distracted the choir. He realized she was waiting and in an offended voice said, "I promised the Lord I'd never touch a drop of moonshine again. I was lost, but now I'm back on the path that leads right up to the pearly gates. Why, I can almost see St. Peter hisself, waiting to whisk me inside and get me settled for all eternity."

Instead of rewarding him with a nod of approval, she took out a piece of paper and a pencil. "The first thing we should do is present them with pamphlets that tell all about the joy of salvation and the perils of damnation. The ones that show interest can be invited to a special Sunday evening service. This is when you'll have to take over, Brother Verber. These aliens need personal counseling to be guided right up to the baptismal font, and you're the logical one to provide it."

"You want me to counsel aliens?" he said, so startled a muted belch slipped out.

"You are our spiritual leader, aren't you? Why don't you put together a study plan and I'll look at it later this afternoon? I should think the best approach is a mixture of prayer, Bible stories, and soul-cleansing confessions." She thrust the paper in his hand. "Here's a list. I need to run along and have a word with Perkins's eldest about dusting the baseboards."

Brother Verber was gazing at the list as the door of the rectory closed. The words were blurry and hard to make out, but he figured he'd be in trouble if he didn't figure out how to offer salvation to heathen aliens. He tried to imagine what it'd be like kneeling next to a slimy purple creature with things

sticking out of his head. The picture was so awful
that he hurried to the bathroom and wrapped his
arms around the commode. He made it just in time.

Darla Jean came into the kitchen and dropped the
laundry basket. "I'll fold the sheets and towels
later," she said to her mother, who was studying a
recipe card. "I'm supposed to meet Heather and
Gracie at the Dairee Dee-Lishus."

"Are you sure you're not meeting that Pellitory
boy?"

Surprised that her mother had even heard her,
Darla Jean flinched. "I just told you that I'm
meeting Heather and Gracie. Are you accusing me
of lying?"

"I happened to run into someone who saw you
riding around with him last night."

"So?"

"So you weren't listening to music at Heather's
house, young lady. That Pellitory boy has a bad reputation, as you know perfectly well. His family
doesn't even go to church, and that oldest boy is
doing time at the state prison for stealing cars. I
wouldn't be surprised if Reggie joins him long before graduation."

"We just rode around for maybe an hour."

"Your pa wants to have a word with you when he
gets home this evening. If I was you, I wouldn't
make any plans for after supper, not even with
Heather and Gracie." Millicent put down the card
and opened a cabinet. "Did you put the sugar back
where it belongs?"

Darla Jean didn't answer, not out of disrespect but
because she was running upstairs to her room.

* * *

Dahlia popped a cookie in her mouth as she turned the page of *Rosemary T. and the Extrinsic Paradox*. Most of it was hard to follow, what with all the words so long they liked to run off the page. Rosemary had warned her about them when she'd loaned Dahlia the book, even admitting she couldn't understand some of 'em herself.

The story was plain enough, though. Rosemary had been in high school, taking piano lessons on Saturday mornings and working every evening at her pa's grocery store. According to the photograph, she'd been a mousy little thing with braces on her teeth and plenty of acne.

Then one night she was walking home all by herself when a beam of light trapped her and carried her into the sky.

Dahlia couldn't help breathing hard as she read the account of what the aliens did on the cold metal table. By the time she finished the chapter, her hand was shaking so hard she nearly spilled her orange soda. The aliens had erased every bit of Rosemary's memories about the gawd-awful ordeal before they set her back on the sidewalk. The only reason Rosemary had ever suspected anything was that she'd gotten in bad trouble when she arrived home at midnight and couldn't explain why she was so late. Two hours of her life had disappeared right out from under her.

Dahlia tried to think if she herself had ever experienced a blackout. There were plenty of times when things were murky, especially when she and Kevvie had been making deliriously passionate love. But if she'd been beamed out of bed, it seemed like he would have said something when she got back or at least the next morning while she gave him his breakfast.

The terrifying thing was that the light in the sky had been so familiar. She figured her memories had been erased just like Rosemary's, and seeing the light was sort of like a nudge from the past. Her mind made up, Dahlia crumpled the can and tossed it with the others. The only way to unlock the secrets was to beg Dr. Sageman to hypnotize her.

I was too miffed at Ruby Bee to go to the bar and grill for supper. After I'd turned off the coffeepot in the back room and made sure the doors were locked so Bigfoot couldn't steal my radar gun, I tucked the tabloid under my arm and headed for my apartment, where I would heat a can of soup just to show her I was unwilling to be manipulated. It might have been interesting to listen to the crackpots debating the merits of the incident, but I had my pride.

I was so busy congratulating myself that I crashed into Jules Channel, who was standing in the road and therefore in peril of being clipped by a chicken truck.

"Look at that," he said before I could offer an apology or a word about pedestrian discretion. He pointed at the inky silhouette of Cotter's Ridge.

Being a professional, I grabbed his arm and pulled him to a safer place. "Look at what?"

"Just above the tree line."

I found myself looking at three glowing orange globes. I didn't have any idea how far away they were, so it was impossible to estimate their size. "They look like pumpkins, don't they?" I said. "What do you think they really are?"

"I have no idea. They don't appear to be moving."

"No," I admitted, "but that doesn't prove anything. Could they be helicopters of some sort? The sheriff borrows one from the National Guard every now and then to search for marijuana fields in the national forest. I don't know why they'd be hanging over the ridge in the dark, unless they're being used for a training operation. The Farberville airport's not too far."

"I've never seen a helicopter with an orange light," said Jules, sounding unconvinced. He might have been planning to elaborate when the lights vanished as if they were targets in a shooting gallery.

Two seconds later I heard the telephone ringing inside the PD.

SIX

◆

"I don't know, Harve," I wailed into the receiver, barely—but just—resisting the urge to hammer my heels on the corner of the desk to underscore my frustration (which was on par with your basic two-year-old's in a grocery store checkout line). "From listening to people, you'd think Orson Welles had presented a broadcast about killer metallic spiders from Mars. Ruby Bee and Estelle are calling me every other minute for an update. The two tabloid reporters finally gave up pounding on the PD door and went away, but only as far as Raz's cabin, where they're taking pictures of him and Marjorie. Traffic's a gawd-awful mess and getting worse. Jim Bob set up a roadside stand at the edge of his parking lot to peddle box lunches and maps to Raz's place. Brother Verber's passing out flyers that invite all aliens to the Sunday evening service and potluck supper at the Assembly Hall. Some of the teenagers are driving around town with green faces and purple hair."

"So explain these orange lights and everything will simmer down."

"I can't explain these orange lights, you jackass! They glowed, and they disappeared. I called the National Guard headquarters this morning. They swore they didn't have any helicopters out last night, but the military has been known to lie. I have a call in to a meteorologist at one of the Little Rock television stations on the off chance there may have been some unusual atmospheric activity. Can you find out if some nearby air force base is testing a secret weapon in"—I couldn't prevent myself from rolling my eyes—"Stump County?"

"There aren't any nearby air force bases. Maybe you ought to consider the possibility that they qualify as UFOs. The term means 'unidentified flying objects,' doesn't it? You got to admit you haven't identified 'em."

I was not in the mood for his pretentious logic. "Do you want these sightings to be the result of visits by little green men, Harve? Well, you're more than welcome to them. I'll send over a report and let you take the center stage when the media descend like wolves. I'm not sure what effect this may have on your chances in the next election, but—"

"Like you said, all you've got are some lights," Harve said soothingly. "It's a damn shame the tabloid reporters are in town, but this doesn't mean either of us has to pander to them. Let them make up their stories. Keep refusing to comment."

I carried the telephone with me as I went to the back room of the PD and poured a cup of coffee. This was a morning that required serious caffeine. "They glibly interpret a refusal to comment as a refusal to deny the more sensational details. I'm damned if I do and damned if I don't, and I'm damned unhappy about my options. All I want is a prosaic explanation for the crop circles and the odd lights we've been seeing."

Harve chuckled. "Don't forget the third cattle mutilation in the last month. Want the particulars?"

"I want to be beamed up," I said, then banged down the receiver. Okay, I told myself, some peculiar things had happened, but taken out of context, they didn't add up to diddly-squat. Footprints in the mud. Lights in the sky. Squashed cornstalks. Things that went bang in the dark. Big friggin' deal—all of it. I almost wished I were back in Manhattan, where aberrance was a predictable element of each day's agenda.

On the basis of the number of messages on my answering machine, the orange globes hadn't been missed by more than a handful of local residents. To add to my distress, I was the most credible witness thus far—and I couldn't deny that I'd seen them (unless I was willing to lie like a Pentagon spokesperson, which I was). I'd been sober and skeptical, two attributes lacking in many of the gabbled reports. A widow out on Finger Lane had called to announce she had a dozen globes, all crazed with lust, locked in her basement, and Buckminster Buchanon swore he'd found one in his granddaughter's bedroom. For some oddball reasons, there seemed to be something Freudian about pumpkins.

Maybe it was time to talk to the experts, I thought without enthusiasm. Arthur Sageman was supposed to be a hotshot in such matters, and Hayden McMasterson had implied he could explain away the paranormal in cozy, comforting terms. Jules Channel was roaming around town, but I wasn't sure I wanted another dose of his asperity until I had a reasonable idea or two. Lucy Fernclift seemed more perturbed than insightful.

I walked down the road to Ruby Bee's Bar &

Grill. Arthur Sageman and his contingent were noticeably absent from the group gathered in the bar, but Hayden McMasterson was not. I was disappointed when I came across the dance floor and heard him say, "So there is proof that aliens are present, and have been since the time of the upheavals in the Earth's crust that dragged the lost continent of Atlantis beneath the sea. These upheavals were the result of a shift in the Earth's electromagnetic field because iron is an important element in the composition of the tectonic plates."

Estelle snorted. "Are you saying there are aliens living under the sea?"

"That is the basis of the intraterrestrial hypothesis," he said, graciously gesturing for me to join his impromptu seminar. "As I told Chief Hanks yesterday, ufologists like Sageman are obsessed with the idea that aliens have crossed incomprehensibly vast distances in order to toy with our primitive civilization. They want you to accept that a highly advanced civilization with the technology to supersede the speed of light has chosen to make contact with drunken fishermen in Mississippi and sheep farmers in New Mexico, as opposed to the salient figures of authority like the President of the United States."

"Maybe they're Republicans," Ruby Bee said as she came whipping through the kitchen doors, steamy plates in her hands and her expression guileless. This resulted in much guffawing from the rednecks perched on stools along the bar, most likely because it was the first remark they'd been able to understand in several minutes. I bit back a smile and leaned over the bar to get myself a glass of beer. From within the kitchen I could smell the intoxicating aromas of fried pork chops, biscuits, and apple pie. My animal instincts, if not my expectations, had been right on the button.

Hayden waited grimly until things settled down. "Then allow me to ask you some questions, madam. How can vehicles that have traveled through a continuum of time and space subsequently crash without viable cause? Why would these aliens act as if they're afraid of us? What could they possibly hope to learn from us—when we've traveled no farther than our own moon and failed to find a cure for the common cold?"

"Could be they're after Ruby Bee's recipe for peach cobbler," suggested a scruffy man in overalls and a Red Man cap. Again, this was well received, and I could see Hayden McMasterson's blood pressure creeping upward.

Estelle waved her hand. "I do believe I'm still waiting to hear about these aliens that live under the sea. Are you saying they're responsible for the crop circles?"

"As I explained in *The Vanquished Dynasty,* aliens have been here since the first seeds of life were sown in the Garden of Eden by a superior race. The Star People now reside beneath the crust but sometimes venture among us. They realize we are not sufficiently evolved to interact with them, so they assume our approximate density and shape."

Dahlia Buchanon, who was sitting in the back booth, came close to emptying the joint with a strangled yelp. After everybody'd resumed his or her seat and stopped hyperventilating, she said with great intensity, "And they look just like real people?"

Hayden squinted at her. "Yes, but they are here to help us as we approach the crossroads of total annihilation or an evolutionary leap. Rather than burst into our reality and cause us acute psychological trauma, they have been making known their presence in small yet increasingly complex phases. The crop circles, for instance, may be their way of communicating with us."

"Those three circles? What'd they mean?" demanded Dahlia. Even though her face was shadowy, her round white eyes were visible.

"I'm here to attempt to interpret their message," he replied smoothly. "Sageman wants fragmentary physical evidence that he can distort into a thesis for his next book. I want to tell the truth."

I didn't much care for the expressions on the faces of those staring at him. There was way too much wonder and not nearly enough incredulity. If I didn't come up with some rational explanations before too long, most of the town would have lifetime subscriptions to the tabloids and be worrying about the odds that Elvis might drop by some evening at suppertime.

Before I could decide where to begin my attack on his preposterous theory, the plot thickened. Sageman and the two women from Little Rock came into the bar and grill and froze as they recognized Hayden. Seconds later Jules Channel and Lucy Ferncliff entered and went through the same routine. On their heels was Brian Quint, although he evinced minimal surprise at seeing Hayden and a great deal of distress at seeing the two tabloid reporters standing together. It almost looked as though we had a *ménage à sept* in the making, although I was reluctant to predict the specific couplings.

I took a swallow of beer and waited to see what any of them would do next. Ruby Bee's sudden intake of breath was hard to miss. The scruffy fellow stuck his nose in the scalloped potatoes. Estelle eased off the stool and edged toward the ladies' room, where I supposed she thought she'd be safe if a barroom brawl broke out.

"Oh, Dr. Sageman," Dahlia said, her voice hiccupy with anxiety, "I was hoping you'd show up sooner or later. Please won't you hypnotize me? I was abducted by the aliens, and I have proof I'm having their baby!" She began to howl in a manner that rivaled the fabled banshees.

The tension dissipated. It was the first time I could remember that I'd ever been grateful to Dahlia. I was pretty sure it'd be the last.

"Five dollars iffen you want to take a look," Raz repeated to each person straggling up the hill, "and fifteen to take pictures." By now he had so many jars filled with dollar bills that he dint know what he was gonna do. He also had promises from the two tabloid reporters that he and Marjorie would have their picture on the front covers. The first thing he'd do was have 'em framed and hang 'em in the front room. Visitin' kinfolk would be flabbergasted, and rightly so.

And it was all on account of three circles down in the cornfield. It was almost as rib-ticklin' as the time his cousin Cootie Buchanon had been caught crossing the state line with two cases of hooch in the bed of the truck and a goat named Evangeline sitting beside him in the cab. Marjorie was particularly fond of that story.

Arthur Sageman chortled as they drove back to Maggody. "I certainly nonplussed McMasterson when I identified the underlying fallacy of his theory, didn't I? I could tell the interviewer was impressed, and poor old McMasterson looked as though I'd hailed on his parade. A fine moment for the ETH movement, wouldn't you say?"

Brian dutifully agreed as he pulled into the parking lot of the Flamingo Motel. He wasn't sure Arthur's disposition would remain so gleeful after he saw the segment on the news, in that all six minutes consisted of sputters of outrage, puerile insults, and, toward the end, bodily assault. The interviewer had looked more appalled than anything else, but she'd promised to try to get in touch with the production office of *Strange Stories* since her station was an affiliate.

Arthur adjusted the rearview mirror in order to smooth down his hair. "I'd planned to spend the evening working on my Houston speech. However, Rosemary is running out of abduction stories, and there's something oddly promising about this local girl with her droopy eyes and aura of repressed sexual frustration. It's challenging to envision someone of her magnitude being swept up in a beam of light, but I've never been one to doubt the efficacy of a superior civilization."

Brian cut off the engine and, while Arthur continued to fuss with his hair, knocked on Cynthia's door. She and Rosemary came outside.

Arthur climbed out of the car and said, "I shall work in my room the remainder of the afternoon. Later Brian and I will go to the spot next to the creek where the craft landed last night so that I can supervise the placement of the equipment. Cynthia, you'll need to follow us in Rosemary's car in order to bring me back here. We'll leave as soon as my interview has been shown on the local news."

Cynthia gave him a surprised look. "You're not staying? I would have thought you'd want to be there in case our extraterrestrial friends return. You're the person most qualified to welcome them to our planet. Surely even those from the far reaches of the universe are familiar with your reputation, Arthur."

"Oh, they are," Rosemary added, hopping up and down like an anemic cheerleader. "They questioned me about you, wanting to know if you were sincere in your belief that they come to us in a spirit of harmony and love. I assured them that you were."

Arthur attempted a modest laugh. "Of course I am, Rosemary, but I feel it's more important to do what I can to help that poor, tortured girl. Besides, it may not be the right time to experience a close encounter of the third kind with this unknown race. The fact that they caused the explosion last night might imply they're—"

"Hostile," murmured Brian, "or dangerous?"

"Neither hostile nor dangerous," Arthur said sharply, wishing he sounded bolder and more confident. "In *Communications with the Universal Community,* I made a very compelling argument that the extraterrestrials are unresolved how best to initiate contact until they've completed an extensive psychological profile of our species via abductions. Brian will make a perfect emissary, and I can better serve our cause by finding out if the girl has had previous interactions in this locale. If she has, it will give us insights into the incidents."

"She's very excited," said Rosemary. "She went home to take a nap in preparation for the session. Should I call her to set a time?"

Refusing to acknowledge the awakening gleam of

cynicism in Cynthia's eyes, Arthur began to issue orders. "Yes, tell her to be here at eight o'clock sharp. I suspect she'll feel more comfortable if you're present to offer encouragement. Cynthia, we'll need to use your room since mine is cluttered with important papers, all the computer equipment, files, notes, and so forth. Brian, see if you can buy extra videocassettes at that supermarket across the road. Should anything of an anomalous nature take place tonight, we must have documentation." He patted his now-perfect hair. "I have an idea tonight is going to be filled with adventure, don't you?"

Rosemary winked, Cynthia blinked, and Brian nodded.

As I locked the front door of the PD, I noticed Jules and Lucy were deep in conversation with my landlord. Roy was slouched in his favorite cane-bottomed rocking chair out in front of the store, but I could tell that he was agitated and that the tabloid reporters were enthralled with what he was saying. I had a gut feeling he wasn't reciting poetry.

"What's up?" I said as I walked across the road.

Roy took a drink of something I doubted was iced tea, wiped his mouth, and waited until I'd joined them. "I meant to come over earlier and tell you about it, Arly," he said apologetically. "Then some tourists from Connecticut showed up, and I got busy with them. By the time they left with two boxes of depression glass and that repulsive faux marble cherub, I'd plum forgot the whole thing."

"What whole thing?"

"Last night about eleven I was driving back here from the picture show in Farberville. As I went past the Assembly Hall, I happened to glance down

County One-oh-two. There was a funny little light that appeared to be flying all around that pasture between Estelle's and Earl Buchanon's houses. You know where I mean?"

I glanced at Jules and Lucy, who were busy scribbling notes. "Was it orange?" I asked Roy.

He took another drink, then leaned back and closed his eyes. "Nope, it was white. I decided to take a closer look, so I drove down the road a short piece, stopped, and rolled down the window. Before I could get a fix on it, that damn thing came diving straight at me. Somehow I got the window rolled up, but my hands were shaking so hard I liked to never have got my truck in reverse. It chased me all the way back to the road. It's pure luck I didn't run down Estelle's sign or end up in a ditch."

"How big was this light?" asked Lucy.

"It's hard to say. When I first saw it, it was off in the pasture. I don't reckon it was bigger than one of those little penlights, but I can't say for sure because I don't know how close it really was."

"Did it make any sound?" asked Jules.

"I might have heard a buzzing noise, but I wouldn't swear to it. It's hard to recall the particulars when you're backing up a narrow dirt road at thirty miles an hour. My neck's still kinked."

I was getting tired of allowing the reporters to conduct the investigation. "Think back, Roy," I said. "There was heavy fog down on County One-oh-two last night, and things may have looked spooky because of the distortion. Couldn't you have seen a planet or a particularly bright star and convinced yourself it was moving?"

"Sure, Arly, and then I convinced myself it was darting around the truck the whole time I was weaving up the road. I convinced myself it was coming after me like a hornet. After all, I just got off the watermelon truck and I ain't never seen fog."

I took the glass out of his hand and took a swig. "Sorry," I said as I returned it to him, then screwed up my face as the cheap whiskey caught up with me. It was not his usual brand. "It's just that I'm having a hard time with all this crazy stuff."

"I've heard it," he said. "That's all anybody was talking about at the barbershop this morning. But lemme tell you something, Arly: What I saw wasn't one of those mysterious orange lights, any more than it was a star. It was something altogether different."

Jules put his notebook in his pocket and said, "Mr. Stiver, could I talk you into letting me take some pictures of you pointing at the pasture? I can't promise they'll make the *Weekly Examiner,* but if they do, we'll pay you fifty dollars."

"The *Probe* can pay seventy-five," Lucy said valiantly.

Roy emptied his glass and stood up. "I don't think so. If you'll excuse me, I'm gonna lock up and go have a couple of beers at Ruby Bee's. Afterward I reckon I'll spend the evening in my room, listening to Beethoven and drinking the remainder of this whiskey."

I turned around and went back to the PD to write up a report. If an alien had stepped out from behind a building, I'd have shot him/her/it on the spot.

"I thought you'd be busier tonight," Estelle said as she climbed onto her stool and automatically reached for the pretzel basket. "Where is everybody?"

Ruby Bee considered pointing out the sheer stupidity of the question but instead sighed and said, "Over at Raz Buchanon's, of course. After everything that's happened there, I'm surprised the tour buses haven't started rolling in. I hear he's raised the price of admission three times today." She glumly assessed the crowd, which consisted of two young married couples in one booth, some strangers eating supper in another, and Jim Bob, Larry Joe Lambertino, and Roy Stiver working on a pitcher in the far corner. Nobody'd put a quarter in the jukebox for a long while, and the ambiance was about as exciting as a canning demonstration at a 4-H club meeting. "There were a goodly number of folks at happy hour, but when it started getting dark, they all left to go watch for flying saucers and shiny white creatures to come out of the woods."

"Did Arly find out any more about those orange lights everybody saw last night?"

"Nobody at the National Guard or the Farberville airport had any suggestions. She called a weatherman in Little Rock and asked him if they could have been weather balloons or stars, but he didn't think so. If she's talked to anyone else, she hasn't bothered to tell me. She didn't show up for supper, even though I went to the trouble of putting aside a piece of lemon icebox pie especially for her. How's that for gratitude?"

"I watched the local news earlier," Estelle said. She paused to reposition a bobby pin, then made sure the spit curls were evenly spaced across her forehead before continuing. "Dr. Sageman said the lights were alien spaceships similar to some seen in one of those South American countries. Dr. McMasterson said they weren't anything more mysterious than clouds catching the last sunlight from the far side of the ridge. Before the interviewer could spit out a word, they were rolling on the floor like a couple of lady mud wrestlers."

"It's funny the way they act around each other, ain't it? After all, they both believe in aliens. They may disagree on where the aliens come from or how they pop up unexpectedly, but you'd think they could work out something." She was going to expound when she saw Cynthia Dodder enter the barroom. "Come join us," she called.

Cynthia took the stool beside Estelle. "Dr. Sageman has appropriated my motel room for his session. He, Rosemary, and the girl are liable to be there for several hours. I sat in the car for a while, but then it began to grow chilly and I'd left my sweater in the room."

"You poor thing," Ruby Bee said, herself having been the victim of gross ingratitude. "Let me get you some hot coffee and a piece of lemon icebox pie."

Estelle moistened her vermilion lips and tried to figure out how to broach the subject tactfully. She finally gave up and said, "What happens in these sessions, anyway? Does he put Dahlia into a trance by swinging a watch back and forth?"

"Not at all," Cynthia said as she accepted a cup of coffee from Ruby Bee. "I've operated the tape recorder in numerous sessions in the last ten years, particularly those with Rosemary and other members of UFORIA. Dr. Sageman has the subject lie down and relax, then creates a mental image of an elevator ascending within a towering skyscraper. When the subject is sufficiently attuned to the image, the elevator doors open and a scene is revealed."

"Gonna be a problem with Dahlia," Ruby Bee said,

setting down the pie and a fork. "If she's ever been in an elevator, it would have been in Farberville. The tallest building ain't more than four stories. The elevator is gonna burst through the roof real quick."

"Have you ever been hypnotized?" asked Estelle.

Cynthia nodded. "I've explored a dozen of my past lives, including one as a courtesan in the court of Louis the Fourteenth and another as a Viking warrior with a bushy red beard and a propensity for pillaging. That was quite an exciting life, I must say. I was the first mate on the ship that discovered the uncharted continent that came to be known as North America."

Ruby Bee and Estelle exchanged looks, but neither of them knew how to respond to an ordinary-looking woman claiming to have a red beard.

Fortunately Cynthia needed no prompting. "Many of my past lives have been riddled with violence. I crossed the Alps with Hannibal and battled the Spaniards alongside Montezuma. During the Civil War I was a beautiful young spy who was captured and hanged by General Grant's forces. Only recently has my karma become such that I can live in peace and heighten my awareness of cosmic truth."

"We need another pitcher!" Jim Bob shouted.

Ruby Bee was secretly relieved to abandon the conversation and take it to him. "You ever talked to that woman?" she asked as she made change from her apron pocket.

Jim Bob looked over his shoulder. "Over at the SuperSaver a couple of days back. She know anything about all these lights?"

"She hasn't said much."

Larry Joe ran his fingers through his stubbly hair. "Joyce sure had a lot to say after her and the kids saw those orange lights last night. The house was pitch-dark when I got home, and they were hunkered under the kitchen table with my shotgun. I had to put in a new dead bolt this morning."

"But you got to admit," Jim Bob said as he deftly refilled his glass, "that this is bringing in the tourists with their fat wallets and their healthy appetites. I saw all those cars in your parking lot this afternoon, Ruby Bee. Even Roy here agrees that business has picked up in the last three days."

Roy nodded, but he didn't seem nearly as enthusiastic as Jim Bob. "I suppose it has."

Ruby Bee shrugged, then went back behind the bar and listened halfheartedly as Cynthia described her life as an Apache chief. Mostly she was wondering why every last one of Cynthia's so-called past lives was more exciting than a Technicolor movie. Hadn't one ever taken place in a dumpy little town like Maggody?

Estelle was eating it up, though, and Ruby Bee was too gracious to risk offending a customer. Cynthia was in the midst of describing how she'd scalped General Custer when a teenaged boy walked across the dance floor.

He held up an envelope. "I'm supposed to give this to some guy that's staying at the Flamingo, but I don't know what room he's in. His name's Sageman."

Cynthia plucked the envelope out of his hand. "Dr. Sageman is busy at the moment and cannot be disturbed. I'll personally deliver it to him."

"I'm supposed to get a tip," the boy said with a sly grin.

Ruby Bee took a quarter from the cash register and handed it to him. "Now be about your business,

Reggie Pellitory. You know as well as I do that it's against the law for minors to be in here. I got my license with the ABC to think of." She watched him till he was out the door, her eyes narrowed as she recalled the time his no-good brother had busted the jukebox because his girlfriend was dancing with somebody else. None of the Pellitorys had turned out well; before too long they'd be holding their family reunions behind bars.

Cynthia studied the envelope. "What if it's a communiqué from Brian that he's in the throes of a significant encounter with an alien? Dr. Sageman would wish to be informed immediately. Then again, I can't risk interrupting him if it's nothing more than a note of apology from boorish Dr. McMasterson."

Estelle craned her neck to look at the crude printing. It didn't look like any secretary had written it, but she was as intrigued as Cynthia. "I can't see you have any choice but to open it," she said helpfully. "Dr. Sageman would want you to, wouldn't he?"

"Well, then," Cynthia murmured as she slid her fingernail under the flap, took out a piece of paper, and read it to herself. "Oh, my goodness . . ."

"Good news?" asked Estelle, who was doing everything she could to read the letter over Cynthia's shoulder. "Has the alien shown up again at Raz's cornfield?"

Cynthia rubbed her eyes, reread the letter, and stuffed it back in the envelope. "No, it has nothing to do with the crop circles. I'd better—well, take action. Thank you for the coffee and pie, Ruby Bee. I do hope I'll see both of you in the morning. I really must go now. Good-bye!" She hurried across the dance floor and out the door.

Ruby Bee put the plate, fork, and coffee cup in the

sink. "What'd you think about that?" she asked Estelle.

"I think," Estelle said, "that we'd be damn fools to sit here and ask each other questions."

"You got a point." Ruby Bee switched off the neon lights on the wall above the bar, snatched the pitcher out of Larry Joe's hand, and explained that she was closed for the night. After some arguing, the married couples staggered away, and the strangers left submissively. Jim Bob was grumbling, but he, Roy, and Larry Joe went off to conduct the town's business elsewhere. Minutes later she and Estelle were out in the parking lot of the Flamingo Motel. The car that'd been parked in front of No. 2 was gone, but the lights were on.

They were on in No. 5, too, and peeking out from beneath the door was the very envelope Cynthia had read in the barroom. It took no time at all to inch it out and open it.

"Oh, my gawd," gasped Estelle.

Ruby Bee was made of sterner stuff. "There's no time to waste," she said. "Your car or mine?"

SEVEN

◆

At a quarter till ten I was putting the final flourishes on the report when a car squealed to a stop in what must have been a fine display of roiling dust and smoking rubber. A door slammed. Nanoseconds later Ruby Bee stumbled into my office.

"Thank gawd I found you!" she said, her hand clutching her bosom. Her dress was torn and splattered with mud, and her hair looked as if she'd come too close to a ceiling fan. I could see her teeth chattering and almost hear her knees knocking. "This is an emergency! Come on!"

"What's wrong?"

"There's no time to explain. Cynthia Dodder's in my car—unconscious, blue, barely breathing. I'm afraid she's had a heart attack or a stroke. In any case, we got to get her to the hospital, and it's too risky to move her to your car!"

I grabbed my car keys and followed Ruby Bee out the door. "Keep up with me," I said. Praying that my siren and cop lights were working, I got in my car, hit the switches, and turned onto the highway. I would have alerted the dispatcher, but the radio had succumbed to a staticky death months earlier. Two out of three is respectable.

We averaged sixty miles an hour and a thrill a

minute, but Ruby Bee stayed on my bumper all the way to the emergency entrance of the Farberville hospital, where medical personnel briskly took charge. Once Cynthia had been whisked away on a gurney, I sank down on a bench, crossed my arms, and took a look at Ruby Bee and Estelle. Neither's pallor was significantly better than the patient's. Their arms and legs were covered with oozing scratches, and mud from their shoes had sullied the antiseptic floor of the waiting room. As noted previously, Ruby Bee's hair was in a bad way, but Estelle's beehive was at a precarious pitch and only a bobby pin away from catastrophe. No respectable cat would have bothered to drag them in.

"Would you care to explain?" I asked.

Ruby Bee opened her purse and pulled out her wallet. "I need a can of soda pop before I can begin to try to tell you what happened. What about you, Estelle? I got plenty of quarters."

A solemn young nurse came into the waiting room, faltered as she saw my badge, then resumed her proficient demeanor. "Is one of you a relative?" We shook our heads. "Do you have information about Ms. Dodder's health insurance? I need to start the paperwork immediately so that she can be admitted to the intensive care unit."

"How is she?" asked Ruby Bee.

The nurse's smile was encouraging, if also synthetic. "The doctors are with her now. We'll monitor her very carefully until we can transfer her upstairs, but I really need personal and insurance information. Perhaps she has various cards in her purse?"

"There wasn't any time to grab her purse," Estelle said, then inexplicably began to snivel. The only other time I'd ever seen her do so was on a night when sherry had loosened her tongue and she'd hinted darkly about a forbidden relationship in the past. "We dragged her all the way back to the car and raced to Maggody, terrified she was gonna die before we made it. The last thing we were worrying about was her purse!" She collapsed against Ruby Bee's shoulder and began to sob.

"I must start the paperwork," the nurse murmured unhappily. "Hospital regulations."

"Let me talk to them for a minute," I said. When she fled toward her office, I said, "You dragged her all the way back to the car? Just where were you-all?"

Ruby Bee peered around Estelle's hair. "By Boone Creek, downstream from the low-water bridge. Maybe a hundred yards as the crappie swims." She began to thump Estelle on the back. "Gracious, the way you're carrying on! Why don't you go to the ladies' room and splash some cold water on your face?"

I held up my hand. "Wait a minute. What were the three of you doing by the creek? Wasn't it a little dark for a picnic?"

"It might have been."

"Don't start this! Cynthia Dodder is in critical condition, and the last thing I need is for you to turn evasive on me. This is not the worst place for me to choke out some answers. After I get finished, they can wheel you upstairs and feed you intravenously until you recover."

Estelle released her stranglehold on Ruby Bee and sprawled into a molded plastic chair. "We saw an alien, if you must know, Miss Hulk Hogan. A big silver one that shimmered in the dark. It was the scariest thing I've ever seen, as sure as I live and breathe. I liked to have a heart attack myself when it came walking across the creek, its arms stretched out like it was aiming to grab us."

"On top of the water," said Ruby Bee.

I did some sprawling of my own as I tried to make sense of their story. I would have had more luck putting together a jigsaw puzzle in the dark. "Okay, let's go back to the beginning. Why were you there?"

Ruby Bee's eyes were flickering, and I could tell she was debating how much of the truth I deserved to hear. It was a dilemma she'd faced in the past; I usually came out on the short end. "Around nine o'clock Cynthia was in the barroom having coffee—and a piece of lemon icebox pie, I might add—when a local boy brought a note for Dr. Sageman. She opened it in case she might need to interrupt him while he was in the middle of hypnotizing Dahlia. All of a sudden she dashed out the door and drove away. Being naturally concerned, Estelle and I went out to the parking lot, where we happened to see the note stuck partway under Dr. Sageman's door."

Estelle leaped into the narrative. "It said that some kind of shiny disk had crashed in the woods downstream from the bridge. There was even a map showing that weedy old road that goes there."

"We were worried about her safety," added Ruby Bee. "Otherwise, we wouldn't have so much as peeked at the note. It was a good thing we did, wasn't it?"

"Oh, yes," I said without inflection. "So you decided to go there in case Cynthia needed your invaluable assistance. Then what happened?"

Ruby Bee opened her mouth, but Estelle once again cut her off. "Cynthia'd parked just past the bridge, so we left the car behind hers and walked to the creek. It was darker than the inside of a cow, because one of us has forgotten to replace the batteries in her flashlight since Hiram Buchanon's barn burned to the ground. We poddled along for a good five minutes, tripping over branches and fighting back brambles, and finally came to that grassy patch where teenagers have been known to sunbathe without a stitch on. You know the place I mean?"

"I know the place."

"I figured you would," Estelle said, wiggling her eyebrows at Ruby Bee. "Well, we stopped behind some bushes to see what was going on. Cynthia was looking down at something on the ground when there was a loud snap-crackle-pop across the creek." She paused for dramatic effect, noticed I was not appreciative, and continued. "Out of the woods came this big silvery creature, with arms and legs and regular stuff, but with a round head. Its eyes were shaped like almonds and pitch-black. There was no trace of a nose and nothing but a little hole where its mouth was supposed to be."

"And it was glowing like an old-fashioned lantern," Ruby Bee said, finally getting her turn. "It looked right at us, lifted its arms, and came lurching across the creek. There was enough moonlight to see real plainly that its feet were a good inch above the water. I can't begin to describe how petrified I was, especially when Cynthia screamed and fell down in a heap like a rag doll. My blood was roaring so loud I couldn't hear myself think!"

I was puzzled by their earnestness. They, along with Cynthia, had been frightened by something, although I wasn't buying a luminescent silver creature that walked on water. "Then what happened?" I asked cautiously.

Estelle pulled out a tissue and blew her nose. "The creature stopped right in the middle of the creek, like it was startled. Ruby Bee and I managed to get Cynthia's arms draped over our shoulders and carried her up the road as fast we could go, all the while looking back to make sure it wasn't coming after us and trying to keep our own selves from gettin' hysterical. It took forever and a day to get to the car, lemme tell you."

"And you drove to the PD," I said. I suppose I should have come up with a barrage of questions, but I was too perplexed to do anything more than stare at the dingy green wall and try to assimilate the scene they'd described. It played like a low-budget movie.

The nurse reappeared. "I have to get the information before we can move the patient upstairs. By law, we must provide emergency treatment, but that's all."

I stood up. "I'll drive back to Maggody and see if I can find her purse. Do you remember if Cynthia had it with her down by the creek?"

Ruby Bee and Estelle held a whispery conference, then agreed that she had. Maybe.

"Wait here," I said. "I should be back in an hour. One of you needs to call Dr. Sageman and the other woman from Little Rock to let them know about this."

Ruby Bee grabbed my hand. "I don't want you to go there by yourself. We didn't make up this crazy story, and we sure didn't share a jar of Raz's moonshine on the way to the bridge. I don't know how to explain it, but there was something menacing the way that creature came at us. It wasn't anything like that cute E.T. in the movie. Call over to the sheriff's department and get somebody to go with you, honey."

I left before she could elicit a promise from me. I didn't know who was working the second shift at the sheriff's department, but my ears began to tingle as I envisioned the hilarity my request for backup would bring, especially when I got to the part about the luminescent alien with a bad attitude and a light step.

By the time I reached the turnoff to County 102, I'd come up with the most obvious explanation: The three women were the unintentional victims of a hoax perpetrated by the high school kids. Estelle had said that a local boy delivered the envelope addressed to Sageman. I made a mental note to get his name when I returned to the emergency room. Rousing him from bed and demanding the names of the conspirators would provide some measure of vindication for the uproar.

A white subcompact was parked beyond the bridge. I grabbed my flashlight (I myself replace batteries weekly out of sheer boredom) and took a quick look. The keys were in the ignition, but Cynthia's purse was not in sight. I reached through the open window and grabbed the car keys, then walked down the overgrown road. There were signs of Ruby Bee's and Estelle's hasty retreat: scuff marks and footprints in the mud, broken weeds, trampled branches, even a scrap of material from Ruby Bee's dress dangling on a thorny bush.

I came to the clearing and stopped. The moonlight glittered on Boone Creek. Nocturnal birds were making their usual racket, accompanied by tree frogs and cicadas. Some unseen animal rustled in the leaves. A car rumbled down the road, splashed across the bridge, and continued on its way toward Hasty. A bullfrog harrumphed plaintively.

This was not the spookiest milieu I'd ever been in, but it made the list. I swept the light along the far side of the creek, saw nothing, and continued into the clearing. Only then did I see the body.

Biting my lip and trying to keep the flashlight from sliding out of my sweaty hand, I edged forward. Brian Quint lay on his back, his arms and legs extended as if he were preparing to make an angel in the snow. His face was no longer pale; it was as red as a cherry. I dropped to my knees and futilely tried to find a pulse in his neck. His chest was still, his skin cool to the touch, his muscles flaccid. I pulled back an eyelid and shone the light. There was no response.

I rose and flashed the beam on the surrounding grass. At what appeared to be precise intervals were short burn marks. I confirmed that they encircled us, and Brian lay in the middle. Cynthia's purse was nowhere to be seen.

It was time for some backup, and I didn't give a rat's ass if my call entertained the whole damn county.

I drove back to the PD and called the sheriff's department. The dispatcher was as skeptical as I'd anticipated but finally agreed to call the sheriff at home and send a couple of deputies to the bridge to protect the scene until everybody descended. I found the telephone number of the hospital and, after wandering through a labyrinth of extensions, managed to get through to Ruby Bee.

"They say she had a heart attack but is stable for the time being," she said in response to my question. "I tried to get hold of Rosemary and Dr. Sageman, but nobody's answering in either motel room. I can't think where they'd be." She covered the receiver and had a short conversation, then said, "Estelle says they might have gone over to Raz's. That alien we saw tonight was most likely the same one everybody saw two nights ago beyond those circles in his cornfield."

"Perhaps." I hung up and went back to my car. In my absence some considerate soul had rolled up the sidewalks and turned off the lights at the pool hall and the SuperSaver. There were a couple of people inside the Suds of Fun, woodenly watching their laundry churn as if Jay Leno were in there, too. There were no cars parked on the road in front of Raz's shack. A light was on inside it, but I doubted he was having a nightcap with Dr. Sageman and Rosemary Tant.

For some reason, Dahlia's house was lit up like a convenience store in a high-crime neighborhood. I pulled into the driveway, took a deep breath, and then went to the front door and knocked. When there was no response, I knocked more firmly and called, "Dahlia, it's Arly. I need to talk to you."

The door inched open, and one eye regarded me. "What do ya want?"

"Can I come in?"

She opened the door and stepped back. "I reckon so, but I don't see what business it is of yours. You can't arrest 'em after all."

I perched on the arm of the sofa and waited until she'd slammed the door and locked it. "Arrest who?"

"Those little gray men, that's who. You can't even arrest somebody in the next town. Why do you go and think you can arrest somebody that lives so far away you'd die of old age before you ever got there?"

It took me a moment to figure out what she was talking about. The fact that I *could* figure it out was more than a little disturbing, but I put it aside for later analysis. "Listen, Dahlia, I'm not here because of anything you came up with while you were hypnotized. I need to find Dr. Sageman and Rosemary Tant. Did one of them bring you home?"

"That fellow with the ponytail gave me a lift. The whole way he kept pestering me with questions, when it was all I could do not to burst into tears on account of the awfulness that happened to me."

"Are Dr. Sageman and Ms. Tant at the Flamingo?"

"They were when I left ten minutes ago," she said, beginning to quiver. "For once I'm glad Kevvie has to work late. I don't know how I'm gonna tell him—"

"I have to go," I said quickly. I patted her on the shoulder, let myself out, and drove back to the motel. There were lights on in all of the units except for Ruby Bee's. Having no idea where to find anyone, I knocked on the door of No. 2 and hoped for the best.

Rosemary Tant opened the door. "Has something happened to Cynthia?" she asked before I could get out a word. "She took my car earlier this evening, but I expected her back by now. Something's wrong—I can feel it!"

Omitting the where and the why, I told her that Cynthia'd had a heart attack and was at the hospital. She was frantic to be taken there, but I told her I had to stay in town and suggested she make arrangements with Dr. Sageman. I left her twisting her hands in the doorway and drove back to the low-water bridge just as Harve climbed out of his four-wheel.

"So what have we got this time?" he asked. "Little green corpses?"

It was not the time for flippancy. "No," I said as I turned on my flashlight. As we walked down the path, I told him everything that had happened, then added, "The medical examiner is the one to make the call, but it looks as though the victim died of carbon monoxide poisoning. His skin's bright red."

"Is his car parked down there?"

"I wish it were, Harve, but it's not."

"So where'd the carbon monoxide come from?"

"That," I said grimly, "is a damn good question."

Eilene Buchanon had been watching the light flitter around the pasture out back for more than half an hour. Earl was upstairs, snuffling and snoring like a rusty chain saw, and she hadn't thought twice about waking him. He'd just tell her to mind her own business, then flop back over and bury his head under the pillow. She had to admit he was a steady provider and a God-fearing Christian, but no one had ever complimented him on his perceptiveness. If he had an imagination, he'd hidden it under a bushel basket since the night she met him at the county fair.

She took his heavy jacket from a peg, slipped it on, and went out to the back porch for a better look at the light. There was something fancy-free about it. It was hard to track when it shot upward against the stars, but each time she thought it was gone for good, it would come swooping down and start cutting wide circles above the alfalfa.

On the far side of the pasture, Estelle's house was dark. Eilene wondered if Estelle was standing on her back porch, watching the light and wondering what it would be like to have such freedom. She recalled Dahlia's remark about being invited to climb inside the mysterious black limousine. There was something inviting about the light, too.

Eilene reminded herself she was a good wife, a dedicated mother, and, most recently, an exemplary mother-in-law. She fixed biscuits every morning and clipped coupons as if they were original works of art. She wrote weekly to Earl's mother in Hot Springs. She turned the mattresses every spring, canned tomatoes every summer, and resigned herself to football every fall. But there was one thing she couldn't deny: This little light wanted her to come out into the night.

Dawn came and went without fanfare. I was slumped at my desk when Jules Channel tapped on the PD door and let himself in. He tried to dazzle me with a smile, but I was way too tired to be dazzled by anything short of the Hope diamond. Sleep deprivation will do that to me every time.

"Coffee's in the back," I said ungraciously.

"No, thanks. I just heard some really strange stories over at the deli in the supermarket. Is it true that Cynthia Dodder had a heart attack last night by the creek, and later Brian was found dead there?"

"It's all true." I went into the back room and refilled my cup. I stalled for a minute, hoping I'd hear the front door close, then reluctantly returned to my desk. "I'd just as soon you didn't write this up for your tabloid. No one deserves to have his or her obituary next to a story about killer parakeets."

"I agree with you, and we don't run that kind of story anyway. The downbeat stories are the exclusive property of the legitimate papers; we exist only to amuse. Besides, Brian was a nice kid. Just because I work for a sleazy outfit is no reason to assume I'm a sleazy person."

I considered apologizing but instead said, "Did you know him well?"

Jules shook his head. "Not really. We ran into each other when he and Sageman were investigating UFO sightings, but that's about all. Can't Sageman help you?"

"He and Rosemary stayed at the hospital until a couple of hours ago. I'm going to take their statements later this morning. It was a long night for everybody involved, and there's no reason to rush into this until I've got some idea of where I'm rushing." I yawned so broadly that my eyes watered. "And I need a lot of coffee before I produce any ideas whatsoever. Now, if you don't mind, I have work to do. . . ."

Once he was gone, I drove to Reggie Pellitory's mobile home in a corner of the Pot o' Gold. This time I wasted no time with a timorous tap. About the time my fist was beginning to throb, the door opened.

"Who're you?" said a man in stained boxer shorts, acting as though we'd never met despite our encounters at the pool hall and one memorable night when I'd knocked him upside the head with my flashlight and booked him for drunk and disorderly. He'd done thirty days, and I'd enjoyed every one of them.

"You know who I am. Let me talk to Reggie."

"He ain't here."

I didn't bother to smile at the monosyllabic wonder. "Where is he?"

Pellitory leered at me. "I dunno why your tail's in

the water. Reggie ain't done nothing. Last night about nine he came home, tossed some clothes in a sack, and then him and his cousin Herschel took off for Tulsa to see the tractor pull. The finals is today."

"Do you know where he's staying in Tulsa?"

"With his Aunt Gwennie, like it's any of your business. You can call her if you like. She's an elementary school secretary, so she doesn't work on the weekends."

"Why do you know what time he left town last night?"

"I noticed on account of *Strange Stories* just came on. I was real curious to see if there'd be anything about Maggody. You see those jack-o'-lanterns over Cotter's Ridge a couple nights back? I hear tell they was flying saucers."

I asked for Aunt Gwennie's telephone number, although I had a feeling she would confirm Reggie's arrival. He was still part of the conspiracy, however, and I wanted names. I was convinced that whatever he and his friends had concocted, perhaps innocently in the beginning, had evolved into murder.

Or something.

I went back to the PD, started another pot of coffee, and dialed the number Reggie's father had given me. A woman answered. After I'd identified myself and ascertained she was the aunt, I asked her when Reggie and his cousin had arrived the previous night.

"A few minutes before midnight," she said without hesitation. "I waited up for them because I didn't want to leave the front door unlocked. We've had some prowlers in the apartment complex."

"Was this a last-minute visit?"

"Initially they'd planned to come earlier so they

could see more of the competition, but Reggie called yesterday afternoon and said he had to work late."

I asked to speak to him and waited several minutes, entertaining myself by imagining how I'd explain the size of the long-distance bill at the next town council meeting.

"Whatta ya want?" Reggie began with all of his father's eloquence.

"You delivered a note to Ruby Bee's Bar and Grill last night at nine o'clock. Who gave it to you?"

"I don't remember."

"You'll have to do better than that, Reggie. Otherwise, I'll call the Tulsa police and ask them to take you into custody as a material witness and hold you until I find time to come fetch you. You'll miss the finals of the tractor pull and at least two or three days of work."

"You cain't do that."

I probably couldn't, but neither one of us had gone to Harvard Law School. "Oh, but I can—and I will, too. Maybe you weren't quite awake earlier. Has your memory improved?"

"Yesterday I was in the break room at the Super-Saver. Kevin Buchanon came in and gave me an envelope with my name on it. Inside it was another one with some guy's name, a note telling me to deliver it to him at the motel at exactly nine o'clock, and a fifty-dollar bill. The note said if I did it, I'd get another fifty in the mail."

"That's a lot of money for a simple errand."

"No shit."

I wrote Kevin's name on a piece of paper and drew a circle of question marks around it. "Are you sure you weren't supposed to do anything else in order to get the second payment?"

"Yeah, I was supposed to get rid of the note."

"Did you?" I asked, crossing my fingers, toes, and eyes. "If I see it for myself, I'll be a lot more inclined to believe your story, Reggie."

"It's in my car. I was gonna throw it away when we stopped for beer, but I forgot about it. I can bring it to you when we get back tomorrow."

I agreed and hung up, disappointed that I hadn't ended up with a tearful confession of pseudo-Martian malfeasance. Tulsa was a solid three-hour drive, and unless his aunt was lying, Reggie couldn't have been at Boone Creek at nine-thirty, when Ruby Bee and Estelle arrived, or during the ensuing hour and a half, when Brian Quint arrived. Kevin was incapable of the duplicity required to glow in the dark; he may well have had problems turning on a light switch. He would have to wait, however; I'd promised Harve that I'd return.

I drove down County 102 and parked among all the official vehicles. A deputy with a styrofoam cup of coffee and a doughnut watched me intently as I took off down the road.

Harve was puffing away on a cigar butt. He'd found time to shave and put on a fresh shirt, but his eyes were as red as mine and his face creased with exhaustion. "Hey, Arly," he said as I skirted the clearing. "Did everybody get home last night?"

"As far as I know, everyone is sleeping soundly in his or her assigned bed. I'll start taking statements shortly." I looked at the spot where the body had lain until the paramedics carted it away only a few hours before sunrise. "Any word from McBeen yet?"

"No, but it's early. Presuming he agrees with us that the cause of death was carbon monoxide poisoning, he's gonna have some tough questions about the logistics. You come up with any brilliant theories?"

I leaned against a tree and regarded the clearing through grainy, heavily lidded eyes. "We seem to be missing some of the more common elements in a carbon monoxide-related death, like a garage or an enclosed room. You saw for yourself that no car has driven down the road recently. We'd be hard pressed to find an outlet for a faulty space heater. I suppose these burn marks have something to do with it, but damned if I know what. Did you get plenty of pictures of them?"

"Yep, we did. They're twelve inches long and twenty-four inches apart. The circle's not perfect, but it's close. We crawled over every inch of the area this morning. No one found anything more remarkable than footprints, and most of them are likely to belong to your mother, Estelle, or Cynthia Dodder, the victim, and you."

I looked down at the nearest mark. "What could have made this, Harve? No, don't answer that. I'm knee-deep in speculation as it is." I went to the edge of the creek and tried to envision a silvery stalker. The width of the water varied, but the narrowest spot was four feet across and several inches deep. "Have you checked out the opposite bank?" I called.

"For extraterrestrial footprints on the gravel bar? Yeah, Les went over there and looked around, but he didn't find anything. Unlike this alien, he got kinda wet crossing the creek. I sent him home to change into dry shoes. One of the new boys found an illegal garbage dump up near where the white car is parked. He found all kinds of things like washing machines, tires, a toilet seat, odd lengths of lumber, beer cans, and so on. He made a list, but it doesn't make fascinating reading." He pushed back his hat and wiped his forehead. "We don't have shit to go on, Arly."

I told him about the light Roy Stiver had seen in the pasture alongside County 102. "First the crop circles," I said, bending back fingers as I went along, "then the bang and the bobbly light, the orange lights that even I saw, Roy's light, and finally whatever Ruby Bee, Estelle, and Cynthia saw last night."

"And Brian Quint. Either he saw it or it saw him first. And don't forget the cattle mutilations. I sent some tissue samples to the lab in Little Rock. I expect I'll hear from them in a week or so, and I'm gonna be surprised if they come up with any explanations."

"There is a straightforward explanation, dammit, and I'm going to find it and make sure the television station puts it on the air—with updates at six and ten!"

I mean, carbon monoxide in the middle of the woods? As we so quaintly say in the South, that dawg won't hunt.

EIGHT

◆

"Dr. Sageman," I said, "there has been a death. I realize that you're in a hurry, but I have questions that must be answered."

He stopped toweling his hair long enough to give me a wounded frown. "What happened was an appalling tragedy, Chief Hanks. Brian Quint was by no means just a valued employee, but also a close friend and a confidant, and I am deeply distraught over his death. If I had not agreed to meet with an assistant producer from *Strange Stories* at the Farberville airport about the possibility of narrating a segment, I would be prostrate with grief. I regarded Brian as the son I never had. In fact, I'd come to think of him as my successor as director of the ETH Foundation."

"I need information about him so I can notify his family—unless you've already done it."

"His father died years ago. His mother lives in Long Beach, and I spoke with her before I took a shower. I didn't know what to say about the cause of death, so I merely said it was an accident and assured her I would take care of the arrangements." He dropped the towel and sat on the corner of the bed, his bathrobe gaping to expose a hairless, freckled chest and a faint ripple of ribs. His aristocratic accent was replaced with gravelly anxiety as he added, "You will get to the bottom of this, won't you? If Brian was killed, inadvertently or intentionally, during a close encounter, all of us in ufology must rethink our supposition that the extraterrestrials come in peace. The Majestic Twelve commission will have to cast off the mantle of secrecy. The conspiracy must be exposed so that we as a race can unite in our response to this impending peril."

I had no idea what he was talking about, but I nodded and said, "What do you know about Brian's background?"

"He sent a résumé when he applied for the position, but I don't have it with me. I seem to think he grew up in the San Fernando Valley and went to one of the California universities to study business, or perhaps marketing. He did public relations for various computer companies, edited in-house publications, and became interested in ufology after attending one of my seminars. We began a correspondence, and two years ago, when my former secretary resigned, Brian expressed eagerness to work for me. I was desperate since much of my research was on computer files. I prefer to dictate my books and then revise them after they've been processed in the computer and printed out. I myself am what you might call electronically challenged." He gave me a sheet of paper. "I've written down his mother's address and telephone number. Brian was single, with no serious romantic entanglements. Last year, after his apartment was burglarized for the third time, he moved into the guest cottage on my estate in Topango. The city lights are less obtrusive back in the canyon, and one feels much closer to the celestial presence."

"Let's talk about last night. You left him setting up equipment by Boone Creek?"

"That's correct." Sageman went to the dresser, picked up a comb, and somberly studied himself in the mirror before attacking his hair with the fervor of a cosmetologist. Between incursions with the comb and spritzes of hair spray, he said, "A few minutes after seven o'clock Cynthia and I left him to document any unusual activity in the vicinity. Brian was a very conscientious investigator, Chief Hanks. I trusted him. If I'd suspected there was physical danger, I would have insisted on staying with him. There was no reason to think so, and I felt it was more important to examine the possibility that aliens had abducted a local girl."

"Did you?" I murmured, then sat back in my chair and gave him lots of time to stew. He was jittery; that was obvious. But I didn't know why, any more than I knew the origins of the strange lights or how best to interrogate the world's foremost authority on extraterrestrial encounters—depending on whom you believed these days. I wasn't inclined to believe much of anyone.

"Okay," I said, "what did you do after you came back to the Flamingo Motel?"

"The subject was already here and eager to begin her exploratory session. She, Rosemary, and I adjourned to the middle room in the opposite building. She was remarkably flexible. In many cases I must endure the more insignificant and tedious past lives in order to win the trust of the subject and coax—"

"When did the session end?"

"Around eleven, I should think, but you should ask Rosemary. I find clocks and watches distracting.

Time is hardly linear, after all, but exists in an autonomous dimension—"

"Then why didn't you answer the telephone when Ruby Bee called sometime between ten-thirty and eleven?" I said. Despite my southern upbringing, I'd become amazingly adept at interrupting these people, all of whom teetered on the brink of delivering a lecture, complete with footnotes, with minimal or nonexistent provocation. The idea of attending a weekend conference with hundreds of them had less appeal than root canal work.

Sageman returned to whatever mundane dimension we were in and gravely considered my question. "The telephone did not ring. The subject was in a deep trance, but Rosemary will confirm it. She never left the room."

"Why did Dr. McMasterson drive Dahlia home?"

"How else could we send the girl home? Cynthia had Rosemary's car, and Brian had the one that we rented at the airport. Hayden McMasterson is an idiot, but he is not a lout. I explained the situation, and he readily agreed. An hour later he was kind enough to take Rosemary and me to the hospital." He noticed my expression. "Does this perplex you, Chief Hanks?"

It did, but I wasn't sure why. "I'm still trying to get a picture of what happened immediately after the session. Dr. McMasterson left with Dahlia. What did you do then?"

"I went into my room, rewound the tapes, and began to listen to them while making some preliminary notes. As soon as possible I'll schedule a second session with the subject. There is a wealth of explicit and vivid material here—all distinctly erotic. I fully intend to make this abduction the core of the Houston lecture and of my next book. The correlation with the crop circles makes it unique."

"Why didn't you read the note and go racing to the site of the crash?"

"Because there was no note. Had I known of the purported crash, I would have found a way to get there. I've dedicated more than twenty years of my life to the cause of ufology, but I've never once been privileged to see a spacecraft. Can you imagine how frustrating it is always to be the bridesmaid and never the bride? I want to see one, dammit! I want to go inside and marvel at the technology, soak up knowledge, share their vastly superior conceits, communicate with them at a level far beyond that of a simpleton witness." He began to pace as best he could, considering the confines of the motel room. A new direction was called for every four steps or so. "Don't they know that I'm the leading authority? Why don't they contact me? I am Arthur Sageman, not some fisherman in Mississippi! They should contact me!"

I slipped out the door, then paused in the parking lot and wasted a few minutes trying to decide if he was certifiable. Odds were good, but as far as I could tell, my opinion of him had nothing to do with Brian Quint's death.

The bar and grill was redolent of freshly baked biscuits and frying bacon. I poured myself a cup of coffee, then sat on a stool and wrote up the interview with Arthur Sageman. He'd last seen Brian at seven o'clock and subsequently had been in the company of Dahlia and Rosemary Tant. The former was too witless to lie, and I could think of no reason for the latter to do so. There was no pressing reason to suspect any of them, for that matter. Or anybody else.

Ruby Bee came out of the kitchen, carrying a plate heaped high with just about everything near and dear to my heart. "I called the hospital," she said. "Cynthia's out of danger, but they're gonna keep an eye on her for the next few days. I told Rosemary I'd give her directions to the hospital so she can sit and visit for a spell."

"She can't have her car until it's been finger-printed." I shoveled a forkful of buttery grits into my mouth, fantasized fleetingly about heaven, then swallowed and said, "Last night you and Estelle were caught up in the drama of tracking Cynthia to this clearing. Never for an instant would I suggest you imagined this apparition, but isn't it possible you saw something a whole lot less incomprehensible and allowed your imaginations to run wild?"

She shook her head. "I knew you were gonna ask me that question, so I gave it some careful thought. Estelle and me may have had some flights of fancy in the past. We may have gotten in the way of your investigations on occasion, too. But all the way back to Maggody, we talked about what we saw, and we're both real firm in our minds about it. The creature was close to seven feet tall. It was shimmery. When it came across the creek, its feet were well above the water. I'm sorry if you don't believe us, but we can't change our story 'cause it's the gospel truth."

The gospel according to St. Sageman anyway. Rather than risk having my plate snatched from under my nose, I settled for a noncommittal shrug. "I just spoke to Dr. Sageman. He claims the telephone never rang last night. Are you sure you dialed the right number?"

"Are you implying I don't know the numbers of

the units . . . or that I'm so crazy that I made up the story about calling, too?"

"No, of course not," I said, prudently holding the edge of my plate. "He also said he didn't find this note about the crash. After you read it, did you put it back under his door?"

"I told Estelle to put it back, but she said we might need the map if we missed the road. I said that was ridiculous because it was the first road past the bridge, but she said—"

"Do you still have it?"

She took a folded paper from her apron pocket, dropped it in front of me, and exited through the kitchen doors.

Despite the fact at least four people had handled it, I opened it with the tip of my knife. The printed message read: "I saw a silver disk crash two nights ago in this location." The map was neatly drawn in black ink, with the main road, County 102, and Boone Creek labeled, and a dotted line indicating the old logging road. A trite X marked the spot.

Although I doubted any telltale fingerprints could be lifted, I refolded it and put it in my shirt pocket, planning to drop it off at Harve's office later. I sopped up the last drop of gravy, then resumed my duties as chief of police and protector of the populace. I did so walking across the parking lot to knock on Hayden McMasterson's door (No. 6, if you're keeping a chart).

"I was just about to leave," he said as he brushed past me, staggering under a burden of camera bags, a tripod, and exotic paraphernalia. "I have permission to enter the field this morning. The only way to determine the validity of the configurations is to dowse them and locate the energy lines. If I'd been there last night, I could have checked for radioactivity, but it dissipates quickly. Oh, dear, did I forget the Geiger counter?"

"Wait a minute," I said, cutting off his route back inside the motel room. "I want to talk to you."

"I must photograph this quintuplet formation for the *Chronicle of Cosmic Inquiry* and for my presentation at the Houston conference. My editor has agreed to delay production of my new book, *Concentricity and Conception,* so that I can add a chapter. My publicist has already approached the major network talk shows, and for once they're willing to examine the slides and consider me as a potential guest."

I thought about grabbing his ponytail to command his attention but settled for blocking the doorway. "Dr. McMasterson, do you recall who I am?"

"You're the police chief."

"Very good. This means that if I get testy, I can shoot you and claim self-defense. I can throw you in jail for pissing me off. I can confiscate your camera and your Geiger counter. The Supreme Court may come down on me one of these days, but in the meantime, you really should take your foot off my foot and pay a little bit more attention to what I'm saying."

"Sorry," he said, stepping back and wiggling his nose at me as if I were an unfamiliar—but not necessarily repugnant—smell. "I'm so tremendously excited. Have you heard about the configuration?"

"Have you heard about Brian Quint?" I countered.

He crumpled like a wet towel. "I never knew Brian well, but I did see him at conferences and sightings. He had a very distinctive bluish green aura. My wife adjusted it for him at the last MUFON conference, and afterward he hugged both of us and said he felt much more euphonious. It was a very special moment for everyone in the room." He began to cry, at first with constraint but then with such emotion that I found myself patting his back, murmuring encouragement—and feeling acutely uncomfortable. I'd never encountered a male in Maggody who cried or would be caught dead in the embrace of another male. Physical contact within the gender is pretty much limited to smirky nudges and fistfights.

"It's okay," I said numerous times, then went into the bathroom and dampened a washcloth for him.

He was fingering his crystal when I returned. "Brian," he said, accepting the washcloth with a rueful smile, "was a dynamic young man, filled with promise. He'd fallen for Arthur's delusions, but at times I sensed that he might be salvageable."

"Why did you think that?"

"He had no choice but to be drawn into the asinine theories of the ETH enthusiasts. He was paid to do so, after all, and paid very well. Given time, he might have seen the fallacies and come over to our side. He called me at the institute to tell me about the crop circles and to urge me to come, which tells me that he suspected my intraterrestrial hypothesis might better explain the phenomenon."

"Dr. Sageman doesn't seem to agree," I said neutrally.

"Brian wanted to learn the truth. In Denver he made a very astute comment about the likelihood of alien input on the Aztec calendar. It predicts eclipses with uncanny accuracy."

I hastily changed the subject. "Where were you last night from seven o'clock onward?"

"Right here. I've already started my next book, which will explore the mysterious events in Maggody. I'm thinking about calling it *Intraterrestrial Intrusion*. Do you think that sounds too threatening?"

"Not at all, Dr. McMasterson. Did you have any conversations on the telephone?"

"I called my wife to share my feelings about the crop circles. This latest manifestation makes it all the more exhilarating, doesn't it? It's the closest I've ever come to being in the immediate area when the phenomenon actually transpired. When I was there earlier this morning, I could still feel the fallout from the ionization."

"Wait a minute," I said, rubbing my temples. "What latest manifestation?"

The glint in his eyes was almost blinding. "Two new circles formed during the night. They extend on a perpendicular axis from the middle of the original circles. The pattern is growing in complexity and beauty." His face froze with horror, and his voice rose a full octave as he said, "Does this have something to do with Brian's death? There's never been any documented evidence that the intraterrestrials have harmed anyone. They move among us in a quintessence of love, guiding us with various revelations until the time comes that we are ready to accept them."

I stood up. "At this point I'm trying to get a picture of what happened to Brian. If I interrogate any aliens, I'll let you know what they say." I stopped in the doorway. "You were working in this room at eleven o'clock when Dr. Sageman asked you to take Dahlia home, right?"

"I could hardly refuse. Frankly I was curious

about what had transpired during the session. There are rumors afoot that Arthur is running out of subjects. His last two presentations at conferences were essentially identical, and sarcastic comments were heard in the lobby afterward. If he doesn't come up with some fresh material, he may find himself paying the registration fee and sitting in the audience."

My instincts said "run," but my mouth said, "Did Dahlia provide fresh material?"

"I've listened to tapes of Arthur's sessions. He's very adept at leading the subjects exactly where he wants them to go. From what Dahlia said in the car, I suspect she cooperated so well that Arthur could barely get in a word. Her purported experiences are interchangeable with Rosemary's. I asked her if she'd read any of the books, and she admitted that she had. Arthur encourages his subjects to do their homework before the sessions."

I went to my car and made a few notes, then decided to escape the madness for a few minutes by driving out to the place where Brian had set up the equipment. I did so without enthusiasm, since it occurred to me I'd failed to investigate the incident. I'd dismissed it as mass hysteria, but a slew of more ominous incidents had taken place since then.

The rental car was parked behind the Esso station, its windows up and doors locked. The car keys had not been found in Brian's pockets. They were not in the ignition, but they could have been stuck in a camera bag.

I slithered down the slope and walked upstream, this time unencumbered by television reporters, sightseers, and yellow tape. The camera bags were in a tidy row near the tripod. I glanced through the camera, which was aimed at Raz's field, then found binoculars hanging from a branch and took a better look. As McMasterson had promised, there were two recent arrivals linked to the originals. I raised the binoculars and tried not to groan as I counted a dozen people behind the barbed wire fence. Raz was apt to be by the gate, his cheek bulging with chaw and his pockets with money.

There were no oversize footprints in the mud, nor were there any new burn marks. The flattened weeds had recovered. I searched all the bags and found a second camera, lenses, film, cassettes, a camcorder, a tape recorder, drawings and diagrams of the circles, a notebook filled with scribbled numbers, a rolled-up jacket, and three 100 percent natural granola bars.

What I did not find were car keys or a note similar to the one addressed to Dr. Sageman. At seven o'clock Brian had begun setting up the equipment. If he'd been below the low-water bridge two hours later, when Cynthia, Ruby Bee, and Estelle arrived, he surely would have made known his presence. Therefore, I decided (albeit tentatively), he had not arrived until after they left at approximately nine-thirty.

I'd found his body at eleven. At some point during the hour and a half Brian had abandoned a lot of equipment and gone downstream. Had someone arrived with the story about the crashed disk and then offered him a ride? Why hadn't he stopped to tell his employer?

The equipment was too valuable to remain where it was, and I had no reason to think we needed to do a detailed investigation of the area. Scowling, I repacked all the bags and made three trips to my car, then went to the rental car and peered through all the windows in hopes I might spot the car keys. The town budget had not yet been able to supply me with the gadgetry to unlock a car door, so I wrote down the license plate to pass on to the rental agent, then drove back to the PD to get started on a third pot of coffee.

"They've started killing people," Mrs. Jim Bob said, her lips so tight she could barely squeeze out the statement. It wasn't exactly an accusation, but there were overtones. "Last night down by the creek they killed an innocent young man. I tried to warn everybody that these aliens were likely to be immoral and without regard for human life. I did my best."

Brother Verber shifted uncomfortably on the pew as hazy memories fluttered through his mind. "If that young man was innocent, what was he doin' by the creek? It seems to me it's more likely that he was down there for one reason, and one reason only. He sweet-talked an innocent young girl into fornicating on a blanket with him, and the Good Lord decided to smite him."

"With poisonous gas? The Good Lord works in mysterious ways, but in this case a bolt of lightning would have been more fitting." She paused to savor the image of cremated flesh, then noticed his distress. "Did you go traipsing alongside the creek last night, Brother Verber?"

"Why, Sister Barbara," he said as sweat trickled down his back and spread beneath his armpits, "I have been devoting all my time to the preparation of a plan to convert the heathen aliens to Christianity. I saw in the *Probe* that over at the Vatican there's a team of astromissionaries getting ready to go forth and spread the Gospel. I was thinking I might write a letter to the pope hisself and see if he wants a look at my lesson plans. I don't want to sound immodest, but I found some real clever ways to link Noah's ark with their flying saucers."

She wasn't convinced, but she didn't really have time to explore the matter further because it was almost time for Sunday school. "I have come to you for guidance about another matter of spiritual concern. It's of a delicate, personal nature and requires the utmost confidentiality." She looked over her shoulder to make sure no one had crept into the Assembly Hall, then lowered her voice and said, "It has to do with Jim Bob."

"Sister Barbara," he said, squeezing her knee to comfort her in her time of trouble, "I am so sorry to hear that. Every time I think we've got Brother Jim Bob all straightened out and heading down the glorious sunny highway to heaven, he takes a detour." He squeezed her knee some more so she'd find inner strength. "Has he been making indecent demands on you? Shall we pray before you commence to tell me what disgraceful and decadent things he's made you do in the name of holy matrimony?"

She tried to ease her knee free, but he was hanging on like a clamp and breathing right in her face. "I'm starting to suspect Jim Bob has made some kind of deal with Raz Buchanon—and what's the first word that comes to mind when you hear Raz's name?"

"Marjorie?" Brother Verber hazarded, more than a little disappointed to have the subject of lasciviousness (or maybe perversity) yanked out from under him like a throw rug.

"Moonshine. Lately Jim Bob has lied about working late at the SuperSaver, which is not uncommon behavior on his part when he has a hussy waiting for him in a trailer somewhere. However, earlier this week, when I happened to be parked across the road, I saw him drive away right as it started getting dark. I decided to follow him. He went by the Pot o' Gold, but he didn't turn in there."

Brother Verber's eyes were wide with disbelief. "He didn't? Praise the Lord, Sister Barbara."

"I had to stay back a goodly distance so he wouldn't notice me," she continued, her voice increasingly tight. "When I got to the top of the hill by the Stonecrop County sign, his car was gone. He turned on one of those logging roads. And we both know where those logging roads go, don't we?"

"To Cotter's Ridge?"

"We already were on Cotter's Ridge at the time, Brother Verber. Everybody in town knows that Raz Buchanon runs his still up there. I'm afraid that Raz is so busy with those folks wanting to gape at the circles that he asked Jim Bob to help him with some deliveries."

"I am shocked. Jim Bob certainly lacks your fine-tuned morality, but the thought of him delivering moonshine to men who'd as soon spend their paychecks on devil's drink as take care of their wives and children—oh, the pain you must be feeling!"

He was right about that, since he was squeezing her knee so hard she was about to cry. Mrs. Jim Bob had to remind herself that she couldn't do that because she was strong and brave and pure of heart, to list only a few of her virtues. "I don't know what to do," she said with a slight wince. "If I confront him, he'll deny it, just like he always does. But moonshining's a federal crime, and if he gets arrested, the judge could slap him with a fine that'd make us bankrupt. We could lose the store, the house, my Cadillac—everything!"

Brother Verber released her knee so he could clasp his hands. "What a painful, painful picture you're painting, Sister Barbara. Let's get down on our knees and pray that the Good Lord will see fit not to let Jim Bob get caught by the revenue agents and end up causing you to lose everything you've worked hard for all these years." He hit the floor like a load of concrete, positioned his hands on the back of the pew, and squeezed his eyes closed.

"I'll pray from the pew," she said as she rubbed her tender knee. She lowered her head, closed her eyes, and prayed fervently that she could find a lawyer to transfer all the assets to her name before Jim Bob was arrested.

Thus the only person with open eyes in the Voice of the Almighty Lord Assembly Hall was Lottie Estes, who was in the storeroom. She'd been sorting through sheet music for the eleven o'clock service when she first heard voices, and not wanting to interfere with spiritual guidance, she'd kept quiet. Quiet as a church mouse, you might say.

"It is so kind of you to give me a ride to the hospital," Rosemary Tant said as she waved out the car window at a child on a bicycle. The child, a mutant Buchanon, raised a finger in response before pedaling away on a bicycle I would have bet my paltry paycheck was stolen.

"I need to speak to Cynthia," I said, "and this gives us an opportunity to discuss what happened last night. The crime squad should be finished with your car by noon. I'll pick you up later and take you to get it."

"I still cannot believe that nice young man passed away. He was always so polite to me, as if I were someone special, and after a session he'd pour me a cup of tea without me so much as saying a word. Last year we had a session in which an alien used me as a vehicle to speak directly to Arthur about turbulence on a distant planet from within the constellation Canis Major. I was absolutely exhausted, and Brian—"

"You were in the room during Dahlia's session," I said. "Did anything unusual occur?"

"There is nothing usual about a session that uncovers an abduction," she said carefully. "It is always fraught with profound and raw emotions. Although Dahlia was understandably fearful before we started, she did remarkably well. Arthur was especially pleased when she described the interior of the spacecraft. Many of us have had identical experiences, which goes to prove we are not dreaming or relying on our imaginations."

"Ms. Tant, I'm not interested in what was said last night. I need to know what happened between seven and eleven o'clock. The session began at seven?"

"About then, yes."

"And at eleven Dr. Sageman asked Dr. McMasterson to take Dahlia home?" I watched her nod. "During that time did you see or hear anyone out in the parking lot?"

"I didn't hear anyone, and I was sitting with my back to the window, so I couldn't have seen anyone. I was not only running the tape recorder but also making little sketches and drawings as Dahlia went along. I use colored pencils because so often there are bright lights in certain arrangements."

"Oh," I said as we passed the Farberville airport. A plane came roaring down at us in a kamikaze fashion, cleared the roof of the car by a few feet, and bounced onto the runway. "Your car was parked right in front of the unit you were in. Didn't you hear anything when Cynthia drove away?"

"Oh, I certainly heard the car. You asked me if I heard anyone, so I assumed you meant persons."

"Did Dr. Sageman mention it?"

"He was irritated because the noise startled Dahlia while she was at a very significant moment in her narrative, and she came very close to tumbling off the bed. When we heard a second car, he went so far as to step outside to find out what was going on."

"How long was he gone?"

"Only a minute or two." She leaned over and put her hand on my arm. "Cynthia is the bravest woman I've ever met, and she is dedicated to the discovery of the truth. She personally investigated more than forty sightings last year, often unaccompanied and late at night."

"There were that many sightings in Arkansas last year?" I asked, surprised.

"Who knows how many there were? Not everyone is willing to risk being embarrassed and ridiculed by their neighbors, as well as by the media. I only allowed my story to be made public when Arthur convinced me I was helping other people with the same traumatic scars. Despite my shyness, I've lectured at many of the conferences and was once the after-dinner speaker. I was so nervous beforehand that I couldn't eat a bite."

I realized I wasn't having much success keeping

her on the subject. "And the telephone never rang during the session?"

"I don't believe so, but my mind had blended into the narrative, and the images were flowing through me so rapidly that I could barely get them onto the paper. My fingers were so stiff this morning I could barely dial the telephone to let the membership know about Cynthia."

"When the session ended, did Dr. Sageman go to Dr. McMasterson's room?"

"Yes, while I combed Dahlia's hair and tidied her up as best I could. The session was difficult, and she was quite damp from tears and perspiration. Dr. Sageman returned to escort her to Dr. McMasterson's car. I made a little joke and . . ."

I glanced at her as she dribbled to a stop. Her mouth was open as if the next word were actually on the tip of her tongue, but her forehead was creased, and her eyes seemed unfocused. "And?" I said encouragingly.

"I'd planned to finish my sketches," she said with a shrug of her bony shoulders, "but Arthur was eager to see them and asked to take my notebook. I was preparing to take a shower when you knocked on the door with the news about poor Cynthia. Now, if you don't mind, I'd like to meditate until we get to the hospital so I can fill Cynthia's room with curative energy."

There was no point in trying to converse with a woman who had wrapped her arms around her knees and was humming loudly through her nose. I was just relieved she didn't float out the window. I had enough problems as it was.

NINE

◆

I left Rosemary sitting cross-legged and droning like a demented bumblebee in the ICU waiting room and entered Cynthia's curtained cubicle. She looked fragile, but her color was much better than I'd last seen it, and she turned her head as I came around the curtain. The tube taped to her nose and wires slinking out from beneath her gown were disconcerting, but green lines blipped across monitor screens with comforting regularity.

"Ms. Dodder," I said, "I need to ask you a few quick questions, if you feel up to it."

"All I feel is foolish. I've been waiting for forty years to see an alien, and when I did, I panicked and had a heart attack. I have no choice but to resign as president of UFORIA. I have disgraced the organization and the ETH movement as well as myself."

"I don't think you disgraced yourself. Ruby Bee and Estelle were absolutely terrified, too. It's a natural reaction to something so unexpected and menacing."

"I suppose so," she said without conviction. Her eyes closed, and her lips began to move, as if she were composing her letter of resignation.

"Did you hear anything after you parked and started down the path?" I asked. "A car door or maybe voices?" What I wanted was a description of insolent adolescent voices, but it didn't seem professional to prompt her—unless she needed a little help.

"I heard nothing out of the ordinary until I arrived at the open area and saw the burn marks. They appeared to be similar to markings found in Arizona five years ago. I was trying to recall the particulars of that encounter when there was a sharp noise from across the creek. I looked up and saw the alien advancing across the surface of the water." Her hand rose unsteadily as if to ward off the memory, then fell back into the rumpled sheet. "I remember nothing else until I regained consciousness here. I shudder to think what would have happened had your mother and her friend not been there. It's possible I would be many light-years away from Earth by now and in the clutches of that horrible creature and his shipmates."

I managed a smile, told her Rosemary would be in to visit, and went back to the parking lot. It was Sunday; that meant the public library would be closed. The Thurber Farber Memorial Library on the campus would not be closed, however. I decided to drop the note off at the sheriff's department on my way back to Maggody and headed for the stacks to do some research, feeling sophomoric in both senses of the word.

"Dahlia!" Kevin said from the other side of the bathroom door. "Please come out of there, honeypot. You must have an awful crick in your neck from sleeping in the tub all night. I'm here to protect you from whatever it is that's upsettin' you. I'm your lawful wedded husband for better or worse."

He stopped, thinking it couldn't get much worse than this. It'd been half past midnight by the time he'd dragged home from the SuperSaver, all because Jim Bob had ordered him to wax the floors and the buffer'd gone loco and knocked down a ten-foot-high pyramid of paper towels. Then he'd found Dahlia locked in the bathroom, moaning and sobbing—and refusing to explain why. The bed had been mighty cold and lonesome without his tawny temptress.

He had a flash of insight. "Is it female trouble? Do you want me to get my ma so you kin talk to her?"

"Go away."

"Are you sure I can't fix you some breakfast?" He persisted, his ear pressed so hard against the door he could hear her despair. "Or better still, I kin run down to Ruby Bee's and fetch a plate of biscuits and gravy, with a side order of ham."

"Go away, I said!"

Kevin was so bewildered that he went into the living room and flopped down on the recliner. His beloved bride had never passed up biscuits and gravy, even the time that she'd had stomach flu so bad she could hardly lift her head and had to be fed like a baby bird.

He finally called his ma to say that they wouldn't be comin' over for Sunday dinner. Eilene sighed, but she didn't say anything. Dahlia's outburst in the bar and grill had been repeated, with varying amounts of elaboration, all over town and most of the county. For all she knew, they were discussing it all the way up to Kansas City, Missouri. Some of the less perceptive men (her husband and her son being prime examples) might have missed hearing about it, but she wouldn't be surprised if it showed up in Brother Verber's sermon.

"What do you think those three are up to?" Ruby Bee whispered to Estelle, jabbing her thumb in the direction of the last booth.

"They are drinking coffee, Ruby Bee." Estelle didn't bother to look over her shoulder at Jim Bob Buchanon, Roy Stiver, and Larry Joe Lambertino. They'd been muttering at one another for the best part of an hour, and Ruby Bee'd been asking the same question most of that time. Estelle's answers had been fanciful at first, but eventually she was reduced to stating the obvious.

"Like I can't see that for myself, Mrs. Optometrist?" Ruby Bee picked up the coffeepot and headed for them, determined to worm something out of them. "Y'all ready for another warm-up?"

Their heads jerked up as if they'd been caught sneaking a smoke behind the gym. Jim Bob and Larry Joe were dressed for church, but Roy was in his overalls on account of claiming to be an agnostic (which, according to Eula Lemoy, was related to an Episcopalian).

Jim Bob put his hands over a piece of paper in the middle of the table. "We sure are," he said.

Ruby Bee took her time replenishing their cups, all the while trying to get a peek at the paper. She even considered spilling some coffee on Jim Bob's hands so he'd move 'em real fast. "Is this a town council meeting?"

There was a moment of silence in which she could hear Larry Joe's gulp and a faint rumble from someone's stomach. Then Jim Bob said, "No, we have 'em on the first Tuesday of the month. We're talking about our deer camp."

"It's a long time till deer season," Ruby Bee said, making sure nobody missed the sarcasm. "More than six months, ain't it?"

Roy took a noisy slurp of coffee. "It sure is, but we're thinking about how to fix up the trailer so it won't be so all-fired cold next winter. I was just saying we needed to put in some new insulation."

"That's right," croaked Larry Joe as he started spooning sugar into his cup, his hand trembling so hard the crystals dusted the tabletop like an early frost. "You recall the commercials about that pink insulation that you can roll out and staple down? We were wondering how much it cost, and Jim Bob here was writing down some figures."

Jim Bob's hands stayed where they were. "But we don't want folks to know about our improvements, on account of they might vandalize the place out of spite. Folks can be awfully ornery when they're jealous, and deer season brings out the worst in 'em." His companions nodded.

"You can say that again," Ruby Bee said emphatically, then went back to the bar and replaced the coffeepot. "They're up to no good," she said to Estelle. "It's written plain as day all over their lying faces. I wish I could hear what they're saying."

"Maybe you ought to bug the booth. That way you could listen to all kinds of private conversations, go into the blackmail business, and make enough money to retire to Florida and play canasta with skinny bald men in Bermuda shorts. I wonder how much you could get from Moon Pie Buchanon not to tell his wife about him and Cloris? And how about—"

"You have been watching too much television." Ruby Bee stalked into the kitchen to check the cobblers and make sure the cloverleaf rolls were rising.

Estelle was working on a comeback when the cute little dark-haired girl from the tabloid slipped onto the next stool and said, "I heard you saw an alien last night. Could I ask you a few questions about it?"

"Is this for the *Probe*?"

Lucy opened a notebook, then scrabbled around in her purse until she found a pencil. "We're doing a major spread on the recent events in Maggody. We probably won't say anything about the awful accident, though. Our readers don't like that kind of thing." She licked the tip of the pencil, wrote the date in neat round figures, and looked up with a smile just as sweet as cotton candy. "Are you sure you actually saw this so-called alien? Couldn't it have been an ordinary person dressed in a suit, with moonlight hitting the fabric?"

"It could have been," Estelle said, offended by the cynicism in the girl's voice, "but it wasn't—unless this 'ordinary person' figured out how to walk on water and glow in the dark. If you don't mind me saying so, you have a funny attitude for someone who writes stories about singing cows and twenty-pound grasshoppers."

"You don't really believe it walked on water, do you?" Lucy's chuckle wasn't at all sweet. "Are you really that neurotic—or is Dr. Sageman paying you to make up this nonsense?"

"I cannot believe my ears! Where do you get off accusing me of lying, young lady? There are plenty of folks all over the world who've seen flying saucers and aliens."

"And there are plenty of folks who hear cows singing and watch twenty-pound grasshoppers hop across their backyards! And do you know what they are? Wacko, that's what! Brian Quint is dead, just like—" She covered her mouth with her hand, fumbled for her purse, and tried to slide off the stool.

Estelle caught her arm. "Just like who?" she demanded. "What do you know about this murder, Miss Lucy Fernclift?"

"Nothing!"

"Were you talking to Brian Quint in Raz Buchanon's barn the other night?" persisted Estelle, spitting out the words. She would have felt guilty about badgering the girl, but she was still seething over being characterized as a run-of-the-mill wacko. "Ruby Bee and I overheard the two of you. We were crouched behind a bale of hay, but we could hear every last word."

"You let go of me!"

"Estelle!" Ruby Bee gasped from the doorway. "What in tarnation's goin' on?"

Lucy stopped struggling and let her purse fall to the floor. Her face was flaming, but she didn't turn all teary or act like she was indignant and ready to file charges. Instead, she studied the surface of the bar for such a long time Estelle was tempted to nudge her to make sure she was awake.

"How about some coffee?" Ruby Bee said in her kindliest voice. She made sure the threesome in the back booth were still huddled over the table, then poured a cup of coffee for Lucy and set it in front of her. "Would you like a cinnamon roll with that? I made them this morning."

"Why were you in the barn?" asked Lucy.

Estelle slid the sugar bowl and milk pitcher down

the bar. "We thought we ought to keep an eye on certain folks," she said out of the corner of her mouth, the way the old-fashioned gumshoes did in the movies. "This is our town, after all, and we aim to protect it."

Ruby Bee had to pinch herself to keep from sniggering. "That's right," she added through tremulous lips. A little noise erupted, but she covered it with a fit of coughing.

Lucy added milk to her coffee and stirred it slowly. "Protect it from what?" she said at last. "Flying saucers and singing cows?"

Estelle, who was still in a snit, shot Ruby Bee a dark look, then turned and said, "Why did you offer Brian Quint a thousand dollars?"

"I thought you said you heard every word," Lucy countered. Any air of timidity was long gone; her voice was brusque, and her face stony.

"Then you don't deny it?"

"If you try to make something of it, I'll deny I ever set foot in whatever barn you're talking about. If you'll excuse me, I need to take some photographs of the new crop circles and get the film in the mail to my editor. Then maybe I'll drive around and check out the local talent in the pasture. Maybe I'll luck into a bovine quartet practicing 'Moooon River.'"

"Well, I never," Estelle said as Lucy went out the door. "Here we were thinking she was a mannersome little thing, and all the time she's nothing but an uppity, smart-mouthed"—she searched for an adequately derogatory term—"whatever."

Ruby Bee waited for a minute in case enlightenment was coming, then put the coffee cup in the sink and wiped the bar. "She sure did act funny, didn't she? Now that I think about it, she didn't deny she'd been in the barn with Brian. She just said she would deny it. Why do you think she would offer him a thousand dollars?"

"For an exclusive interview with Dr. Sageman?"

"I don't see how that could be. He and Dr. McMasterson seem as eager as hookers to give interviews to anybody they can snag. It'd make more sense if Brian was paying her to do an interview."

Estelle got that expression on her face that meant she had an astonishing brilliant idea, at least in her opinion. "I think we should find out a little more about this Lucy Fernclift, don't you? How do we know she really is a reporter for the *Probe*?"

"I saw her name under the story about the woman who takes her poodle to a tanning salon twice a week."

"You saw her name," Estelle said, waggling her finger, "but you didn't see her picture. How do we know this girl's not an imposture? Maybe the real Lucy Fernclift is trussed up like a turkey and lying in the trunk of a car somewhere—or even worse."

"That little thing's a murderer? I swear, Estelle, that's the silliest thing I've ever heard you say. You need to stop reading tabloids and find a new hobby. Why don't you go to that bookstore in Farberville and see if you can find a book of counted cross-stitch patterns or dried flower arrangements?"

Estelle finished the last of her sherry, patted her hair, and daintily climbed off the stool, never allowing one hint of irritation to flash across her carefully neutral face. "Thank you so much for the advice, Miss Abigail Van Hanks. I do hope that Lucy doesn't come after you with an ax later tonight, but if she does, I'll send a right nice dried flower arrangement to your funeral."

"Hold your horses," Ruby Bee muttered, thinking real hard about all the units out back. "It just happens that Rosemary is at the hospital with Cynthia. Dr. Sageman paid for a car to come pick him up and take him to the airport for an interview. Dr. McMasterson told me he was going to be at Raz's all day, dowsing the circles for electricity. Jules Channel said he was going to try to talk to the sheriff, and now Lucy Ferncliff says she's going to Raz's and then into Farberville to mail the film."

"I must say it's a load off my mind to know where everybody is this morning. I was worried they all were planning to come to my house for Sunday dinner." Estelle brushed the sweet roll crumbs off her pastel blue sweater, flashed her teeth, and made like she was gonna leave.

"So there's not one soul in any of the motel rooms. There most likely won't be anytime soon either."

"So?"

Ruby Bee went around the end of the bar and went to the back booth. "You boys are gonna have to run along," she said loudly so Estelle could hear her. "I need to lock up for a while and see to my customers at the Flamingo. Come on back at noon for dinner, Roy. I'm fixing honey-glazed ham, sweet potatoes, and corn on the cob."

After the town council had left, she opened the drawer beneath the cash register and took out a key. "Well?" she said to Estelle. "Are you gonna stand there like a garden gnome, or are you gonna help me make beds and set out clean towels?"

"What if they come back?"

"Then they'll be tickled pink to have neat beds and clean towels. I have every right to clean their rooms, Estelle. Not even Arly can argue with that. Besides, it was your idea in the first place."

"What was my idea?" Estelle said suspiciously.

"To look for an ax in Lucy Fernclift's room. We might as well check under all the beds while we're at it."

So at eleven o'clock on this pleasant Sunday morning everybody was busy, blissfully or otherwise.

Despite the two new circles in the cornfield, business had trickled off at Raz Buchanon's, but he figured things would liven up after church let out. Taking money from sightseers was damn easier than running the still and driving all over the county at night to deliver the goods, he thought as he sat on an overturned bucket by the gate. If nothing else, it gave him the chance to spend more quality time with Marjorie.

Down in the field itself, Hayden McMasterson was having a splendid time with his dowsing rods. The two teenagers he'd hired to assist him were having a splendid time, too, since they were getting paid five dollars an hour to write down whatever dumbshit things he said and draw dotted lines on his charts.

"Oh, yes!" Hayden said delightedly as the copper rods crossed each other, then whipped out. "This is definitely a three-line ley." He consulted a compass hanging on a leather thong around his neck. "Please note this ley is on a perfect north–south axis and indicate that it extends through that dead oak tree beyond the fence. Correlations have been shown between positive energy lines and damage to trees and shrubs."

"Like wow," said one of the boys.

"Yeah, like wow," said the other.

Hayden tracked the three-ley line to the fence, beamed at the bare branches above his head, and went back inside the largest circle. "The floor pattern follows the swirls, as expected, and the rods are beginning to whirl ever so slightly as I approach the center of the vortex." He glanced up at his assistants. "This concentration of nodal energy has healing power. As I stand here, I feel my inner spirit pulsate with renewed vitality. You're welcome to come and share this with me."

"That's okay," said the second boy.

After a while Hayden lucked upon yet another three-ley line. He waited patiently until it had been recorded, watching the quivering of the rods and trying to recall details of the county survey map. "Are there tumuli in the area?" he called.

The boys looked back blankly.

Hayden resumed searching for three-ley lines.

Over in Farberville at the sheriff's department Jules Channel sorted through photographs of mutilated carcasses. He did so under the supervision of a young deputy who'd been obliged to show up for the early shift after a long, hard, and financially disastrous night at the cockfights across the state line in Oklahoma. The *Weekly Examiner* had a discretionary fund for just such contingencies, or ought to, anyway.

"You'd better get going afore too long," the deputy said, mindful of the time. "Sheriff Dorfer'll kick me out on my butt if he finds out I let you read the files."

Jules opened the third folder and scanned the laborious handwriting. "Less than a week ago," he murmured, jotting down the pertinent data in his notebook. "Has the sheriff discussed these with you?"

"Naw, I mostly work in the jail, except for Sunday mornings. I can't let you stay much longer, Mr. Channel. I've already had one reprimand this month for showing up with a hangover."

"No one reported any lights in the sky? That's odd. What about unfamiliar vehicles in the area?"

The deputy was getting desperate. "You said you'd pay fifty dollars for a picture. Why doncha pick one and leave before anyone else gets here?"

"Look at the exquisite detail in this one," Jules said admiringly. "Your sheriff really ought to consider a new career."

Arthur Sageman sat in a molded plastic chair at the Farberville airport. In the next chair were stacked folders, files, charts, diagrams, and several packets of neatly labeled photographs of the crop configurations. In a box under the chair was the plaster mold of the alien footprint, wrapped carefully in newspaper. In his hand was a handwritten list of the essential points he needed to make during the interview. The general thrust was that he was the most qualified expert to narrate the segment on *Strange Stories,* despite the unpalatable fact that Hayden McMasterson had written several books about such phenomena and he himself had focused on abductions. The issue was as sticky as the floor beneath his feet.

He finally put down the list and went to the American Eagle counter, where a young woman was pecking on a computer keyboard. "Any update on the flight from Dallas?" he asked, turning on the full force of his melodious accent and crinkling his eyes at her. "Surely by now. . . ?"

"All I know is that it's still on the ground at DFW, and they're working on it."

"Please let me know when you find out something," he said, then resumed his seat and mentally reviewed what amounted to a short yet scintillating presentation. He'd had numerous meetings with television producers, and the one thing he'd discovered was the brevity of their attention spans. Three, maybe four words, and their eyes began to glaze over like a mirror in a steamy bathroom.

"Crop circles that kill," he said under his breath, searching for alliterative allure. "A town in terror. Abduction in Arkansas." He decided the ultimate one had the most potential.

Lottie Estes put her heart and soul into the finale of the offertory hymn, then lifted her hands from the piano keys and looked out at the congregation. Several folks nodded appreciatively, but Mrs. Jim Bob didn't so much as acknowledge Lottie's expertise. Neither did her husband, who was hanging his head. Lottie wondered if he was uncomfortable on account of all the sin hovering over him like a black cloud. Why, she herself wouldn't have the nerve to stick her nose in a house of the Lord if she had spent half the night committing a heinous crime. It was like sinning on top of sinning—a double-decker, in a manner of speaking.

Brother Verber cleared his throat as he approached

the pulpit. Announcements had been made earlier, and the first offering taken. Now it was time to start saving souls, to drag the strays back in the flock, to send Satan away with his pointed tail between his legs. He wasn't sure why he felt so uneasy as he spread out his notes, made sure his handkerchief was handy, and set his Bible where it was handy. The seminary had stressed the impact of arranging your props so you didn't have to fumble for 'em later.

"Sometimes we are lost at sea," he began in a deceptively mild tone, like he was offering the blessing at a Kiwanis luncheon. "We can see the sandy beach, we can see the greenery beyond it, we can see the purple mountains' majesty above the fruited plain. Yet we are floundering in a stormy sea, flailing our arms, gulping down salty water, struggling for breath, wondering if our very lives are gonna flash before our eyes as the devil grabs our legs to drag us down into an eternity of damnation."

"Amen," murmured a few tentative voices.

Brother Verber upped the intensity a notch. "Oh, yes, we're floundering something awful in Maggody these days. We're drowning **in** wickedness and lust. Our only hope is to look right here in the Bible and see if the Good Lord can throw us a lifesaver." He held up his Bible and tapped it with his finger, set it down, and flipped it open. Feigning surprise, he goggled, then said, "Why, listen to this right out of Matthew fourteen, verse twenty-four, and see if it don't ring a bell. 'But the ship was now in the midst of the sea, tossed with waves: for the wind was contrary.' "

He gave 'em a minute to appreciate the astonishing coincidence, then switched to a dramatic whisper so they'd have to strain to hear him. "Then it says: 'And in the fourth watch of the night Jesus

went unto them, walking on the sea.' Walking on the
sea, brothers and sisters! Walking right on top of the
sea! Can you believe it? Then it goes on to say:
'And when the disciples saw him walking on the
sea, they were troubled, saying, It is a spirit; and
they cried for fear.' "

"They ain't the only ones," said someone way in
the back. Heads swiveled, but nobody could identify
the guilty party. Let the records show, however, that
if looks could kill, Ira Pickerell would be planted in
the cemetery before the forsythia bloomed.

Brother Verber mopped his forehead and waited
until he felt his soul begin to swell with righteous
indignation. "Then Jesus waved at Peter and told
him to get hisself out of the boat and come for a
walk! Peter jumped right into the water, yessir, and
took off skipping across the waves, just laughing
and looking back at everybody when all of a
sudden—yes, all of a sudden—he got to thinking
about where he was."

"Hallelujah," said the hopelessly confused.

"Right here in verse thirty, it says: 'But when he
saw the wind boisterous, he was afraid.' That's right,
he was afraid just like every other sinner in this very
room who's ever considered what might happen if
he lost his faith at a real bad moment, and Satan
dragged him down!"

Mrs. Jim Bob shot her husband a quick look to see
if he was breaking out in a sweat, but he didn't appear to be doing anything except contemplating the
tips of his shoes. She elbowed him so he'd start paying attention to the sermon, as befitting the husband
of the president of the Missionary Society.

"Are we gonna let Satan drag us down into the
muddy depths of Boone Creek?" boomed Brother

Verber. It wasn't exactly what he meant to say, but he'd lost his place in his notes. "There is sin along the banks of Boone Creek. Jesus has invited us to walk across the water and cross to the shore of righteousness, but some of us won't heed His call. No, some of us are so crazed by lust and the desire to press our naked flesh—"

"You pervert!"

Everybody, including Brother Verber, Jim Bob, Mrs. Jim Bob, Lottie Estes, and Mrs. Ira Pickerell, stared as Darla Jean McIlhaney stormed up the aisle and banged out the door of the Assembly Hall.

"Amen," said a voice in the back.

TEN

◆

After I finished at the library, I dropped by the sheriff's department to leave the note to be examined for fingerprints and started back to Maggody. As I came to the airport, I remembered the locked rental car and pulled into the lot.

A dusty black limousine was parked under a sign that prohibited parking for more than three minutes. The chauffeur, a middle-aged woman with pinkish blond hair, was reading a romance novel and surreptitiously sipping a beer. I went into the terminal, which was hardly grand enough to merit the term, and headed for the rental counters.

"Chief Hanks!"

I spun around and saw Dr. Sageman seated near a plastic plant. "Are you going somewhere?" I asked as I went over to him.

"No, of course not. Surely you remember that I was supposed to meet an assistant producer from *Strange Stories*. His flight has been delayed by mechanical problems. I've been waiting for more than two hours. I think I'll have him paged at the Dallas airport and find out if we need to reschedule our interview. I am not accustomed to be kept waiting like this."

I continued to the rental counter, flashed my

badge, and explained the problem. The agent professed to have never before encountered such a problem. I asked to speak to her supervisor and was told he didn't come in on weekends. I reiterated the problem in simple sentences composed of one-syllable words. The agent suggested I return the following day, but after a few reckless threats from me she went into a back office to call her supervisor for guidance.

Dr. Sageman appeared at my elbow. "I reached my party, and he agreed to postpone the interview until tomorrow. I'll dismiss the car and ride back to Maggody with you."

"Okay," I said, as if he'd asked if I was willing to give him a ride and were awaiting my response. He marched away as the agent returned with a key.

"Don't lose this one, too," she said, viciously snapping her gum as if it were a weapon. "If you do, you'll have to get a locksmith to make new ones at your own expense."

I pocketed the key and went outside, where Sageman waited with an armload of files and a cardboard box. He followed me to my car, fussed with his precious commodities until he was satisfied nothing would fly off the backseat, and then climbed into the passenger's side.

"I'd hoped for a firm commitment," he said as we left the airport. "The producers of *Strange Stories* used to be very keen on UFO sightings, but lately they've been doing a lot on guardian angels and poltergeists. The crop circles caught their interest, though, as did the inexplicable tragedy of young Brian's untimely death."

"You're going to talk about that on television? I

thought he was your surrogate son and heir to the throne."

Sageman pulled off his glasses to flick away what must have been a very small tear. "If his death serves to warn others, it will not have been in vain."

"Let me ask you something," I said as I whipped around a truck, then swerved back into the right lane in time to avoid a bus destined, according to a placard, for Minneapolis. Arkansas's version of life in the fast lane. "You've seen burn marks like those we found, haven't you?"

"I haven't seen the marks, but from what you said, they may resemble those found in Arizona several years ago. A policeman saw a flaming cigar-shaped object go down beyond a hill, drove into the desert to investigate, and came across a craft and two humanoid figures dressed in white. Before he could get close enough to make out any more, the craft and crew departed. Although there were some discrepancies in his later testimony, the sighting was basically validated."

"And you used it in a book," I said.

"I didn't know you were one of my fans," he said, practically purring. If he hadn't been a tad nervous about my driving, he might have pinched my cheek, but his bloodless hands were clutched in his lap. "I was contacted by a local resident who had been driving along the same road when she saw the craft. She pulled over to get a better look. The next thing she knew, she was turning into a gas station four hours later. I was able to help her recover the hours of her life that had been stolen from her, and although her memories were distressing, she was relieved to learn the truth."

"The subject you called Leonard wasn't quite as relieved, was he?"

He averted his face, despite the fact the only thing of interest along the highway was a field dotted with car cadavers. "That was my only failure," he said, sighing. "The boy approached me after a seminar and begged me to take him on as a subject. He was so upset that he could barely speak. Brian advised me not to become involved, but Leonard, as I called him in the book, was so obsessed with recurrent nightmares that I felt it might do him good to bring his fears out of his subconscious so he could deal with them."

"Maybe he should have done that with a psychiatrist," I said coldly. "I checked out your credentials, Dr. Sageman. Your doctoral degree is in education administration. That hardly qualifies you to do intensive hypnotherapy, does it?"

"I am a licensed hypnotherapist, Chief Hanks."

"All you had to do to obtain this so-called license was to send twenty dollars to some outfit in Denver. Plus postage and handling, of course."

"I did extensive independent study."

"For fifty dollars Brother Verber's seminary will make him a bishop. For a hundred they'll make him a cardinal, and for five hundred he can probably be Pope Willard. That doesn't mean he can move into the Vatican and canonize his cousins, does it?"

He huffed and puffed as we drove through a winding valley. Daffodils bloomed around the ruins of a farmhouse, and wild dogwood and redbud trees added patches of color to the placid green mountainsides. I'd returned to the Ozarks to escape the madness that was Manhattan. Now I wondered if I needed to retreat even farther to escape the madness brought into this backwoods sanctuary by people such as my passenger. The Himalayas came to mind.

"I want you to leave Dahlia alone," I said as we passed the Maggody town limit sign. "No more sessions, no interviews for that damn television show, no books, no nothing. If I find out that you've so much as greeted her on the street, I'll find a way to dump you in the county jail for a long, long time. It's amazing how paperwork can disappear, Dr. Sageman. You won't lose four hours of your life; you'll lose four months of it before someone remembers to arraign you."

"She approached me," he said stiffly. "She claimed to have proof."

I turned into the parking lot in front of Ruby Bee's Bar & Grill, continued around the corner to the motel, and braked with unnecessary vigor. "She's done a lot of peculiar things in her day, but I will not tolerate you encouraging her to believe she was kidnapped by aliens and who knows what else. I'm going to her house this afternoon to talk some sense into her thick skull. You, on the other hand, are to avoid her as if she has leprosy. Got it?" I waited until he opened the car door, then added, "And don't leave town again without my permission. I'm investigating a possible murder, and until I find some answers, you may consider yourself a suspect."

He was visibly angry, but his voice was crisp, and his accent thicker than the dregs of a proper teapot. "I shall inform you should I find the necessity to go to Farberville in the morning for the interview. I'm sure it gives you satisfaction to consider me as a suspect in Brian's death. However, you told me you found his body at eleven o'clock. I was with Rosemary and Dahlia up until that time. Even if I had not been, I had no way of knowing about this sighting because I never saw the note with the map. Perhaps you might attempt to discover who stole it from under my door. That shouldn't be too challenging for a police officer of your caliber, should it?"

I sat and fumed while he collected his files and the box from the backseat, then rolled down the window so I could cool off while I drove back to the PD. Once inside, I sat and fumed a good while longer. I knew Sageman was a charlatan, and I knew he knew I knew it (if you can follow that). He was a very rich and successful charlatan who'd written a lot of books and hundreds of articles for pseudoscientific journals. He'd turned Rosemary Tant into a heroine in the field of ufology with such titles as *Abductions and Adolescence, Mother Earth; Father Star, They Come in Darkness,* and *Rosemary T. and the Extrinsic Paradox.* She'd been on the Oprah show, for gawd's sake.

I finally noticed the answering machine was blinking frenetically at me. The last thing I wanted to do was listen to lectures from Ruby Bee, but I hit the play button and sat back while the tape rewound. The first message was from McBeen, the county coroner. His tone was as peevish as usual as he confirmed the cause of death as functional hypoxemia with carbon monoxide as the likely agent. There was also a contusion on the back of the skull from a blow that could have resulted in unconsciousness; internal hemorrhaging indicated it had happened prior to death. The time of death was compatible with the hour and a half that I'd surmised, but as always, McBeen was hanging out in the ball park.

The next two messages were from Ruby Bee, who's convinced I hover over the answering machine whenever she calls, refusing to pick up the receiver simply to annoy her (there is some truth in this). Eilene Buchanon called to say she'd seen a light in the pasture behind her house; her description matched Roy's. Jim Bob wanted an official report as soon as possible. Ruby Bee insisted I speak to her then and there if I knew what was good for me. Four times.

I settled my feet on the corner of the desk and gazed at the ceiling, trying to come up with a theory—good, bad, or marginally probable—that would explain how Brian Quint had received a lethal dose of carbon monoxide in an open wooded area. Or why he was lying in the middle of the burn marks. Or what had made the burn marks. Or what the hell was going on in Raz's cornfield. Pretty soon I had enough questions for a thirty-minute game show, although the grand prize might be a mutilated carcass and a fun-filled trip to a glamorous resort on the back side of the moon.

The tabloids would no doubt claim (in capital letters) that little ol' Maggody was in the midst of an intense extraterrestrial experience—or intraterrestrial, not to slight the ITH enthusiasts. It would make a sensational story. There had been two dozen witnesses when something had taken place across the creek from the cornfield. Almost everybody in town had seen the orange lights. Roy and Eilene had seen the identical white light. An anonymous witness claimed to have seen a saucer crash. Three sober, if highly suggestible, witnesses had seen an alien walk on water. Perhaps all that could be dismissed as pandemic hysteria, but I couldn't dismiss the reality that Brian was dead.

Church had been over for an hour. I decided to go to Kevin Buchanon's house and see what he knew

about the note. For the record he's the quintessence
of the clan's cognitive inadequacies; astronomers interested in studying black holes could save billions
of the taxpayers' dollars by shining a light in his ear.

Raz was too engrossed collecting money from the
crowd to return my wave as I drove by his shack and
parked behind Kevin's car. Kevin himself came out
onto the porch as I came up the walk. "I'm glad to
see ya, Arly," he said, his throat rippling as if tiny
salmon were swimming up it to spawn, "but I ain't
sure what you kin do. I mean, I've been pounding on
the door all morning and begging to be let in, but
she stopped answering me more than an hour ago.
You know how women are."

"I'm not sure what I can do either," I said, "since
I don't know what you're talking about."

He sat down on the top step, propped his elbows
on his knees, and, after a few false starts, cradled his
face in his hands. "Dahlia's all upset about something, but she won't tell me what, and I'm worried
she's gonna do something terrible to herself. My ma
sez to let her be, that she'll get hungry sooner or
later and come out, but the refrigerator and two cab-
inets are empty. She could stay locked in the bathroom for weeks!"

"She won't do that, Kevin," I said, trying to sound
optimistic. I changed the subject before he could
press me for an explanation. "I need to ask you
something. Yesterday you delivered a note to Reggie
Pellitory while he was in the employees' lounge at
the supermarket. Where did you get it?"

"Yesterday?" He scratched his head and swallowed several times. "What time yesterday?"

"I don't know the exact time, and it doesn't matter. Where did you get the note? Did someone give it to you? Can you describe the person?"

His elbows slipped as he recoiled under the pressure of my questions. "I ain't sure what time it was," he said, choking out each word as if it were a hair ball. "I hadn't had my break yet. I was supposed to have a break at four, but then Jim Bob jumped on me because some lady dropped a bottle of ammonia in the housewares aisle. I mopped it up and swept up the glass, but the whole store was stinking to high heaven, and Jim Bob told me to get the fan from the lounge. It must have been going on five before I had a break."

"And took the note to Reggie."

"That'd be right." He grinned, satisfied.

I took a deep breath and reminded myself that valuable information would be lost forever if I strangled him. "Who gave you the note, Kevin?"

"Reggie Pellitory?"

"You delivered the note to Reggie Pellitory," I said, amazed that I could speak through clenched teeth. "Where did you get it?"

"Oh, yeah, I guess I got confused what with all your questions. Jim Bob gave me the note, Arly."

For a paralytic moment I felt as if I'd switched brains with Kevin because all I could do was stare at him with what must have been a truly idiotic expression. "Jim Bob Buchanon?"

"That'd be the only Jim Bob I know. It was awful good of him to give me back my old job, wasn't it? I dint have much luck selling those fancy vacuum cleaners, but I—"

"He's a prince." I went back to the car and drove down the hill to the highway, my thoughts as twitchy as the needle on the speedometer. Jim Bob

Buchanon? If he'd actually seen a spacecraft in the woods, why on earth would he pay Reggie fifty dollars to take a cryptic note to Dr. Sageman when all he had to do was tell him? If for some obscure reason Jim Bob felt the need for anonymity, why hadn't he made a muffled telephone call or slid the note under the door himself?

Hizzoner had demanded a report as soon as possible. I was going to obey orders, but only after a brief detour by the PD to fake a little evidence.

"What's taking Arly so long?" Ruby Bee muttered as she wiped her hands on a dish towel and hung it on a hook. Noon had come and gone, and only a few tourists were still polishing off the last crumbs of piecrust or dawdling over coffee.

Estelle craned her neck to make sure no one was near enough to eavesdrop, then said, "We don't know for sure what we found means anything. There could be a perfectly reasonable explanation. Besides, what's Arly gonna say when you admit we searched the units? You know how poorly she takes it when we go out of our way to help her."

"Who could forget?" Ruby Bee was gonna say more when Jules Channel came across the dance floor and sat down on a stool midway down the bar. He was wearing a white sweater that Ruby Bee would have bet was cashmere; it made a nice contrast with his tan and emphasized the whiteness of his teeth. It occurred to her that she hadn't gotten around to inquiring about his marital status.

"Too late for lunch?" he asked.

Ruby Bee gave him a menu. "How'd you make out with Sheriff Dorfer?"

"He wasn't there. I suppose I'll go back tomorrow

morning and see what I can find out about these cattle mutilations." Jules paused delicately, then added, "You don't know anything about them, do you?"

"Of course we do," said Estelle. "The dispatcher, LaBelle, is one of my regulars, and she sez the sheriff's about to rip out what hair he's got left. The lab down in Little Rock is swamped with more important things—like Brian Quint's autopsy—and may not get around to examining the tissue samples until the end of next week."

"Oh." Jules resumed his study of the menu.

Ruby Bee wasn't sure, but she thought she saw a little smile on his face. She was beginning to get disillusioned with the two tabloid reporters. First Lucy Ferncliff had accused Estelle (and Ruby Bee, by proxy) of lying about the alien at Boone Creek. Now Jules Channel was smirking like he'd heard a dirty joke. It seemed downright hypocritical to write stories about mermaids and naked Pentecostals, then make fun of folks that were as honest as the day was long.

"So," she said casually, fixing to work the conversation around to that very issue before she wasted any time exploring his eligibility, "how long have you worked for the *Weekly Examiner*?"

"A year or so." He ordered the special and coffee, still smiling to himself, then said, "I'd like to interview both of you about what you saw last night. I'd also like to take some photographs of you pointing at the creek. The actual spot's liable to be off-limits, but we can find someplace else with similar characteristics."

Estelle had seen the smile, too. "And lie about it? It seems to me there are folks visiting Maggody right this minute that don't mind that a one whit.

Maybe that goes with living in a big city. Around these parts we may not be college graduates, but we believe in sticking to the truth—for the most part anyway."

"So I've noticed," Jules said, turning serious. "Ladies, I truly believe you saw something last night and you weren't exaggerating." He leaned forward and, in a voice barely audible, added, "But I think Dr. Sageman is behind it."

"You do?" whispered Ruby Bee. At the end of the bar Estelle was too stunned to say much of anything.

"Yes, I do. Even though I work for a tabloid, I'm still an investigative reporter. I want to get to the bottom of this as much as you, and I want to know what happened to Brian Quint." He sat back up and shrugged. "The problem is, my hands are tied. Whenever I approach Sageman, all I get is a restatement of his dogma that we're being visited by extraterrestrials. He's not fooling me, though; I'm convinced he knows more than he's telling us."

Estelle abandoned her stool and moved next to Jules. "He told me that there was a government conspiracy," she said breathlessly. "It goes all the way back to the late 1940s, when a flying saucer crashed in New Mexico and the military hushed it up. The day after the crash was reported, men from a nearby army air force base came and loaded up all the scraps. Then an officer announced that it was nothing but a weather balloon."

"He also said that ever since then," contributed Ruby Bee, "the government has been collecting debris from crashes—along with alien corpses—and keeping them in an underground laboratory out in the desert."

Jules shook his head wonderingly. "Sageman told you this? I'm really surprised, since . . ."

"Since what?" demanded Ruby Bee and Estelle, not precisely in unison but damn close to it.

"He works for military intelligence. I can't divulge my sources, but I was told by a Pentagon official that Sageman is on a top secret commission that investigates UFOs and reports directly to the President." Jules glanced around the barroom to make sure no one with a cloak and dagger was lurking in the shadows. "This underground facility does exist. The workmen who built it were told that they and their families would suffer if they ever admitted knowledge of it, but I found a painter who was willing to talk. One day he got off the elevator on the wrong floor and saw what at first he thought was a regular hospital nursery with incubator lights and cribs. Then he realized the inhabitants were small gray humanoids with black, almond-shaped eyes."

"Like what we saw," said Ruby Bee. She had to lean back and fan herself with a menu as she imagined a whole room filled with aliens.

"What we saw wasn't small," protested Estelle. "We both agreed it was seven feet tall."

"These," Jules whispered, "were children." He waited for them to gasp, which they did, then went on. "Sageman is one of the masterminds of the conspiracy. His assignment is to provide disinformation to the public and at the same time destabilize and discredit the UFO movement. If people dismiss all these sightings as craziness, they won't demand to know the truth."

Ruby Bee was fanning herself so vigorously her hair was standing on end. Estelle wasn't doing much better; she tried to take a swallow of sherry, but most of it dribbled down her chin as she stared at Jules.

Smelling their fear, he went in for the kill. "I've suspected this for a long time, but I found proof when I took the job at the *Weekly Examiner*. My editor receives a certain sum of money from the Pentagon for every story about a saucer or a close encounter. Do you remember the stories during the campaign about a goofy alien that was photographed with the major candidates? I got a thousand-dollar bonus for each of them. The one about the President's wife adopting an alien infant was worth twice that."

"Oh, my gawd," said Ruby Bee, who remembered every word of the story because there had been an actual artist's depiction of the alien baby, and it reminded her of her second cousin's son (who'd been expelled from grade school three times and dropped out all together when he was nine).

Estelle managed to swallow some sherry this time. "Why don't you write a story and expose the conspiracy? You could give it to one of the real newspapers or even a television show."

"I need hard evidence," he said. "What's so frustrating is I know where to get it, but not how. Sageman keeps everything on computer disks, from dates and numbers to the reports the Majestic Twelve commission submits to the President, and he never goes anywhere without them. If I could get my hands on those disks for even a few hours, I'd take the information to every legitimate news source in the country and force the government to tell us what's going on—before it's too late."

Ruby Bee was having a hard time catching her breath as she tried to sort out what he'd said. It was one thing to listen to Dr. Sageman and Dr. McMasterson bickering about whether the aliens were coming down from the sky or up from the ocean. Dahlia's declaration in the back booth—well, it'd made for some interesting discussion afterward. Even what she'd seen with her own two eyes didn't make any sense. But the man sitting right across from her had proof that UFOs existed and the aliens had made contact.

"Too late?" gasped Estelle.

"Too late to save our civilization," Jules said dolefully. "What if they've come to enslave us? They have a superior intellect and the technology to travel faster than the speed of light. They haven't come here to learn from us; they've come for their own dark purposes." He put aside the menu and stood up, his face scrunched up with pain and his eyes glittery with tears. "I've lost my appetite. Maybe I'll take a drive and enjoy my freedom while I can. It won't be long before . . . we may not be able to do that anymore." He trudged heavily toward the door, encumbered by the incipient shackles of slavery.

Ruby Bee's knees were so wobbly she had to grab the edge of the bar to steady herself. "Wait, Mr. Channel. Maybe I can help you."

He hesitated, then turned around. "I don't see what you can do, Ruby Bee. Unless I have access to Sageman's computer files, we're doomed. It's just as well I never had any children; the thought of them toiling in underground mines on a planet light-years away, bred like cattle, living lives of quiet desperation"—his voice cracked—"it's too horrible to bear."

"You said Dr. Sageman travels with all his computer files. I straightened up his room earlier today. He'd moved the furniture around to use the table as a desk. It's a real mess, but next to the computer I noticed a pile of flat plastic squares." She formed a rough shape with her thumbs and forefingers to demonstrate the size. "Would those be what you're talking about?"

"They might be," Jules said as he came back to the bar and reached over it to squeeze her shoulder.

Estelle felt obliged to contribute to the salvation of the planet. "I looked more carefully while Ruby Bee made the beds and cleaned the bathroom. There was a thick pile of that paper with holes along the margins. I didn't have time to do more than glance at it, but what I read had to do with the size and arrangement of crop circles in Raz's field."

"Were there labels on the disks?" Jules asked, staring at her.

Now that she had his full attention, Estelle took her time recalling the scene. "Most of them had stickers with dates or names written on them. I didn't find one that said Maggody, but it may have been in the computer."

One of the women in the first booth was looking at them as if she could hear every word. Ruby Bee went over to the jukebox, dropped in a quarter, and punched the handiest button. An adenoidal wail filled the room as she came back and said, "I reckon I could let you in Dr. Sageman's room. I'll have to go with you, of course, since it's my motel and I have an obligation to my guests—even if they're government agents. One of these days Arly might get around to having babies, and I don't aim to see my grandchildren end up as slaves." She realized Estelle was glowering hard enough to melt wax candles. "You can be the lookout," she said to her in a spurt of generosity.

"When?" demanded Jules.

"I don't know," she said. "We'll have to think of a way to make sure he's out of his room long enough for you to make copies or whatever you need to do."

The three settled down to discuss their strategy as someone in Nashville bemoaned the loss of his truck, his dawg, his job, and his woman (in that order).

ELEVEN

✦

I made sure my badge was nice and shiny before I knocked on Hizzoner's front door. I was hoping to have a private conversation with him, but Mizzoner opened the door and regarded me with what can only be described as ill-concealed panic.

"What?" she shrieked, shrinking into the hallway as if I were accompanied by a gang of glassy-eyed children from *The Village of the Damned*.

It was not the warmest reception I'd ever had, but rather than worry about it, I said, "I'm sorry if I'm interrupting your dinner, but I need to speak to Jim Bob."

Her mouth tightened until her lips were invisible. After a quick glance over her shoulder she came out onto the porch and closed the door behind her. "You don't have any call to speak to him. He's been working hard all week and deserves to rest on the seventh day, just like the Bible says. If you'd attend church more often, you'd be familiar with the notion."

"If I had a deputy, I might be able to take the day off myself. Now that I think about it, there's nothing I'd rather do more than sit in a pew at the Voice of the Almighty Lord Assembly Hall and listen to one of Brother Verber's inspirational sermons. I just know I'd come out with a hymn on my lips and a halo over my head. Maybe I could even come over here after church to have friend children with y'all. Why don't you put in a good word with Jim Bob about increasing the budget so I can afford some of that old-time religion?"

"I will not tolerate sacrilege on the Sabbath," she said, her posture as rigid as a majorette's. If she'd had a baton, she probably would have bopped me on the head, but as it was, she muttered something about mending my ways, shook a finger at me, and started for the door.

I cut her off. "I really do need to speak to Jim Bob for a minute. Is he here?"

"Jim Bob has nothing to do with this."

"Yes, he does," I said, wondering how much she knew about the origin of the note. I'd never thought of their marriage as a close relationship replete with cozy conversations beneath the blankets; they were more likely to have bedrooms at opposite ends of the house, if not opposite corners of the county. "He may not be the one who came up with the scheme, but at some point he became involved."

"You know perfectly well who's behind this. Jim Bob may have unwittingly allowed himself to be used, but anything he did was out of charity, not out of greed."

The conversation was getting so weird I had to resist the urge to step back and check the sky for hovering craft. "Jim Bob did something out of charity?"

"One of the commandments is to love thy neighbor as thyself, Miss Chief of Police. All Jim Bob did was come to the aid of a neighbor who needed a helping hand."

"Who is this neighbor?"

"Are you playing games with me?"

If I was, I wished someone would slip me a copy
of the rules. And a scorecard, for that matter. "I'm in
the middle of an investigation," I said, "and I need
to speak to Jim Bob."

"As soon as he finishes his dinner, he's going
down to the SuperSaver, but I don't want you to pes-
ter him while he's there either. Shouldn't you be
worried about this poor boy's death last night? Murder's a sight more important than whatever little
transgressions Jim Bob may have committed."

I opened my mouth to explain the purpose of my
visit, decided against it, and gave her a meek smile.
"Guess that's what I'll do."

Temporarily thwarted, I drove back to the main
road, sat at the intersection, and watched the stoplight change a couple of times while I contemplated
my next move. I finally drove out County 102,
parked behind Rosemary's car on the now well-
trampled shoulder, and walked to the clearing to find
out how good my memory was.

It proved to be adequate. Brian had not fallen and
hit his head against a rock, unless he'd done so on
the gravel bar twenty feet away. If he'd staggered
into a tree, the coroner would have found bits of
bark in the wound. The weeds were thick enough to
cushion a fall.

The true believers no doubt would claim that
Brian had been clipped on the back of his head by
an appendage on a craft—or attacked by a lurching
silver alien. They would also claim that the burn
marks were evidence that the craft had utilized some
sort of fiery propulsion system—with carbon monoxide as the by-product.

And if the perpetrators were to be brought to jus-
tice, I'd have to serve arrest warrants in the region

of Canis Major. We'd have attorneys from Androm-
eda and a prosecutor from Pegasus. We could round
up jurors from the cast of *Star Wars.*

I walked back to the road and along the shoulder
to the illegal garbage dump. The only thing that
might be classified as a blunt object was a cracked
toilet seat, but it was covered with a layer of dust.
The pieces of lumber were too long to be swung
with ease. Bouncing a tire off someone's head
wasn't likely to do much damage.

It was time to get busy finding out when, how,
and why Brian had left the gravel bar across from
Raz's field. There were only 755 locals and a couple
of dozen visitors (of the terrestrial variety anyway).
Unless Brian had been joyriding in a UFO, surely
someone had seen him between seven and eleven the
previous night.

I headed for the PD to see if Harve could be bul-
lied into sending me a couple of deputies, preferably
with hardy knuckles.

After Kevin had quit trying to talk to her through
the door and left for work, Dahlia came out of the
bathroom, detoured through the kitchen for a can of
soda pop, and went out to the backyard. She
couldn't see Raz's cabin through the brush, but she
could hear car doors slamming and voices calling
back and forth as more folks arrived to stare at the
crop circles. It was a nice enough day, as sunny and
warm as a body could hope for in early spring, but
she shivered as she searched the sky for a flash of
silver that would warn her they were coming for
her—again.

Dr. Sageman promised her that she'd remember
what she said during the session, and as she stood in

the yard, hands on her hips, eyes seeping tears, she did. He'd been real careful not to hurry her along but instead had spoken in a honeyed voice and even patted her on the arm when she got to shaking when the images got so horrifying she couldn't hardly bear 'em.

And the ordeal wasn't over, not by a long shot. She had proof that they'd come for her before, and they'd come back when it was time to retrieve the monster growing inside her. As if on cue, it growled like a fierce wild animal, and she would have fainted dead away if she hadn't realized at the last moment that it was her stomach instead of her womb making its desires known.

There was no way to escape them either. With some coaxing from Dr. Sageman, she'd remembered the tiny metal pellet they'd inserted way up in her nose so they could keep track of her whereabouts. She pinched the bridge of her nose, wishing she could sneeze hard enough to make the pellet come shooting out. But Rosemary had suffered with one, too, and she'd said there was no way short of surgery to get rid of the pesky pellet. All you could do was wait until they were done with you.

There was no place to run, no place to hide.

Wheezing bleakly, Dahlia trudged back inside and went to the kitchen to fix herself some lunch. Kevin wouldn't be back till late, so there wasn't much reason to stay in the bathroom all afternoon and evening. But as soon as his headlights turned into the driveway, she figured she'd have to retreat. Refusing to talk to him was causing him pain, but the truth would squash him like an armadillo on the interstate. She couldn't do that.

* * *

A deputy showed up toward the middle of the afternoon. We arbitrarily divided the town, and he headed for the Pot o' Gold Mobile Home Park and the little subdivision with what the builder called cul-de-sacs and everybody else called dead ends. I worked my way up the hill toward Kevin and Dahlia's house, although I didn't bother with them or with Raz, who was waving his arms and arguing with several gray-haired visitors who must have demanded a senior citizen discount.

No one admitted having seen Brian Quint at either side or in transit. However, every last soul with whom I spoke had heard all about the mysterious death. The hyperbole had reached such epic proportions that husbands were keeping loaded guns by the front door and wives were sharpening butcher knives. In broad daylight, mind you. When it started getting dark, missionaries and door-to-door salesmen were going to discover they were endangered species.

I stopped by the supermarket to see if I could corner Jim Bob. A checker directed me to the office, where I found my potential witness on the telephone. I sat and waited until he banged down the receiver, scribbled a note, and then turned around to glower at me.

"I said I wanted a report first thing this afternoon," he said, his belly inflating and his eyes bulging as if he were a bullfrog. "Maybe you've forgotten that you're employed by the town council, Chief Hanks, but we sure as hell haven't. When's your contract up?"

I unpinned my badge and tossed it at him. "It's all yours—lock, stock, and flying saucer."

"Save the hysterics for when you get a run in your

panty hose," he said sourly. "Tell me what all you found out about the boy that died last night. Then you can get back to investigating and I can run my store—okay?"

I toyed with the idea of stomping out of the room, but I wasn't sure how far I'd get with less than a hundred dollars in my savings account. "If you want an official report, call an official meeting of the town council. In the meantime, I need to know about the note you gave Kevin yesterday afternoon."

"I don't write notes to the stock boys."

I pulled out the faked note and dropped it on his desk. "The X on the map is where I found the body last night," I said, watching for his reaction.

He picked it up and read it under his breath. "You think I wrote this? I didn't see any silver disk crash anywhere, and if I had, why would I write this pissant note and give it to Kevin? I'd be more likely to alert those reporters from the tabloids and call the television station in Faberville, wouldn't I?"

"It was in an envelope with Reggie Pellitory's name on it. Where'd you get it?"

"Oh, yeah," he said, nodding. "It was stuck under the door when I unlocked the store yesterday morning. I meant to give it to Reggie myself and remind him this ain't a damn post office, but I got busy. When Kevin came here to say he'd finished mopping, I gave him the note and told him to find Reggie." Even though he was a Buchanon, he realized the significance of the note and gave me a puzzled look. "Did Reggie show this to the Quint fellow? Is that why he went to the low-water bridge?"

"Reggie was supposed to deliver it to Dr. Sageman," I said evasively. "I'm still—"

"Yeah, I talked to Sageman the other afternoon, and he said he's going to give a real important lecture about the circles and all this crazy shit at some conference and maybe even write a book about 'em. Those tabloid reporters are eating it up, too. Next week when their stories come out, we're going to be flooded with tourists." He picked up my badge and tossed it back at me. "Make sure your radar gun's working, Chief Hanks; you might hand out enough traffic tickets to justify the salary we pay you."

"It won't take many," I said, then went back outside, no more enlightened than I'd been. Despite Mrs. Jim Bob's odd remarks, Jim Bob didn't seem to know much about the note. Concluding that she must have been referring to one of his innumerable torrid affairs with women in double-wide trailers, I repinned my badge on my shirt and drove over to Elsie McMay's house to ask her if she'd seen Brian Quint the previous night.

Estelle came into the barroom and took her customary stool. "Dr. Sageman's still in his room," she reported. "I peeked through the window and saw him lying on the bed. I could hear Dahlia's voice, so he must be playing the tape from her session. I'd sure like to hear what all she had to say about being kidnapped by aliens."

Ruby Bee set down a glass of sherry. "You'd think that if the aliens were so all-fired intelligent, they'd have picked someone easier to beam up. If they're really making women pregnant with their babies, like Rosemary says, it seems to me they should have ruled out anyone with a drop of Buchanon blood. Her grandfather was a double cousin Buchanon on his mother's side. He lit so many fires that his wife had to follow him around day and night with a fire extinguisher."

"This ain't the time to worry about family trees," Estelle said. "We promised Jules we'd figure out a way to get Dr. Sageman out of his room. Short of starting a fire ourselves, I can't think of anything. He looked real comfortable and liable to stay there the rest of the afternoon, particularly since he doesn't have a car. He's not the sort that'd hitchhike—or get picked up if he tried."

"Is Rosemary's car still parked by the low-water bridge?"

"It's not in the parking lot, and she told me that Arly offered to drive her to the hospital this morning. Even if we went and fetched it for Dr. Sageman, that doesn't mean he'll go someplace else so we can sneak Jules into the room to copy the files."

Ruby Bee tried to think of a plan while she took a fresh pitcher of beer to some truckers in one of the booths. "What if," she said as she returned, "we fetch the car and leave it in front of Rosemary's room? Then we tell Dr. Sageman that we heard there was another cow cut to ribbons way on the other side of Emmet. We can give him the wrong directions and have him driving all over the county till dark."

"We don't have a car key, for one thing. Are you aiming to hot-wire it?"

"There was a key on the dresser in her room," Ruby Bee countered. She took a room key from the drawer and put it down in front of Estelle. "You go get it while I get those fellows cleared out. I'll be ready to go as soon as you get back."

Estelle picked up the key. "I'll do it, but don't think you can order me around like I'm some kind of private in your personal army, Mrs. Patton." Having made her point, she stalked across the dance floor and continued out the door without so much as a glance over her shoulder.

She slowed down once she came around the corner. Dr. McMasterson's car was gone, but Lucy Fernclift's was parked in front of No. 3. Jules's car was in front of No. 4, but she didn't worry about him since he was the one wanting to get inside Dr. Sageman's room. The curtains were wide open in No. 5, which meant Dr. Sageman might see her. If Jules was right about him being in government intelligence, she might end up in the dungeon of the underground laboratory, making small talk with the painter that'd blabbed about the alien babies.

None of the private eye shows she watched so faithfully had dealt with this particular dilemma. The worst danger came from Dr. Sageman, she decided. If he stood up, there was nothing she could do to avoid being caught, but as long as he stayed on the bed, she figured she was safe.

She walked briskly to the door of Ruby Bee's unit, trying to act like she had every right to be there. Then, when no one opened a door or shouted out a window, she scurried to No. 2, unlocked the door, and ducked inside.

Once she'd caught her breath, she headed for the dresser and grabbed a key. She was on her way back across the room when the door opened. The sight of the gun pointed at her face set her heart to thudding so wildly that it was a marvel she didn't keel right over on the avocado shag.

I reconnoitered with the deputy late in the afternoon. He admitted he'd had no luck; I admitted the same, thanked him, and let him escape to the poker game in the back of the sheriff's office. There was a message on the answering machine, but as soon as I determined it was from Ruby Bee, I turned it off and called the hospital in Farberville. Rosemary answered the phone in Cynthia Dodder's room and agreed to wait in the lobby for me.

The telephone rang before I could leave. After a brief debate I warily picked up the receiver.

"Didn't you get my message?" Ruby Bee took off belligerently. "It's a good thing I didn't hold my breath while I waited for you to call me back!"

"I'm on my way to the hospital to pick up Rosemary. I'll call you when I get back." I did not add that weather conditions in hell would have an influence on the alacrity with which I'd do so.

"Estelle has disappeared."

"Maybe she was beamed up to give the crew haircuts," I said. "I told Rosemary—"

"This is not the time to make stupid jokes. Estelle has been gone for more than an hour, and you need to stop smarting off and find her before something terrible happens."

"An hour's not very long. How do you know she didn't remember she needed to run an errand in Farberville or drop by Elsie's for coffee and cookies?"

Ruby Bee snorted like a jumpy horse. "For one thing, her car is parked out in front of the bar and grill. I don't reckon she walked all the way to Elsie's house."

I hoped Rosemary would find a way to amuse herself in the lobby because there was no way I could get off the telephone until I heard the entire story. "Tell me what happened," I said.

"She went to one of the units to get something. It shouldn't have taken more than a minute or two. I waited for a while, then closed up and went to look for her. She's not anywhere to be found."

"Couldn't she have gone inside to talk to someone?"

"I asked Jules and Lucy, but they haven't seen her. Dr. Sageman's taking a nap. Dr. McMasterson's gone, but I used my key to look inside his room. She's not in my unit either."

"What about Rosemary's unit?"

"She isn't in there. It's like she really was kidnapped by aliens right there in the parking lot. I know Estelle can be irritating at times, but she's been my best friend for more years than I care to recollect, and you have to find her."

I tugged on my chin for a moment, then did some quick calculations. "Okay, you call everybody you can think of and make sure she isn't buying a lamp from Roy or giving an emergency manicure. It'll take me an hour to fetch Rosemary. If you haven't heard from Estelle by the time I get back, I'll start looking for her."

"She could be dead an hour from now!"

I repeated my instructions, hung up in the middle of her sputters, and went out to my car. Across the road Roy was helping a tourist load an armoire into the back of a station wagon. The Suds of Fun was surrounded by unfamiliar cars, and farther down the road the parking lot at the SuperSaver was filled to capacity. Jim Bob had been wrong about one thing; tourists weren't waiting for stories to appear in the *Probe* and the *Weekly Examiner.* One of the minor mysteries was how they'd found us since Maggody doesn't always appear on maps. Have a look if you don't believe me.

I wasn't too worried about Estelle, although I was more than a little curious about Ruby Bee's off-handed explanation that Estelle had gone "to one of the units to get something." It was challenging not to suspect they were running an unofficial investigation of their own. In the past they'd ended up in so much hot water that they could have filled all the hot tubs in Hollywood.

Grumbling to myself, I started for the hospital.

Joyce Lambertino marched into the living room and turned off the television. "I just heard the most peculiar thing from Saralee. You'd better listen."

"Can't it wait until the game is over?" asked Larry Joe. "It's the eighth inning, and the score's tied."

"This family's safety is more important than a bunch of filthy, overgrown boys that seem to take pride in spittin' and scratchin' in front of a camera. You need to hear what Saralee told me while she was drying the dishes."

Larry Joe thought about arguing, but Joyce looked pretty determined to have her say. "What did she tell you?"

"She woke up real early this morning and went into the kitchen to get some cereal. She heard funny noises out in the backyard, so she peeked out the window over the sink, thinking it was a stray dog or even maybe be Raz's sow. What she saw was a great big hairy creature dressed in rags and rooting through the garbage can for food. She ran back to her bed and hid under the covers till she heard us get up."

"Saralee watches way too many scary movies for an eleven-year-old. I haven't heard of anyone seeing a bear lately, but I'll ask around at school tomorrow."

"It was a hairy man," Saralee announced as she

came into the living room. "It wasn't any stupid old bear."

"Were you wearing your glasses?" Larry Joe asked her in the same voice he used when he was grilling his third-period shop class about missing socket wrenches.

"I know what I saw, and it wasn't a bear. Bears don't wear overalls except in picture books."

"Then it was a tramp that was hungry. I'll call Arly and let her know he's in these parts, and she can drive him to a shelter in Farberville. Now can I watch the game?"

"It was Bigfoot," Saralee said to Joyce. "If he gets hold of fat little Traci or the baby, he won't need to eat from the garbage can. He'll just rip off their flesh and suck the blood right out of their bones. Larry Junior's safe; he'd taste like green persimmons." She screwed up her face and made some gagging noises to demonstrate how any discerning cannibal would react to a mouthful of her cousin, who was overly fond of punching her when he wasn't yanking her braids until she cried.

"That's dumb," Larry Joe muttered.

Joyce came close to slapping the smirk right off his face. "Larry Joe Lambertino, you get off your lazy butt and go make sure this creature's not hiding out behind the forsythia bushes, waiting for you to leave so he can break down the back door. Then I want you to call the sheriff's department and tell them to get over here to investigate this. I don't know for sure what Saralee saw, but I do know that no one is gonna watch any baseball games until we find out once and for all."

Saralee grinned at him as he headed for the kitchen. Once the back door banged, she said, "Traci and Lissie Milvin took their dolls on a picnic to the other side of the field. They left about an hour ago."

"Oh, no," Joyce said, obliged to sit down as her knees turned to jelly. The walls seemed to turn bright red, and she could almost hear shrill screams of terror and savage growls. "Why didn't you tell me?"

"I just now remembered."

"Go tell Uncle Larry Joe that he needs to find 'em and get 'em back here!"

"Maybe it would be safer to send Larry Junior," Saralee said as she cleaned her glasses on her shirt-tail, settled them back on her nose, and blinked solemnly. She was going to elaborate, but Aunt Joyce was making funny little gulping noises and rocking back and forth like she was on the front porch of the county old folks' home.

She waited for a minute to see if Aunt Joyce was going to do anything else that might be interesting, then went through the kitchen and out to the patio, where Uncle Larry Joe was picking up the scattered garbage. He didn't seem all that pleased when she told him about Lissie and Traci, and the look he gave her was about as nasty as the one Bigfoot had given her when he saw her at the window.

It occurred to Saralee, who was a sight sharper than her relatives, that there might be money to be made. If she went inside, no way Aunt Joyce would allow her to leave, so she went through the carport and cut across the neighbor's yard. She was trying to decide how to spend her windfall as she trotted down the road toward the highway and the Flamingo Motel.

TWELVE

$\blacklozenge$

"I noticed Dr. Sageman's written several books about your abduction experiences," I said to Rosemary as I drove back toward Maggody.

"Four," she said promptly. "The newest one is by far the most insightful. The second caused an incredible uproar."

"How did you get hooked up with him?"

"It was through Cynthia. She convinced me to attend a UFORIA meeting, and I ended up joining the group, even though it was naughty of me because I wasn't a believer. Arthur presented a lecture at a conference in Eureka Springs, in which he described a series of past-life regressions he'd conducted with a young man who had come to Earth many times over the last two centuries to bring technological advances. As I sat in the audience, I felt a growing uneasiness that compelled me to have a word with Arthur after his lecture. He hypnotized me for the first time that very evening."

"And you remembered the abduction?"

"Yes, although it was very misty at first. It took many more sessions before the details emerged with any clarity and I was able to acknowledge the sexual assault and its painful consequences."

"Are you aware that Sageman has no legitimate credentials in the field of hypnotherapy?"

She stiffened as if I'd jabbed her; which is what I'd meant to do, metaphorically speaking. "I suppose you found the hearsay about Leonard. I met the boy myself, and he told me he'd been in mental institutions several times while he was in high school and college. He was convinced he was being stalked by invisible aliens. He caused such a disturbance at one of the lectures that he was asked to leave the conference."

"But Sageman went ahead and hypnotized him. Wouldn't it have been better to get him professional help?"

"In retrospect it would have, but Arthur thought he was doing the right thing. There was no way he could have predicted that Leonard would commit suicide."

I did not say that he might have recognized the danger signs if he'd been trained. Instead, I said, "I've ordered Sageman not to have any more sessions with Dahlia. She may not be as unstable as Leonard was, but she's capable of some crazy things. I don't want you to have any contact with her either."

"If you say so," she said with a sniff, then folded her legs and lowered her head.

We rode in silence to the low-water bridge. I parked behind her car and handed her the key. "It may be a little dusty from the fingerprint powder," I said.

"I fail to understand why they went to all that trouble," she said, still angry over my dictum. "Cynthia was on the way to the hospital long before Brian Quint was asphyxiated by the alien craft."

"The crime squad didn't find anything," I admitted. "Sorry about the inconvenience."

She forgave me enough to nod, then got in her car. Once she'd started the engine, I turned around and drove to the bar and grill to find out if Estelle was back on her stool, sipping sherry, sucking pretzels, and plotting to make my life miserable. And if someone offered me a grilled cheese sandwich, I wouldn't refuse it.

Ruby Bee was out the door before I'd switched off the ignition. "What took you so long?" she demanded. "You promised you'd be back in an hour, missy—not an hour and a half."

"I had to drag Rosemary out of the hospital gift shop before she cleaned them out of kidney stone key chains. Then I took her to get her car and came here." I touched her shoulder. "No sign of Estelle?"

"No, and I must have called everybody in town. Eula Lemoy's line was busy for so long that I finally drove over to her trailer and made her stop talking to her sister in Arkadelphia long enough to answer my question. I even went out to Estelle's house to make sure she hadn't gone there for some senseless reason. I had Jim Bob page her at the supermarket, and looked for myself at the launderette and the pool hall."

"We'll find her," I said.

"Why don't you get a dog from the police like you did last winter? He can pick up her scent from her purse and follow her trail from the parking lot."

I winced as I remembered my canine chum, Larry. "Let's not go that far just yet. You said that Estelle went to get something from one of the units. It wasn't yours, was it?"

"No, it wasn't mine. We decided to do Rosemary

a little favor by fetching her car for her. Estelle went to get the key."

"I had the key up until ten minutes ago. Cynthia left it in the car when she went to search for the crashed spacecraft."

"So it was the wrong key. The important thing is to find Estelle before something terrible happens to her. I don't understand why she went off without telling me where she was going. It's been nigh onto three hours since she disappeared."

I was on the verge of repeating my promise to find her when Saralee Lambertino came around the back of the car. "What room are the tabloid reporters in?" she asked Ruby Bee, apparently too intent on her mission to dally with any standard pleasantries.

"Why do you want to know that?"

Saralee bared her shiny braces. "Because I got a story for them, and they might pay me."

"What story?" I asked as calmly as I could.

"I ain't telling anybody else till I talk to the reporters. I hear they're offering folks a hundred dollars. I may just buy myself a chemistry set and learn Larry Junior a thing or two."

Ruby Bee grabbed a blond braid. "Listen here, young lady, I'm not in the mood for any sass from the likes of you. You spit out whatever it is, or I'll march you inside and find a pair of scissors."

"Bigfoot was rooting through the garbage early this morning," she said sulkily. "I saw him out the kitchen window."

"Bigfoot," I echoed without enthusiasm, but without much astonishment either. It'd been that kind of week.

"That's who I saw," she said, then elaborated with a description of the visitor and what she seemed to hope was happening to her cousins at that very moment. She did so in such a matter-of-fact voice that both Ruby Bee and I were reduced to gaping at her, our expressions equally appalled.

"When I left, Uncle Larry Joe was gonna call the sheriff," Saralee concluded, scowling. Her face brightened. "But even if he did, it may be too late by now."

I reminded myself that I was standing in a parking lot on a sunny afternoon, in the company of my own mother and a disconcerting but basically unremarkable child. We were not on a Hollywood set, nor were we in any danger of being wafted upward in a beam of light. This may have taken a moment, but I eventually said, "Saralee, I want you to go home and stay there. If I find out you've been spouting off any more of this grisly nonsense, I will show up and personally stuff you in the garbage can. Headfirst, too."

She must have heard the sincerity in my voice because she had enough sense to march off in the direction she'd come, her braids swishing rebelliously.

Ruby Bee waited until Saralee was out of earshot, then said, "There's something I might ought to tell you. Estelle and I were in Raz's barn the night the alien appeared, and—"

"The barn?"

"It seemed like a good idea at the time, although I'd be hard pressed to explain it now. Anyway, we overheard Lucy Fernclift trying to bribe Brian. She as much as admitted it this morning."

I sat on the hood of the car and demanded the entire story. There wasn't much to it, I'm sorry to say, but I was starved for anything remotely resembling a clue. What she told me barely qualified.

"Now," I said, "you are going back inside in case Estelle calls to explain where she is. I'll interview all your charming guests out back, and if no one has any information, I'll ... think of something else." I paused and added, "If Harve calls wanting me to beat the bushes for Bigfoot, tell him I'm busy."

I marched off much as Saralee had, although my pinned bun was incapable of swishing in any fashion whatsoever. I did a cursory search of Ruby Bee's unit, finding nothing more incriminating than a stash of candy bars adequate for a very lengthy hibernation and a dog-eared paperback with a cover that featured a tawny young hero with unlikely convexities.

Rosemary had not returned to No. 2, but the door was ajar. I went inside and glumly regarded stacks of folders, clippings, notebooks, and other evidence that UFORIA had launched a full-scale investigation of the crop circles and ensuing crap. I'd done enough research at the library to be aware how seriously a hefty percentage of the population took the subject. Controversy still raged about incidents from almost fifty years ago, with accusations and counteraccusations and gnashing of teeth. Children and grandchildren of purported eyewitnesses were hot property, as were photographs of smudges of light. It was possible Maggody was going to become the next supernova.

There was nothing of significance in the room. I went on to No. 3 and knocked. Lucy Ferncliff opened the door and recoiled in much the same way Mrs. Jim Bob had earlier. "What do you want?" she said.

"I'd like to ask you a few questions." I stepped around her and waited until she closed the door. "Where were you last night from seven until midnight or so?"

"Right here. I worked on my story about the crop

circles, then took a bath and read." She edged in front of the table. "I heard about the terrible accident," she continued, "but I barely knew Brian. I first met him the day we all arrived."

"You didn't go down to the creek last night in case you could get a scoop for the tabloid?" I persisted, intrigued by the beads of sweat on her upper lip. "If the alien had returned, you might have been in contention for a Pulitzer."

"I needed to spend several hours on my story. This assignment's important to me, and I don't want to blow it."

"I suppose not," I said as I glanced around for evidence of her selfless devotion to exploitative journalism. Leather bags and camera equipment were piled precariously on a chair; two conventional bags were set by the closet. A laptop computer and notebooks were on the dresser. A current issue of the *Probe* lay in the middle of the bed. And on the bedside table was a copy of one of Sageman's books.

I reached around her and picked it up. "Doing a little background reading?" I asked.

She looked very much as if she wanted to snatch the book out of my hands. "You may have gathered from what I said earlier that I have some reservations about the ufology movement. This furor over so-called abductions may be truly dangerous. I'm thinking about doing a spec piece for one of the legitimate magazines. If Sageman agrees to an interview, he'll be featured."

"One of these days he'll be indicted for quackery. It's too bad Leonard's family never sued him."

"I've been told he requires signed legal forms that absolve him from responsibility. He and a few others in the field are making a lot of money with their books and lectures. Usually he charges a fat fee for the sessions, and there are a lot of people who are willing to pay it in order to become members of the elite. Some call themselves selectees. Isn't that cute?"

The contempt in her voice was hard to miss, but also hard to explain, considering her chosen profession. "Do you enjoy working for the *Probe*?" I asked bluntly.

"Of course I do, and the pay is excellent. Are you thinking of applying for a job?"

"Maybe so. Why don't you give me your editor's name and telephone number? I'll give him a call."

"I'm not allowed to do that."

"No problem. All I have to do is look through an issue and find the information. I'll bet there's even a toll-free number for people who've found demons in the toilet bowl and want to share their stories with the entire country." I picked up the paper and opened it. "Yep, here it is, right next to a story about a woman with taste buds on the bottoms of her feet."

"I may have exaggerated when I claimed to be on the staff, okay? I've done some free-lance articles and have filled out an application for a full-time job. The editor's promised to make a decision based on my coverage of the story here."

"Is that why you tried to bribe Brian in the barn?"

Her cheeks turned pink, maybe even fuchsia. "I wanted to get access to some transcripts of Sageman's hypnotherapy sessions in order to compare them with what he used in his books. Brian agreed to copy a file for me."

"Did he?"

She shook her head. I dropped the paper on the bed and went to the door. "I have a feeling I'm going to want to talk to you later, so stick around."

"May I go to the Dairee Dee-Lishus, or should I stay here and wait for bread and water?"

"Sure, but the only thing you can get that's not swimming in grease is a cherry limeade. Just don't leave town without telling me." I gave her a chance to suggest I have a nice day, but she didn't appear to be in all that balmy a mood.

Perhaps her colleague would be, I thought as I went across the lot and knocked on the door. Jules opened it rather abruptly, then managed a smile of sorts.

"Anything wrong?" he asked.

I was beginning to feel as popular as a chaperone at a junior high dance. "I'm just asking a few questions about last night. Where were you?"

"I went to the cornfield and interviewed a few people, then drove into Farberville to go to a movie. I got back here at midnight and went straight to bed."

"You weren't worried that you might miss an alien invasion?" I asked.

Jules nudged me inside and closed the door. "I hate to break this to you, Arly, but there may not be such things as flying saucers. Ninety-five percent of UFO sightings are nothing more than aircraft or natural phenomena. The remaining five percent initially elude an explanation, but witnesses are so eager to see something strange and exciting that they distort—"

"I don't need a damn lecture! You cause enough grief as it is. Don't compound it with this sanctimonious and condescending attitude about the very people you're exploiting to make a buck!"

He had the wisdom to back into a corner before I

degenerated into physical violence. "You're right. It's a very bad habit of mine, and I apologize."

"Me, too," I said, slumping against the wall as my petulance dried up. "I'm frustrated because I can't seem to get anywhere near solving Brian's murder. No one seems to have a motive. If Sageman had been the victim, I'd be knocking on McMasterson's door—and the other way around, too." I stopped and thought about what I'd said. "Someone did try to lure Sageman down there. If he hadn't been in Cynthia and Rosemary's room, he would have been the one who went racing to investigate the crashed disk."

"He wasn't in Cynthia's room," Jules said.

I blinked at him. "Yes, he was. The session started right after seven and ended at eleven. Rosemary said he went outside, but only for a couple of minutes."

"Well, someone was in there for at least an hour. I could hear an occasional noise through the wall—a glass knocked over, a mutter every now and then. I'd heard about the session, but I assumed it had been canceled."

I sat down on the corner of the bed, crossed my arms, and looked up at him. "You said you were in Farberville last night."

"After I finished my interview with the amazing Raz Buchanon and his wonder sow Marjorie, I came back here to take a shower. It was about eight o'clock. Minutes later I heard Sageman—or so I thought—go into the room. The light was on when I left half an hour later."

It was refreshing to find someone who'd seen something, even if it didn't make a whole helluva lot of sense. "What about cars in the lot when you left?" I asked. "Was Rosemary's car here?"

"Yes, and McMasterson's car was here, too. The light was on in his room, but the curtains were closed. I was a little bit surprised he'd come back so early. He's quite capable of lying in the middle of one of the crop circles all night to be one with his beloved intraterrestrials."

"Maybe I'll ask him," I said as I stood up. "Was Lucy's car in front of her room?"

He nodded. "I asked her to go to a movie with me, but she said she was going to wash her hair. I haven't heard that one since high school."

"Better luck next time," I said ungraciously, then went outside and surveyed the parking lot. Rosemary had returned and presumably was inside her room. Lucy had gone, presumably to the Dairee Dee-Lishus. McMasterson's rental car was at the end of the building. I headed for his door but hesitated as I went by Arthur Sageman's window and saw him asleep on the bed, a yellow legal pad on his chest. His glasses had slid to the tip of his nose, where they hung at a precarious angle. He might know who'd entered his room or could offer a motive. And I had no compunction about interrupting his pleasant little siesta. In fact, if I'd had a bazooka, I might have blown down his door just to see how high he'd jump.

Pounding would have to suffice. I raised my fist, then stopped as I heard Dahlia say from inside the room, "Don't you dare do that, you runt. You're gonna be mighty sorry when Kevin finds out about this."

"Take it easy," Sageman said soothingly.

Dahlia screamed. I banged on the door and rattled the knob, but it was locked. She screamed again. I looked through the window. Sageman lay as serenely as a daydreamer in a field of buttercups.

"Don't touch me, please," Dahlia whimpered. "I'm a respectable married woman."

I rapped on the glass with enough fervor to wake the dead, or so I thought. I tried the knob again, then picked up a rock and was about to smash the glass when Hayden McMasterson stumbled out of his room.

"What's going on?" he demanded.

"I don't know, but I'm going to find out," I said grimly, then hit the window. The nature of glass being what it was, shards splattered on my hand, wrist, and forearm. There were more of them than seemed possible from a single windowpane. And boy, oh, boy, were they sharp little suckers.

Jules Channel came out of his room as I watched bubbles of blood appear on my skin. "What the hell?" he said hoarsely.

Hayden grabbed my shoulder just as my knees folded. "I don't know," he said to Jules. "Help me get her inside my room and I'll get a towel for the bleeding."

Jules took my other arm. "She was behaving normally a few minutes ago," he said to Hayden.

"You monster!" squealed Dahlia.

I wrenched myself free. "We've got to get in the room!"

Hayden took a key from his pocket and handed it to me. "Try this," he suggested.

My whole arm was throbbing as I jabbed the key in the lock, twisted it, and yanked open the door. "Dahlia?" I called as I checked behind the door, then dashed for the bathroom. As I came out, I heard

Sageman say, "I want you to relax now. Let the image slide away from you."

The problem was that he hadn't moved his lips or anything else and appeared to have slept right through the commotion. A green light flickered on the tape recorder on the bedside table as Dahlia moaned uneasily. Jules and Hayden were watching me from the doorway, their expressions carefully neutral despite the fact I was behaving like someone with a bee in her bonnet—or someplace a sight more uncomfortable.

I turned off the tape recorder and bent down to have a closer look at Sageman. I then stood up, sighed, and left the room, collecting my would-be keepers along the way. "Sageman's dead," I said flatly. "Both of you wait in your rooms. I need to make a call."

"Dead?" croaked McMasterson. "Are you sure?"

"I'm sure, and this time we're not going to worry about hostile aliens, unless one got hold of a gun." I locked the door and went across the lot to call Harve from Ruby Bee's unit.

Mrs. Jim Bob drove toward Cotter's Ridge, her chin stuck out so far she could barely see the road. Jim Bob's truck had already turned off by the time she came around a curve and spotted the county line sign. It was the exact same place she'd lost him a few nights back, which had to mean something.

She pulled over. Right across from her was a road of sorts, more of a trail than anything else. Even though it was getting dark, she could see that the weeds were flattened. Someone had driven that way—and Jim Bob was the obvious candidate.

There could be only one reason for him to be up

on the ridge after dark, she decided as she rolled down her window and strained to hear the sounds of a truck engine back in the woods. He was on his way to Raz's still to load up jars of Satan's poison. It was only a matter of time before Arly caught him in the act of committing a felony; she wouldn't hesitate for a second before bringing in the federal agents, who'd indict Jim Bob and seize everything that wasn't nailed down, then come back for everything that was.

There was only one way to save herself from poverty, disgrace, and the terrifying specter of knowing she'd be the laughingstock of the Missionary Society and the Extension Club (for starters). She was going to have to catch him in the very act of loading his truck, force him to see the wickedness of his ways, and order him to destroy the still and whatever jars of moonshine Raz had amassed.

Mrs. Jim Bob had a pretty good idea where the still was on account of an incident awhile back. What had happened had been Brother Verber's fault, naturally, and she herself had been nothing but an innocent victim of circumstance.

The thought of making Jim Bob destroy the still brought a thin smile to her face. Once he was done, all covered with sweat and panting from the exertion, his mouth dry, his hands blistered, why, she'd tell him in no uncertain terms to sink to his knees to beg her forgiveness and pray for mercy. By the time she was satisfied with hearing his confession, his knee would ache so bad he'd limp for a month of Sundays. He'd also think twice before sneaking off to do loathsome things with a hussy.

She eased her car over the rutted shoulder, wincing as something scraped, and slowly drove down the poor excuse for a road. Branches clawed the car and slapped at the windshield. The increasing darkness seemed to fit her mood.

"Jim Bob Buchanon," she said aloud, "you're gonna pay for this particular transgression like you've never paid before—or my name isn't Barbara Anne Buchanon Buchanon."

Tightening her grip on the steering wheel, she continued into the woods.

THIRTEEN

◆

"So, should we put out an APB for Bigfoot?" asked Harve as we watched the paramedics carry out a body bag. "Larry Joe Lambertino swore he came callin' this very morning."

The parking lot was crowded with official vehicles, but we had only a few spectators thus far. The media appeared to be taking the day off; tomorrow they'd come slithering onto the scene to interview the likes of Saralee Lambertino and Raz Buchanon.

"Why not?" I said. "He's probably a hit man for the Martian Mafia."

McBeen came out of No. 5 and joined us. "Right offhand I'd say death is a result of the nasty hole in his right temple. A small-caliber bullet, almost no external bleeding but lots of damage inside the cranium. It's still in there somewhere. All I can say at this point is that he died several hours ago." He glared at my blood-speckled arm. "I suppose you want me to patch you up, but I'm not gonna do it. Take two aspirin and call somebody else in the morning."

I waited until he got in his truck and drove away. "He's not exactly a kindly old country doctor, is he?" I said to Harve, who was trying to fire up a wet cigar stub. Once he did, I ran through everything I'd found out during the day, which didn't amount to squat. "I briefly questioned everybody before you arrived. No one admits having spoken to Sageman after I brought him back here in the middle of the afternoon. He must have settled down in his room to work and was listening to Dahlia's tape when someone dropped by. Estelle's disappearance may be related."

"Uh, Harve," said one of the deputies, pointing at Cotter's Ridge and gulping, "you might want to take a look up there."

My stomach filled with undiluted acid as I turned around. This time there were four orange lights above the tree line, aligned and bobbing merrily.

Harve yanked the cigar out of his mouth. "What the hell are those?"

"Obviously they are some kind of spacecraft piloted by a whole gang of seven-foot silver aliens. They probably dropped off Bigfoot when he started stinking up the ship or forgetting his table manners. Don't forget the ones coming out of the ground from Atlantis to make swirls in the corn and cut up cows. At this rate we're going to have so many aliens in Maggody that we'll have to start looking into public housing. The Voice of the Almighty Lord Assembly Hall will have to put in some more pews and order some extra hymnals. Any more questions, Harve?"

He gasped as the lights disappeared, then got his cigar back in place and slapped me on the back. "Glad to know you've got everything under control. Be sure and give me a call when you've rounded 'em up."

"I'll be sure and do that. In the meantime, why don't you give me some help with the investigation, dammit?" I paused as I saw Ruby Bee arguing with a deputy who was brash enough to think he could dissuade her from entering her own parking lot. The sight was more unnerving than a bunch of stupid orange lights. "Maybe we'd better try to get a dog from the Farberville PD to search for Estelle," I said in a more reasonable voice. "It's late now, but I'll call first thing in the morning."

Harve had seen Ruby Bee, too. "Tell ya what," he said hurriedly, "one of the boys will stay here the rest of the night, just to keep all these aliens from tampering with the scene. I should have a report in the morning about the weapon and whatever fingerprints were found."

He scuttled away before I could express my dissatisfaction with his offering, which was so meager even Brother Verber would have turned up his nose at it. I made a dash for the door of No. 5, but Ruby Bee cut me off.

"What is going on now?" she said, her fingernails biting into my arm. "Is it true that Dr. Sageman was murdered in his room? And what about Estelle? Why aren't you doing something to find her before she's murdered, too?"

I told the deputy I'd be back, then hustled Ruby Bee to her unit and sat her down on the sofa. She finally quit barking at me, accepted a glass of water, and slumped back into the upholstery. I returned to the tiny kitchenette and washed off the blood.

"I bet I know why Dr. Sageman was murdered," Ruby Bee said from the other room. "He worked for a top secret government intelligence agency that collects evidence from crashed flying saucers. They're holding live aliens in an underground laboratory somewhere in the desert."

I stayed at the sink, letting the water run over my

hands. The damage appeared to be superficial, but a few of the punctures were still oozing tiny beads of blood. I had a feeling my heroism wasn't going to win me any citations. "Gee, that's good to know. Did you read this in the *Probe* or the *Weekly Examiner*?"

"It's the honest to God truth, and the proof is inside Dr. Sageman's computer files. All you have to do is find the right one and read it for yourself. This conspiracy is putting the entire human race in danger. Maybe Dr. Sageman decided to tell what he knew, and someone killed him to silence him."

"Then you don't think Bigfoot did it?"

"I wish you'd listen to me! One of the folks staying at the Flamingo Motel is a spy for the government. There's something real fishy about Lucy Fernclift. As for Rosemary, she could be putting on an act. For all we know, she could be a trained killer. She could even be in cahoots with someone else, like Dr. McMasterson."

I dried my hands and came to the doorway. "Do you remember when Doowadiddy Buchanon used to call me every other day to report that Nazi storm troopers were hiding in his root cellar? The term for that is 'paranoia.' "

"Don't get smart with me. You just go ask Jules Channel if you don't believe me. This very morning he told Estelle and me the whole story."

"Maybe I'll go get my thumbscrews and do just that," I said in a sinister voice. I left her glowering and went over to McMasterson's unit. It hadn't been all that long ago that I'd implied he would be the logical suspect if Sageman turned up dead; now seemed like as good a time as any to find out if I was right.

He looked downright ill as he let me in. "I tried to surround myself with a protective force field, but I still feel vulnerable to all this negativity. You feel it, don't you?"

"No," I said. "When I saw you this morning, you were going to examine the new crop circles. How long did you stay there?"

"Until three o'clock or so. There was such cosmic intensity that I found the experience as exhausting as it was exhilarating. There are half a dozen three-line leys, which means the circles are potent with powerful nodal energy. I'm confident we'll be able to establish a link with area tumuli." Before I realized what was happening, he put his arms around me and enveloped me in a warm, hairy hug. "I wish you'd come with me to the circles and allow yourself to absorb their healing powers. We'll be safe there, and our auras will be strengthened."

He was squeezing me so tightly I could barely breathe. The smell of musk oil was overpowering, and his ponytail was tickling my nose. I finally resorted to grinding my heel into his bare foot. Once he quit hopping around and yelping, I said, "Trust me when I say I am not a New Age person. I like my aura just the way it is, thank you, and prefer it to remain this way right into old age. You said you came back in the middle of the afternoon. Did you see or hear anything?"

He sat down and examined his foot. "I heard car doors slam, but I was so involved with my writing that I didn't even glance out the window. I'm composing a series of quatrains to celebrate the circles and welcome our intraterrestrial forefathers." He let his foot fall and gave me a sullen look. "Not that you'd be interested."

"Did you hear anyone in Sageman's room last night?"

"I don't think so." He fingered his crystal as if seeking a second opinion. "No, I didn't hear anything, but as I said, I was writing. Creativity produces an altered state of consciousness in which one's psychic energies—"

"Jules Channel said he heard someone go into Sageman's room at eight o'clock. Were there any respites from your state of altered consciousness when you heard anything at all?"

"No," he said firmly.

I warned him not to leave town and went back outside, where the breeze smelled of nothing more cloying than fresh manure. Who could have been in Sageman's room? My eyes wandered down the row of units as I made a list. McMasterson claimed to have been in his room, Lucy Fernclift in hers. Brian was at the creek. If Jules was guilty, why had he told me? Sageman and Rosemary were busy with Dahlia. Cynthia had told Ruby Bee and Estelle that she'd sat in the car until the chill drove her into the bar and grill, and as best I could recall, that had been at eight o'clock. Someone had been waiting for her to leave.

I must have made a little noise because the deputy stepped out of the shadows.

"Deputy Whitbread here," he said, visibly disappointed I wasn't being ravaged by Bigfoot. "Is everything okay, ma'am?"

I waved at him, stuck my hands in my pockets, and leaned against the weathered wood while I mentally reconstructed the scene. Then, berating myself for not noticing the glitch earlier, I went back across the lot and knocked on the door of No. 2.

Rosemary yanked me inside and locked the door. "This is so terrible! I'm so upset that I don't know what to do. Arthur was such a dear man . . ." She turned away and grabbed the edge of the dresser. "And I'm frightened," she admitted almost inaudibly, her shoulder blades jutting underneath the thin fabric of her robe. "First Brian and now Arthur . . ."

I patted her on the back and assured her the deputy was on duty. "I have a question about last night," I continued. "You were sitting there when you heard a car door slam. Arthur looked out the window, then went outside. Why did he do that?"

"To see who was leaving, I suppose."

"Even though it meant interrupting the session?"

"He was gone only a few minutes," she began defensively, then shook her head. "It did seem odd. Dahlia was at a very significant moment in her narrative, and I was surprised when Arthur told her to retreat and fill her mind with neutral images."

"Did he say anything to you before he left or when he came back?"

"Not that I recall. We finished the session, and then he brought Dahlia out of her trance and said he'd contact her about scheduling another session."

I went outside. Sageman must have seen a light in his room, I thought as I stood next to Rosemary's car. He'd gone outside to see who was there and then returned shortly thereafter and said nothing to Rosemary. Who could it have been, and why hadn't he mentioned it?

I trudged across the road and up the steps to my apartment. As I reached for the doorknob, I heard a noise from below. I peered over the rail and saw Jim Bob come out the back door of Roy's apartment, pause to take a piss, and climb into his truck. He turned on the headlights as he pulled onto the road and drove out of view.

It was so uninteresting that I opened a can of chicken soup and turned on my tiny portable television set to watch the talk show guests make fools of themselves. And started thinking about Bigfoot, who was making a fool of yours truly. And came to the conclusion he wasn't the only one.

Dahlia found a stump and sat down to rest. It was spooky all by herself in the woods, especially when the moon went behind the clouds and the shadows got black as the inside of a rain barrel. It was noisy, too, with the birds squawking and the leaves crackling, and the night air was getting a mite crumpy.

Taking a sandwich from the sack, she wiggled around until she was comfortable and took a bite. She was going to need her strength when she finally arrived at the top of the ridge. She'd seen the orange lights and knew they'd be there, waiting for her. Why else would her nose have started tingling so bad it liked to explode?

She popped the last of the sandwich in her mouth, licked her fingers, and set the sack in her lap where she could reach the cookies without having to root for 'em. Kevin would be getting home from work afore too long, she realized with a nervous belch, and the first thing he'd see was the note she left on the kitchen table. He'd probably double over with pain when he read how she'd gone up to confront her kidnappers and do what she had to do.

Which she would figure out by the time she climbed all the way to the top of the ridge. The trail was a sight worse than she remembered it, but it had been a long while since anyone had gone by the ramshackle remains of Robin Buchanon's shack. Most likely the outhouse had collapsed by now, as well as the barn and the rickety fence. All of 'em had been held together with nothing more than spit and a prayer.

Not that aliens would care. She ate another sandwich while she tried to recall if the flying saucer she'd been in had a bathroom. Surely it did if they traveled all those light-years from another galaxy. They couldn't count on finding gas stations along the way.

She lapsed into worrying some more about Kevin and how he'd react to her note. Finally, when she'd finished the last sandwich, she struggled to her feet and resumed her hike up the side of the ridge. It was so treacherous she wondered why they were making her hike rather than beaming her up like they'd done before. It didn't seem mannersome.

Mrs. Jim Bob felt like she was riding a three-legged mule. The car bucked and shuddered, and all the warning lights on the dashboard were blinking so brightly that she wanted to close her eyes. The interior was filled with an acrid smell that made her eyes water and her throat sting, but it only got worse when she rolled down the window.

It was all Jim Bob's fault, she reminded herself as she narrowly avoided a fallen tree trunk. He was gonna regret the day he was born. Here she'd been doing her Christian duty to save his immortal soul from bankruptcy, and he didn't have the decency to drive slow so she could catch up with him.

She hadn't known the woods could be so dark and unfriendly. Whenever the moon came out from behind the clouds, it cast an eerie light that reminded her she was at the mercy of whatever was lurking behind the bushes. Like heathen aliens, she thought as she let go of the steering wheel long enough to make sure her door was locked.

The front of the car dipped so abruptly her head jerked forward and hit the steering wheel. Gasping, she tried to regain control, but the car crashed into a spindly oak tree. Branches fell across the windshield. Seconds later smoke drifted out from under the hood like Satan's furnace had been fired up.

She cut off the engine, but that didn't seem to help. The smoke was getting so thick she could barely see. The lights on the dashboard blinked in farewell and went out. The headlights followed suit.

The sudden blackness added to her fright. She scrambled out of the car, falling onto the ground in a confusion of arms and legs, and crawled as fast as she could away from her car. The smoke came after her, as did the sound of sizzling.

She grabbed a branch and got to her feet. The most important thing was to get away from the car before it exploded, even if it meant plunging blindly into the woods.

Praying the Good Lord was on duty, she plunged blindly into the woods.

Larry Joe sat at the kitchen table, his shotgun propped within easy reach. The test papers from his fifth-period class (Auto Repair II: Carburetors and Combustion Systems) were all graded, and the results posted in a spiral notebook. He'd tried to read one of Joyce's paperbacks, but his eyes kept drifting closed. Besides, he wasn't sure he liked all the references to hard bellies and throbbing manhood. It made him wonder what all went through Joyce's mind when she was in bed with him. Which is where he wanted to be, instead of sitting in a cold kitchen with nothing but an occasional cockroach to keep him company.

Down the hallway one of the kids was snoring steadily. Another had padded to the bathroom and returned to bed without bothering to check on the well-being of the lonely sentinel in the kitchen.

Larry Joe went to the window and looked out at the backyard. If Bigfoot was hiding behind the for-sythia bushes, he was doing so good a job of it that he hadn't disturbed the dog asleep on the patio. The garbage cans had not been tumped, or the dog's bowl emptied, or the plastic birdbath disturbed.

He was about to go watch television (with the sound turned off, of course) when he saw movement out behind the carport. The dog raised its head, then dashed off in the opposite direction with its tail be-tween its legs. There was something there all right. And it was coming toward the house.

Larry Joe'd always thought the best way to die was in your sleep or maybe with your loved ones gathered around the bed. He'd been obliged to play football in high school and go drinking with the boys after the games, but he'd been careful to be the one to drive home. After graduation he'd been se-cretly relieved when the army doctor found a hair-line fracture that hadn't healed like it was supposed to. These days he hunted with Jim Bob and some of the others, but he kept close to camp and even vol-unteered to stay back and cook. He made sure Joyce had the tires rotated every year.

His hand was damp as he picked up his shotgun and slipped out the back door. It was still there, whatever it was. He eased around the barbecue grill and tried to see into the inky shadows.

Light from the utility pole caught a hairy shoulder. Without stopping to think, Larry Joe raised his shotgun and fired.

The blast almost knocked him off his feet, and the sound roared in his ears like a freight train bearing down on him. Inside the house the kids began to scream. And the damn dog, wherever it was, began to howl.

I made a detour by the PD to get my gun, then went to find Deputy Whitbread in the motel parking lot, where not a creature was stirring. He'd retreated to the relative warmth of his car and with reluctance rolled down the window as I approached.

"Something wrong, ma'am?" he whispered.

"What's your first name?"

"Ed, ma'am. Actually it's Eduardo, on account of my grandfather being from—"

"Here's what I want you to do, Ed," I said hastily. "Turn on the police radio and get into a loud conversation with the dispatcher about a three-car wreck over in Emmet. After a minute or two tell her that you're on your way. Switch on your headlights and drive all the way down to the fence, turn around, and peel out of the lot." I considered the scenario. "And hit your siren as you go past the bar and onto the road. Got it?"

"A three-car wreck in Emmet? Was anybody hurt?"

"Improvise, Ed."

"But Sheriff Dorfer told me to stay here until someone relieves me at seven."

I crossed my fingers. "I just spoke to him from

my apartment," I said, doing my best to radiate sincerity. "He okayed all this."

Deputy Whitbread scratched his head and squirmed. "Maybe I ought to confirm your orders, ma'am. Sheriff Dorfer—"

"Is already back in his bed, putting his icy feet on Mrs. Dorfer and fighting for his half of the blanket. He won't feel kindly toward you if he has to get out of bed again and go all the way to the living room."

Deputy Whitbread squirmed awhile longer, then agreed to do as I said. I slipped into No. 5 and watched through a slit in the curtains as he feigned an argument with the dispatcher, who kept demanding to know what in thunderation he was talking about, and eventually drove off. To my surprise, he even remembered to turn on the siren (it had been a long list to keep in mind).

I used my flashlight to collect the tape recorder and make my way into the bathroom. It wasn't the most comfortable place to sit, but I had no idea if I would end up waiting all night for someone who'd failed to appreciate the opportunity provided by Deputy Whitbread's departure. There may have been something a tad undignified about sitting on a toilet in the dark, my gun on the edge of the tub and the tape recorder in the sink, but the word "dignified" wasn't one I'd have chosen to describe the week.

Once the tape was rewound, I lowered the volume and began to listen. Dr. Sageman's voice was crisp as he announced the data regarding the session, then seductive as he led Dahlia through a series of images involving an ascending staircase. Before too long she was begging to be allowed to rest, claiming she was tuckered out worse than a fiddler's elbow, but he kept urging her to climb to the next flight. He eventually had to agree that she could have an orange soda pop before she went on, but refused to allow her any cream-filled sponge cakes.

I quit smirking when she said, "It's midnight, and I'm in my bedroom now. I don't know if I ought to wait up for Kevvie, 'cause he's been working late every night this week." She wheezed sadly. "There's no reason to bother. Most nights he's too tired to . . . see to my needs. He used to be so eager that those old bedsprings would get to squeaking and I was worried we'd wake up the preacher, but—"

Dr. Sageman cleared his throat. "So you're climbing into bed all by yourself, right? You've got the pillow under your head and the blankets tucked under your chin. It's nice and warm, isn't it? Lift your head and look around. Are there any strange lights shining through the bedroom window?"

"A white light," she said, beginning to snivel. "I ain't never seen anything like it before."

Her story got more and more ludicrous, as Dr. Sageman steadily fed her images whenever she faltered and corrected her whenever she strayed. In the background Rosemary made little clucks of approval whenever Dahlia rescinded a description in order to agree with Sageman.

Before too long Dahlia was aboard the spacecraft and surrounded by silver men who jabbered at one another as they examined her. I was so enthralled that I nearly fell off the toilet when I realized I'd heard a noise at the front door of the unit. Unprofessional on my part, I suppose, but nevertheless true.

I fumbled until I found the button to turn off the tape player. It was too bad I couldn't turn off the thudding in my chest; it was so loud I could have led the Salvation Army band. Reminding myself that I had my gun (and all three bullets), I eased open the bathroom door just as someone came into the room. A flashlight beam illuminated the rumpled bed, then moved to the table and bobbed about until it came to rest on a plastic box next to the computer.

"Looking for something?" I drawled as I turned on my flashlight and pointed it at the intruder.

FOURTEEN

◆

Jules Channel's tan didn't look so good in the glare of my flashlight. He stumbled back until he came close to tripping over the corner of the bed, but I wasn't in the mood to do him any favors by pointing out the peril.

"Computer disks?" I said as I came out of the bathroom. "Is that what you were looking for last night when Sageman caught you?"

"What are you talking about?"

It didn't seem like the moment to tell him I had no idea since I was on a wild-goose chase. Maybe I'd caught him. "Just who are you?" I said in a fierce whisper.

"A reporter."

"Yeah, and I'm a trailer park queen who believes everything I read in the *Weekly Examiner* and the *Probe*. Would you like me to take off my socks so you can see the taste buds between my toes?"

"Could we go somewhere and talk about all this?" he said, giving me a weak smile. "I'd better explain a few things."

"Like the government conspiracy and the aliens in some underground laboratory? The only place we're going to talk is the county jail, buster. I don't know what your part in all this is, but by damn you're—"

He lunged at me and covered my mouth. "Sssh! I hear someone outside the door."

I'd have shot him if I hadn't heard it, too. Instead, I grabbed his wrist and dragged him into the bathroom. I was aware of his warmth as we tried to avoid tumbling into the bathtub or falling over each other. I allowed him to put his arm around my waist, even though I knew I'd be irritated with myself later if it turned out he was a murderer. I did jab him with my elbow when he tried to whisper in my ear. I have my limits.

I peeked around the door as the silhouette of a figure moved past the window and approached the table. I removed Jules's hand, took a breath, and stepped out as I'd done minutes earlier.

"Looking for something?" I drawled.

There was a snicker from the bathroom, but I ignored it and turned on my flashlight.

Lucy Fernclift recoiled so violently that she backed into a chair, lost her balance, and, with a yelp of surprise, disappeared behind the edge of the bed. I went across the room and waited until she extricated herself from the tangled mess of wires and cables. She was dressed like a proper burglar in a black sweater and trousers, but her makeup seemed excessive for the occasion.

Rubbing her head, she said, "What the hell do you think you're doing?"

"Holding a press conference, or so it seems," I said without sympathy. "What are you doing?"

She crawled onto the bed, still holding her head, and gave my question a great deal of thought. "I paid Brian for a file, but he never gave it to me. I saw someone coming in here. I was worried about my file."

"And cows sing," contributed a voice from the bathroom. "I'm in the moooood for love . . ."

Lucy swung around. "Who's that?"

I was about to tell her when I heard a noise outside. "Go see for yourself," I growled as I yanked her up and shoved her toward the bathroom.

This time it was seriously crowded. There were more shoulders and elbows than seemed humanly possible, and someone managed to come down hard on my toes. The sink cut into my back, but the toilet blocked a retreat. Jules and Lucy may have showered before bed, but the bathroom was beginning to smell like a junior high locker room.

The front door opened with a familiar creak. I pushed Lucy into Jules (or vice versa), stepped over a knee, and eased back into the front room. For the third time a figure was creeping toward the table.

I was fresh out of drawls. "What do you want?" I snapped as I turned on the flashlight.

The beam caught Hayden McMasterson in a paralytic crouch, although his outstretched hand was shaking pretty hard. He was wearing an ankle-length diaphanous robe with all sorts of cryptic symbols embroidered across his chest, an attire more appropriate for a hippie wedding than a midnight prowl.

"What are you doing here?" he asked weakly.

"I figured that one of you would hear the deputy leave and come creeping in here. Even though I got almost no sleep last night, I decided to wait to find out who it was and arrest him or her for murder. So that's what I'm doing here—sacrificing my health to catch a murderer!"

He seemed startled by my outburst. "I'm really sorry, Chief Hanks. If you'd like, I can give you a body massage with a special herbal oil that my wife makes from—"

"I would not," I said. This time there was so much snickering from the bathroom that it sounded as if squirrels were scampering up the tile walls. I was about to order them out when I heard a soft tap on the door.

"Jesus H.!" I muttered, then grabbed Hayden's ponytail. He was too busy wincing to ask any questions as I steered him into the bathroom. Jules climbed into the bathtub and held out his hand to Lucy, who joined him. Hayden mumbled unhappily as I ordered him to stand on the toilet.

"Who is it?" hissed Lucy.

I didn't bother to tell her I didn't know but instead eased open the bathroom door. Once the figure'd moved in front of the window, I turned on my flashlight.

"Rosemary," I said wearily, "did you happen to notice anyone else heading this way?"

"Not really, but I did hear someone drive off just a moment ago."

It seemed to me that the entire cast was pretty much assembled. I was about to order the others out of the bathroom when I heard a creak outside the door. I hauled Rosemary into the bathroom and shoved her into the mass of bodies, then stuck my head out as far as I dared, expecting to see another silhouette.

The grunts and mutters behind me should have alerted this latest arrival that there was something peculiar going on in the bathroom. I stepped out and was about to repeat some surly variation of my question when I heard a snuffle from beyond the bed. It was as easy to identify as the pervasive stench.

"Oh, my gawd," I said as I slammed the door. I turned on the overhead light, sat down on the toilet, and buried my face in my hands.

Hayden clutched his crystal with one hand and the faucet with the other. "Who is it?"

"Majorie," I said through my fingers, not caring if they heard me.

"Who's Marjorie?" asked Lucy. "Is that the name of the woman with the bright red hair?"

"Marjorie is Raz Buchanon's pedigreed sow," I explained numbly. "One of you forgot to close the door completely when you came inside. She must have nudged it open with her snout."

Lucy started to climb out of the bathtub. "Well, run her off and let's get out of here. This is so ridiculous I couldn't sell it to my editor."

I shifted to allow her to step onto the bathmat. "Go right ahead, but keep in mind that less than a year ago Marjorie chewed the leg off one of Perkins's goats. She tried to do the same to me, too."

"You're afraid of a pig?" Lucy said, laughing in a way I found particularly unendearing. "You grew up with them, didn't you?"

"I grew up with a healthy respect for them."

"So what are we supposed to do?" asked Rosemary.

I shrugged. "Wait until she decides to leave."

Lucy jabbed her finger at Rosemary. "You were the last one to come in tonight, so it's obvious you're the one who didn't close the door."

"All this negativity is making me nauseous," Hayden said.

"Moooonlight in Vermont," crooned Jules from the bathtub, utilizing a bar of soap as a microphone.

Outside the door the snuffles grew louder.

* * *

Kevin's hand shook so bad he could barely read the note his beloved had left for him. How could she think she was having Their baby? And why had They told her to go to the top of Cotter's Ridge? Kevin went into the living room and collapsed on the recliner, his head buzzing with confusion. One question kept repeating itself over and over till he wanted to scream: Who were "They"?

His eyes filled with tears as he pictured her lost in the woods, falling down and fighting the brush, with leaves in her hair and her deliciously dimpled knees all bloody. She'd be at the mercy of the critters on the ridge. Even if he dint know exactly who "They" were, he knew plenty about bears and polecats. Was his lust goddess already nothing but a scattering of gnawed bones? Was her limp, lifeless hand stretched out toward him, like she'd hoped till the end that he would rescue her?

And he would. He leaped to his feet and tried to recall what he might have that would serve as a weapon. His pa made him keep his deer rifle in his bedroom closet at home. The hatchet was so dull it wouldn't slice Velveeta (Dahlia'd tried once). The bow and arrow set had been a birthday present when he was six. Critters weren't likely to skedaddle at the sight of the rubber tip.

He would have to defend his wife with his bare hands, he decided. Why, he'd punch and kick and claw while she climbed a tree, where she could see how courageous he was. Afterward she would wrap his wounds in strips torn from her petticoat, then cradle his face in her lap, allowing him to nuzzle her monstrously warm bosoms while she stroked his forehead.

Armed only with his imagination, Kevin marched out the door and into the night. When he was half-way across the yard, he remembered he'd forgotten to turn off the kitchen light and went back. Dahlia was real stern when it came to wasting electricity.

"You were trapped in the crapper all night?" Harve said, guffawing so loudly I had to hold the receiver away from my ear. "We should have sent the sow up the river when we had the chance!"

"It was not all night," I said. "An hour later Deputy Whitbread got nervous and came back to make sure I hadn't gotten myself killed. He saw the light in the bathroom and had the sense to investigate. I sent him to get Raz, who persuaded Marjorie to accompany him home."

"Why didn't you crawl out the window?"

"Because the window is the old-fashioned kind that only cranks out a few inches."

"What were their excuses for creeping into the room?"

"Each one of them swore he or she had seen someone and wanted to know who it was. I was voted the most likely culprit, which says a lot about my skills as a wily undercover cop. I guess I slept through that class at the academy. What'd you hear from the lab?"

"I just now got the preliminary report from McBeen," Harve said. "Near range with a twenty-two-caliber bullet, powder burns on the skin and on the pillow we found beside the bed. No gunpowder residue on either hand, which rules out suicide even if we'd found a weapon. No signs of a struggle either. Someone he knew came into the room and shot him while he was stretched out on the bed, all nice and comfortable. Otherwise, he'd at least have gotten up. McBeen sent the body on to the state lab, but he doesn't think they'll find anything more."

"Fingerprints?"

"Thicker than flies on a honey spill, and most of 'em too smudged to be of any use. The boys'll keep trying, but don't expect much; that kind of stuff only plays on television. I'll leave Les over there the rest of the day and send somebody else tonight, but we need to get this cleared up, Arly. This ain't the kind of publicity that'll do us any good, not even in an off election year."

"No kidding," I said, then hung up. The day was as dreary as my mood. Rain came down not with any drama but steadily and with no indication it was going to let up anytime soon. Low clouds blanketed the valley. The more prudent drivers were using their headlights.

I opened the telephone directory and was about to dial a number when the door opened and Jim Bob barged in.

"Have you seen my wife?" he demanded.

"Since when?"

"I don't keep track of where she is every minute of the day, fer chrissake. All I know is when I came home last night, she wasn't there, and she wasn't back this morning when I got up. I called over at the rectory, but Verber says he hasn't talked to her since after church. I called some of the biddies, too. No one has seen or heard from her since yesterday evening."

"Could she have gone to visit relatives? Are there suitcases missing?"

"No, there ain't any damn suitcases missing. I already called her aunt down in Eldorado and her tight-assed cousin over in Belvedeer, and both of 'em promised to call if she shows up. Besides, she would have left a note, no matter how pissed she was. She never misses a chance to spell out my so-called transgressions, right down to crossing the *t*'s and dotting the *i*'s."

"Are you sure?" I asked carefully. "Maybe you were out so late last night that she wanted to teach you a lesson."

He loomed over the desk, giving me a view of his gold fillings and reptilian tongue. "What do you know about last night?"

Not nearly as much as he thought I did, I realized. "I saw you leave Roy's around midnight."

"Yeah, that's about right," he said, his expression easing. "Just find my wife, okay? You don't have to be in any big rush about it, but make sure you find her sometime today. I don't relish fixing my own supper after a hard day at the store."

He left, slamming the door so hard the pages of the telephone directory fluttered. I wrote Mrs. Jim Bob's name on a piece of paper and drew a question mark next to it. That being all I could think to do, I pushed the paper aside and called the Farberville Police Department. After some wrangling from both sides, they agreed to bring a member of the canine corps by midafternoon—if the rain stopped.

I flipped to the yellow pages and was about to make a call I should have made weeks earlier when the door once again opened. This time Eilene Buchanon barged in, although with more decorum than Jim Bob.

"Have you seen Kevin and Dahlia?" she asked as she struggled with her umbrella. "Kevin was supposed to help his pa tune up the tractor this morning, and Dahlia and I were going to the Kmart in Farberville to look for fabric for kitchen curtains. I called, but nobody answered, so I finally went over there half an hour ago. Kevin's supper from last night is still in the oven." She took a tissue from her purse and blew her nose. "I'm afraid they've been kidnapped."

I went around the desk and settled her on the chair. "Why would anyone kidnap them?" I asked reasonably. "Maybe they decided to sneak away to a fancy motel for the night and forgot about the plans for this morning."

"Kevin had to work until midnight. He wouldn't agree to go off to a motel when he got home, not at that hour. Anyway, his car's parked in the driveway. How could they have gone off anywhere?" She blotted her eyes, blew her nose again, and attempted to smile. "Earl says I'm being silly, but I can't help worrying about them, what with all the crazy things happening and the way Dahlia's been carrying on since that doctor hypnotized her. Maybe you ought to find out what kind of ideas he put in her mind."

I told her about Sageman's murder, which didn't much improve the situation, and promised to do what I could to find the errant couple. After she left, I added their names to the list, wondering how the dog handler would react when I mentioned how many residents I'd misplaced in less than twenty-four hours.

I waited a minute in case anyone else wanted to barge in, then dialed the number of the one establishment in Farberville that provided limousine service. When a woman answered, I identified myself and asked who had arranged for a limo several weeks earlier.

"I'll have to hunt through the files," she said lugubriously, as if their files extended back to the advent of the horseless buggy. "We're busier than you'd think. It'd be easier if you knew what day it was."

I'd already tried, but I could think of nothing memorable that had happened beyond the gossip concerning the mysterious limo itself. I couldn't even remember what had been the blue plate special. "It would have been during the day," I said, "and you can't have too many customers wanting to come to Maggody."

"Is it true y'all are being overrun with flying saucers? My brother-in-law saw one back some years ago, when he and his eldest boy was out fishing over near Hog Scald Holler. They was—"

"The limo?" I said.

Papers shuffled in the background. I was about to give up when she came back on. "Yeah, this is likely to be the one you want. It was a fellow from California. Mervine fetched him at the airport in the morning and took him back later that same day. It doesn't say where they went, though."

"What was the name?"

"The name on the credit card receipt is kinda smeary, but it looks like Andrew Sageman. Wait—Arthur, now that I look at it. Visa, if you're interested."

I rubbed my forehead. "A tall man with white hair and an accent?"

"How should I know, honey? Mervine was the one that drove him. It must have been while I had that recurrence of the shingles and thought I'd die."

"Did Mervine also pick him up out here two days ago?"

"Lemme ask her." She covered the receiver and had a lengthy conversation with the unseen Mervine. "Naw," she reported, "Mervine thought it was odd on account of it being the same name, and she's real sure it wasn't the same feller. She was right miffed at the feller from two days ago. She was supposed to take him back to some motel, but he dismissed her at the airport and only paid for half a day. Here I'd scheduled the car for the whole day like he asked. What if someone else—"

"Can Mervine describe the first man she picked up at the airport?"

"Lemme ask her."

I waited an interminably long time, straining to understand the muffled exchange. I was reduced to gnawing on the pencil and spitting out bits of painted wood when the woman said, "Mervine ain't real positive, but she thinks he was young and sickly, like he had tuberculosis. She thinks he had blond hair. She drove him all over Maggody, up and down dirt roads till she liked to overheat the engine, and finally over to a café in Hasty. She came back for him in an hour, then took him back to the airport. He gave her a nice tip, though."

"Thanks," I murmured.

"Glad to be of help. Next time you need a limousine, just call us and we'll give you the best deal in town, ya hear?"

I thanked her again and replaced the receiver. So Brian Quint had come to Maggody several weeks ago. He'd cruised around town in the slinky black car for most of the day, then quietly flown back to California.

Before I could concoct any explanations for his visit, the telephone rang. I let the machine answer it, listened long enough to determine that Ruby Bee was still worried about Estelle, and dashed out to my car, where I'd cleverly left my umbrella. As I drove toward the north end of town, I remembered that I had the surveillance equipment in my trunk that I'd planned to return to Sageman. Now I'd have to sort through his papers and find a contact at his foundation to advise me about his and Brian's effects. I may have slept through that class, too.

The rental car appeared undisturbed. I unlocked the door and searched through the clutter for a note or map that might have lured Brian to the low-water bridge. My posterior was thoroughly soaked by the time I crawled out, empty-handed and irritated.

Rain slithered under my jacket collar and streamed down the sides of my face as I opened the trunk, but what I saw was responsible for the chill that seized me. Neatly folded was a bundle of shimmery material. Next to it was a portable blowtorch with a bright red propane tank and a blackened nozzle; its label proclaimed it to be a Wonder Weeder (patent pending). A silver motorcycle helmet had rolled toward the back of the trunk. Someone had done a meticulous job painting oversize almond eyes and a round mouth.

Here I'd been searching the unfriendly skies for our alien when he'd been in the trunk all along. It was a little late to be fastidious about fingerprints, so I pushed the fabric aside and found boots that had been spray-painted to match the rest of the costume. They were of an unremarkable size and had no discernible tread. Under them was some kind of flat flashlight pack and, more ominously, a length of garden hose and roll of electric tape.

I knelt at the back of the rental car. The scratches on the tailpipe were barely visible, but the accumulation of crusty grime had been disturbed. It seemed I'd found the murder weapon. Now all I needed was to put it at the scene of the crime. Brian Quint could have driven it to the low-water bridge, but he'd been in no condition to drive it back to the Esso station.

Someone else had done that.

After some more thinking, I drove back to the PD and called Harve to tell him about the likely source of carbon monoxide. He put me on hold while he arranged for the rental car to be examined, and I was doodling on the margin of my missing persons' list (and wishing I could add myself) when the door opened and Reggie Pellitory shuffled in.

When Harve came back on the line, I told him I'd call him later and gestured at Reggie to sit down.

"I brung the note," he said, dropping it on my desk. "I got to be at work in an hour. Jim Bob'll have my ass in a sling if I'm late."

"Don't count on getting the second fifty-dollar payment," I said.

"It wasn't my fault I didn't deliver to the guy in person. That bitch at the bar grabbed it out of my hand and said she'd see to it. I deserved the rest of the money since I missed the semifinals of the tractor pull. I been waiting all year for that."

"I've learned how the note got to you, Reggie, but I don't know why. Who would expect you to cooperate?"

"How should I know?"

"Try to help me out here. Someone knew your name and where you worked, and the same someone assumed you'd do an errand for money. Who was it?"

"Like I said, how should I know?"

"Did you see that black limousine that drove all over town a few weeks ago?"

"I was over in Farberville bailing out my pa." He shifted a wad of tobacco from one cheek to the other and glanced around for a coffee can. The previous chief of police had provided several of them, but I'd unwisely insisted on a more classy ambiance. Hence the stains on the floor.

"You related to Raz Buchanon?" I asked idly.

"Hell, no—and I'll beat the shit out of anyone who sez otherwise."

I decided not to offer any editorials about the Pellitory ancestry and let him leave while I nurtured a couple of novel notions. Harve would have to wait for my call until after I had a little talk with Raz. Unless I was on the wrong track (and I'd been on often enough to recognize every pothole), consanguinity wouldn't enter into it.

Conspiracy was a whole 'nother ball of wax.

"That's right," Ruby Bee said, glad she wasn't paying for the long-distance call. That man on the other end spoke so slowly that the words came out like tree sap. She reminded herself to be charitable, since he was so far south he was likely to slip off the tip of Florida, where he'd disappear forever into the Bermuda Triangle. She tried to match his tempo as she repeated, "A dinosaur ate my car."

"What kind?"

"A Chevrolet."

There was a moment of silence. "What kind of dinosaur?" he asked at last.

Ruby Bee racked her mind for fancy dinosaur names, but the only one she could think of was that fat purple one that sang sugary songs and was on every twin sheet at Kmart. "I was too terrified to notice," she said, opting for the offense. "You would have been, too, if you'd gone out in your backyard and seen this monster picking his teeth with your windshield wipers."

"I'm sure I would have. Can you describe the dinosaur for me? Color? Size? Was it alone or were there others in the yard? Did it attempt to attack you?"

Ruby Bee wished she'd chosen an easier premise, but it was too late now. "I thought maybe you'd want to send someone to interview me. I could do better if I was interviewed in person, and I wouldn't mind a bit if the reporter wanted to take my picture. In fact, I'd be real proud."

"The *Weekly Examiner* conducts its investigation by telephone, and we prefer actual artist's depictions to photographs. Just tell me about this astonishing ordeal with as much description as you can provide. If we use the story, you'll receive a check for fifty dollars ten days after publication."

"You never send reporters?"

"Never."

Ruby Bee hung up and went to the window to stare at the door of No. 4, where someone claiming to be a tabloid reporter was staying. Maybe he was the secret agent for the government, she thought as she clutched the collar of her robe more tightly. He'd tried to trick her and Estelle into helping him steal Dr. Sageman's files. When that had failed, had he crept into his room and killed him?

More important, what had he done with Estelle?

Saralee had to wait until Aunt Joyce went to lie down before she dared make the call. Traci and the baby were in the living room watching cartoons; she didn't know where Larry Junior was, but she hadn't seen him for more than an hour. Uncle Larry Joe had gone off to a town council meeting, even though Aunt Joyce had pitched a fit. When he insisted, she'd thrown a plate of French toast at him and called him a yellow-bellied coward. Traci and Larry Junior both had burst into tears, and the baby had choked on a Cheerio and turned blue. All in all, breakfast had been lively at the Lambertino house.

She closed the kitchen door and dialed the toll-free number. When a woman answered, Saralee got down to business. "Bigfoot tried to break into my house last night."

"How old are you?"

"Old enough. I was the one who saw him first. He was digging through the garbage out in the backyard. He looked right at me with these red eyes that glowed like they was on fire. I was so scared I wet my pants."

The woman sighed. "Sorry, but we've got enough Bigfoot stories for the rest of the year."

"He came in a flying saucer," Saralee added desperately. "They must have set him down in the pasture behind the house. Everybody in town saw the lights."

"I did half a dozen flying saucer stories last month. Now if your great-grandmother was pregnant, the *Probe* might be interested."

"But I saw Bigfoot myself! He was right on the patio, trying to get inside and kill me. My uncle shot at him last night. If you was to send a reporter, I could show him where it happened and let him take my picture." She paused, then gave it her best. "And pictures of the bloodstains. My uncle winged him and blood splattered everywhere. The dog's still missing, and the cat's nothing but clumps of fur and pink guts."

"We do all our interviews from right here in the office, and we have a great big file of photographs. You have an exuberant imagination, sweetie. Give us a call after you graduate from college."

Saralee banged down the receiver, checked to see that Traci was still staring at the television, and went to see if Larry Junior wanted to play Bigfoot Meets Barbie.

Raz was standing on his porch as I parked. From my perspective, the side yard appeared as empty as his expression—and his pockets. His cheek was a different matter, but it would take full-scale military intervention to change his repugnant habit.

"Business trickled off?" I asked him in a touching display of neighborly concern.

"Reckon so."

"Maybe that's why Marjorie got bored and went wandering last night."

Something not unlike apprehension flashed across his face. He inched away from me and shook his mangy head. "I dunno what got into her. Most times she's real content to watch old movies, but long about midnight she turned restless and snuck out. Mebbe it was on account of the moon."

"Or maybe you went over to the Flamingo Motel

to do a little business," I said, forcing myself to bear down on him despite my inherent aversion to lice and everything about him. "Maybe you wanted to find out how to increase ticket sales by adding more circles or arranging for another explosion across the creek." I poked him in the chest. "You didn't know that Dr. Sageman was dead, did you? You put Marjorie in the truck and drove over to see if he had any new suggestions. When the deputy drove away and folks started prowling all over the parking lot, you thought you'd better wait to see what happened. Marjorie decided to go see for herself." I poked him again, this time nearly hard enough to send him off the edge of the porch. "Then the deputy returned and you hightailed it back to your shack. Sure enough, Deputy Whitbread showed up a few minutes later and asked you to coax Marjorie out of the motel room."

He held up his hands. "I don't know nuthin' about that, 'specially the explosion. I liked to jump out of my skin."

"Listen up, Raz Buchanon, those crop circles didn't simply appear one night in your field. I already know that Brian Quint came to Maggody a few weeks back. He drove all around town until he spotted the perfect site and someone who was shifty and degenerate enough to go along with his scheme. He told you how to construct the crop circles, didn't he?"

"It may have been something like that," Raz whined into his whiskers. "But it weren't illegal, Arly. I never said that there was flying saucers out in the field. Iffen folks wanted to have a look for themselves, they were free to do it." He sent an arch of tobacco juice toward the field and tried to look remorseful. "Not free, mebbe, but nobody made 'em pay."

"How'd you make the circles?"

"I went along the other side of the fence and propped a ladder on the top strand. Then I crawled down the rungs into the field, strapped boards on my feet, and started walking in circles. That young feller told me about putting a stick in the middle and holding onto a string so's the circles would be round. I measured the strings real careful before I started." He hooked his thumb beneath his overall strap and puffed up like a bedraggled rooster. "I did a goddamn good job, too. Fooled you, dint I?"

"You sure did, Raz. You also fooled the tabloid reporters, the representatives from UFORIA, the woman from the television station in Farberville, and Dr. McMasterson, to name a few."

"And that Sageman feller," he added with a cackle. "He promised to talk about me at some conference in Texas next month. He had slides of me and Marjorie that he was gonna show, and he even said he might write about me in a book. The only book that you ever find the Buchanon name in is a family Bible, and that ain't common."

"Then Sageman didn't realize the crop circles were faked?" I asked, surprised. "Why did you go to talk to him last night?"

"I went to get my money from Quint. I dint hear till this morning how the aliens murdered him out by the low-water bridge. You catch 'em yet?"

"I'm getting close," I said, then went back to my car. His assertion that he hadn't done anything illegal was apt to be true. Fraud was a factor, but he'd never claimed that extraterrestrials (or intraterrestrials) had made the circles. Somewhere in the

Constitution is the inalienable right to make fools of ourselves by jumping on whatever bandwagon we wish. All Raz had done was charge a small fee for the privilege. It paled in comparison with what McMasterson, Sageman, and scores of others had been doing for decades.

I suppose Abraham Lincoln was right when he claimed you can't fool all of the people all of the time. Then again, he'd never come to Maggody.

FIFTEEN

◆

Brother Verber licked the stamp and reverently placed it on the envelope. He wished he knew the zip code for the Vatican, but surely those Italian postmen would know where John Paul's house was, him being the pope and all. He didn't know how much postage he needed either. It'd be mighty embarrassing if his letter arrived with a few pennies due, but the Catholic Church had so much money they had boxes of it in the basement and gold fixtures in all the bathrooms (or so he'd heard from a Baptist preacher over in Berryville who'd seen a movie called *Nasty Habits* three times).

He made sure his return address was easy to read, then said a little prayer concerning future financial prosperity and tucked the envelope in his pocket. He'd been so busy with his letter that he'd kinda forgotten about Brother Jim Bob's call earlier. Now he got up from the dinette and gave the matter his full and undivided attention while he poured a glass of wine and stood at the window, watching a haggard dog slink across the grass and disappear behind the Assembly Hall. According to Brother Jim Bob, Sister Barbara had done much the same, except in her car, of course.

Absently sucking a drop of wine off his lip,

Brother Verber thought about her plight. Maybe having to face the possibility of destitution and disgrace had driven her away to live out her final days in desolate, tacky motel rooms without cable. Or even worse, she might become a bag lady who wheeled her pitiful possessions in a grocery cart from garbage can to garbage can, subsisting on moldy bread crusts and limp lettuce leaves. Her skin would grow wrinkled, her hair gray and scraggly, and her body so skinny that her breasts would shrivel up like empty burlap bags.

He battled back tears as he refilled his glass. She'd come to him for advice, and he'd flat out failed her. It was as much his fault as it was Brother Jim Bob's that her breasts someday would no longer be a glorious tribute to God's handiwork (comparable to round ripe melons such as your catawbas and honeydews).

He sat down on the sofa to pray for guidance and a little help remembering the exact details of what Sister Barbara had said about Jim Bob's plummet into perdition. Guidance was not forthcoming, but he finally pulled together most of the conversation.

The root of evil in this case was Raz Buchanon's still up on Cotter's Ridge. If there wasn't any still, there wouldn't be any moonshine. If there wasn't any moonshine, Jim Bob wouldn't be able to deliver it, and there wouldn't be any revenue agents wanting to seize Sister Barbara's cherished possessions. She'd return all bright-eyed and bushy-tailed and brimming with eagerness to aid him in his war against Satan. Her honeydews would inspire them into every battle.

He'd found the still in the past. The situation had been awkward, but there wasn't any time to dwell on it (although Sister Barbara had looked real fetching in that scarlet nightie and cute lil panties, not to forget the peekaboo bra with the tantalizing black strap straying down her satiny shoulder).

Brother Verber told himself that all he had to do to save saintly Sister Barbara was to go find the still and make sure he destroyed it once and for all. He drained the glass and rose unsteadily to his feet. He was almost to the door of the rectory when he had a less pleasant memory of the incident on the ridge when he'd rustled up a skunk with a real poor attitude. He detoured to his bedroom and collected his raincoat and boots, then put on the plastic pith helmet, just in case.

Humming "Onward Christian Soldiers" to strengthen his resolve, he marched out to his car. Like the post office, he was committed to deliver rain or shine. In his case he'd deliver eternal salvation rather than picture postcards and reminders from the rural electric cooperative.

I headed out to the north end of town to make sure Harve's boys were photographing and fingerprinting the guilty car. As I approached the SuperSaver, however, I braked so abruptly I was nearly rear-ended by a dump truck and swerved into the parking lot.

Eula Lemoy, Elsie Buchanon, and Lottie Estes stood in a line on the sidewalk beneath the overhang. Each held a cardboard sign attached to a stick (broom, yard, and hickory, respectively). The words were written in the impeccable penmanship of a schoolteacher, and offered the same sentiment: DON'T BUY GROCERIES FROM A MOONSHINER!

I rolled down the car window. "How y'all doing?"

"Fine, thank you," Eula said without turning her head. "How are you today?"

"Fine." I finally pried my hands off the steering wheel and got out of the car to join them, although I made sure I stayed out of whacking range. "If you don't mind me asking, what's this about?"

Eula smiled grimly. "As any fool can see, we're picketing the supermarket." Farther down the line Elsie and Lottie nodded in agreement.

"Jim Bob may not be an ideal role model, but he's not a moonshiner," I said.

"I happen to know for a fact that he's delivering moonshine all across the county," Eula countered. "Lottie heard it from Mrs. Jim Bob's own lips, and they were in the House of the Lord at the time."

Lottie's smile was no less grim. "We are doing our civic duty by letting the God-fearing citizens of this town know about it."

"So they won't go spending money in an establishment owned by a sinner," added Elsie. "It's our obligation as Christians to battle demon whiskey."

No cars were pulling into the lot, but I suspected the rain was doing more to deter potential shoppers than the three self-righteous demonstrators. Through the plate glass I could see the sinner under discussion. He had the look of a starving piranha in a fishbowl as he stared out at us.

I hastily said, "What did Mrs. Jim Bob say that led you to believe her husband's running moonshine?"

"He's been going up to Cotter's Ridge at night," Eula said. "She followed him, but she lost him on the trail that goes to the still."

"She did?" I said, recalling the conversation I'd

had with her after church. It made a lot more sense, even if her assumption made none at all.

"It's about time you got here," Jim Bob snarled as he came out the door. "These women are disrupting my business and trespassing! I want you to file criminal charges and get them the hell off my property." He stabbed his finger at Eula Lemoy. "If I've a mind to, I can file a civil suit for libel."

"Slander is the correct term," Lottie informed him with the perfect degree of superciliousness to escalate the situation seriously.

I got in front of her before we had a demonstration of bodily assault. "If you're not helping Raz with his deliveries, then what have you been doing on the ridge at night? Courting Bigfoot?"

He chewed on his lip, then caught my arm and dragged me away from the demonstrators. "I went up there to investigate those orange lights," he said in a low voice, glancing everywhere but at me. "I was thinking I could make a fortune if I captured one of the aliens. I'd parade it on shows like *Strange Stories* and *Good Morning America* and eventually sell it to some outfit like Sageman's foundation for enough money to retire to Florida."

I gave him an admiring look. "It was pretty brave of you to go there alone. I'd have been scared the alien might have turned me into a very small pile of ashes."

"Roy and Larry Joe went with me, and we took shotguns. A dead one wouldn't have been worth as much as a live one, but we figured we'd come out okay."

"Did you go there last night?"

"Roy and me did. Larry Joe's wife had some screwy notion that Bigfoot was in their yard, and she wouldn't let him set foot out of the house. We tromped around for a couple of hours, but we didn't find anything."

"And went to Roy's to sit around and congratulate yourselves?" I suggested.

"I just said we didn't find anything, dammit."

"I didn't say you did." I went over to the women, who'd been watching our private discussion with intense interest. "I'm afraid that you really are trespassing on Jim Bob's property. I'm all for you continuing to picket, but you'll have to go down to the edge of the road."

"In the rain?" Eula said with a gasp. "We'll get drenched, and none of us can have her hair done till Estelle turns up. Why, I'm presiding over a tea for the Veterans' Auxiliary on Wednesday."

"I have a wedding tomorrow morning," said Lottie.

"I'm recovering from a head cold," added Elsie, coughing delicately.

"I guess that's a sacrifice you'll have to make in order to do your duty as God-fearing Christians," I said as I got back in my car. I looked in my rearview mirror as I drove away. Hizzoner stayed on the sidewalk, a worried expression marring his already unattractive face. The demonstration appeared to be over, at least until the sun came out.

Instead of going north, I drove to the Flamingo Motel and found Les, who was huddled in the doorway of No. 5. I ascertained that the current residents of the other units were safely stashed in their respective rooms, went inside to get the tape recorder, and then went to the door of Ruby Bee's Bar & Grill. The Closed sign was in place, but I continued inside.

The lights were off, and it took me a minute to

spot Ruby Bee on the end stool. "Did you find her?" she asked in a dispirited voice.

"Not yet. I need you to do something for me." I set down the tape recorder and two plastic cassettes. "I listened to most of the first tape. Finish listening to it, then put in the second tape. If you hear anything besides Sageman, Dahlia, and Rosemary spouting nonsense, make a note of where it is in the tape so you can tell me later."

"How's that gonna help Estelle?"

"Trust me on this. By the way, do you know who Reggie Pellitory is dating?"

"Darla Jean McIlhaney. Her ma's dead against it, but she can't seem to put a stop to it. Estelle said Millicent has grown so many gray hairs that coloring them was worse than painting an old barn. Darla Jean's pa is threatening to send her away to live with her aunt in Cedar Rapids. That's in Iowa, I think. Millicent wasn't sure."

"I'll be back after a while."

"There's something you ought to know," Ruby Bee said, still talking as if she had one foot in the grave and Vincent Price were hanging on to the other one. "It's about Lucy Fernclift."

"I already know. After you listen to the tapes, you'd better switch on the lights and dust the drawing room. As soon as I run one little errand and make a couple of telephone calls, we're going to have an old-fashioned denouement."

The rain had not eased up, but I was feeling much brighter as I drove to the McIlhaneys' house. It took Darla Jean less than ten minutes to burst into tears and confess to almost everything but burning down Hiram Buchanon's barn (she hadn't been born). I was glowing as I drove to the PD.

* * *

Kevin picked his way across the porch of the cabin, making sure he avoided the worst of the rotted planks. Rain splattered through holes in the roof and pinged off his head like marbles. He was shivering so hard he could barely move, but he kept on going, a veritable Energizer bunny propelled by a love that was stronger than any physical discomfort or AAA battery.

He'd been stumbling through the woods more hours than he could keep count. At first he'd called Dahlia's name and paused to shove back branches and search behind bushes for her remains. Once the moon had dropped behind the ridge, there wasn't any hope he could see her lifeless body unless he tripped over it, so he'd save his strength for the long haul up the ridge.

There hadn't been a dawn, but only a faint lessening of the darkness. The rain had started long about then. His progress, which hadn't been all that good, slowed down to almost nothing as the leaves got slipperier and the mud stickier. Water bubbled down the trail, soaking his already icy feet and staining his white socks brown.

Whoever "They" was, Kevin was gonna strangle them when he found them. But first he had to find Dahlia. The note had said she was going to the top of the ridge. The trail went right by the cabin, though, and it was possible she'd decided to rest there. Lordy, he hoped so. The ridge was a good eight miles of scrawny pines, rocks, and skittery slopes. The nearest ranger station was in Stonecrop County.

The cabin door hung on one hinge. He ducked under it and went inside, where it was as gloomy as

Idalupino Buchanon's bomb shelter and stank so bad all kinds of critters must have died there over the winter and were commencin' to thaw. Oddments of primitive furniture remained: a rocking chair made of crudely hewn oak, a lopsided table, a whiskey crate, a sodden braided rug that had lost all its color.

There was a second room where once upon a time Robin Buchanon had entertained paying customers on a mattress stuffed with corncobs. Kevin peered from the doorway, but there was no sign of Dahlia. He returned to the porch to scratch his head and squint at the rain.

A movement in the undergrowth beyond the remains of the fence caught his attention. "Dahlia?" he called hesitantly, unable to make out anything more than a quiver in the foliage. "It's me, Kevin. I'm here to rescue you, my temptress."

The quiver intensified, as did his apprehension. He opened his mouth to repeat her name, but nothing came out. Backing up until he ran into splintery wood, he wiped the rain out of his eyes and tried harder to make out what he'd seen.

About the time he'd decided that his mind was tricking him, he saw the top of a head rise above a bush. The hair was thick and tangled and stood out wildly despite the rain. Two eyes followed, both of them yellow and glinting angrily beneath a low-slung forehead and bristly black eyebrows. The nose was flat, as if it'd been squashed by a brick.

Kevin didn't wait to see what else was gonna appear. He flung himself off the corner of the porch and took off down a path alongside the cabin. He heard a howl that almost stopped him in his tracks, then realized it was coming from his own mouth. In front of him was a thicket of blackberry bushes. He skidded to a stop, glanced over his shoulder, and looked around for a place to hide.

The outhouse was so crooked that it should have blown over in the last williwaw, but it hadn't. Kevin jerked open the door. The high-pitched scream was the last straw. With a gurgle, he crumpled forward in one hell of an impressive faint. If there'd been a row of judges, he would have received all eights and nines.

"I really appreciate you all being here today," I began politely, even though the majority had no choice and the minority would have never forgiven me had they been overlooked. For the record, the majority was comprised of Jules Channel, Lucy Fernclift, Hayden McMasterson, and Rosemary Tant. Arthur Sageman and Brian Quint were present in spirit only. Cynthia Dodder had sent her regrets from her hospital room. The minority was comprised of Ruby Bee and Sheriff Harve Dorfer. There were a couple of deputies outside, but I was in the mood for intimacy. The barroom was the best I could do for a drawing room, since the PD was so small I ran into myself when I paced.

Everybody was sitting on a stool. I played bartender until everyone had his or her request. "There are a few things you don't know," I continued. "For instance, you may not know that Darla Jean McIlhaney has been stepping out with Reggie Pellitory. 'Stepping out' is a euphemism in these parts for behavior that's rarely condoned by the parents of the involved parties."

"What's your point?" asked Lucy Fernclift.

I rewarded her with an insincere smile. "You're probably unaware of the Pellitory family, but they have a well-deserved reputation for murdering their grannies and swinging from low branches when the moon is full."

Ruby Bee sniveled into her sherry. "So?"

"So," I said, enjoying myself immensely, "when a slinky black limo came to Maggody, its occupant searching for local vermin, one of its encounters was with our boy Reggie. Another was with Raz Buchanon, whose credentials are no more impeccable. Deals were struck, instructions and money proffered. Two or three weeks later hell broke out not only in Maggody but also in other parts of the county."

Harve took a cigar stub from his pocket and gazed fondly at it. "Like crop circles and cattle mutilations?" he suggested like a benign priest about to say grace.

I nodded. "Brian Quint started all this with his visit. Perhaps I should have paid attention to the rumors about the limo, but it seemed harmless and was gone by midday. It wasn't harmless, though. His visit set off a series of events that led to Cynthia's heart attack, his own murder, and the murder of Arthur Sageman."

"Poor Arthur," Rosemary said sadly. "He was going to do a final book about my abduction experiences. I believe it was to be titled *Rosemary: Repentance and Redemption.* I've come to grips with my trauma, you see, and—"

Jules cut her off. "Give us a break, okay?"

Hayden cleared his throat and said, "Abductions are a confabulation offered to a sympathetic hypnotist in response to a personal sense of inadequacy brought on by repressed childhood abuse and—"

"Please," snapped Lucy, whipping out a gold cig-

arette case and lighter, "could we avoid this icky
New Age I'm-okay-you're-fucked-up crap and—"

"Shut up!" Harve banged his beer mug on the bar
in case someone wasn't paying attention.

I made sure everyone was before resuming.
"Brian Quint was a very ambitious young man, also
opportunistic and manipulative. Maggody has received some bad press over the last few years. Anyone who chanced upon the stories might easily
conclude that we're the most artless little town in
the world, maybe in the solar system." I paused to
draw myself a glass of beer, even though I was on
duty. Ruby Bee snorted just to let me know she dis-
approved, but I went ahead blithely. "Brian spoke to
the two men I mentioned earlier: Reggie Pellitory
and Raz Buchanon. The former"—I gave them a
moment to sort it out—"agreed to mutilate cattle for
a fee and do some other tasks later. The latter was
tickled pink to find out how to make big bucks by
stomping down a few cornstalks and standing aside
to watch the gawkers stream through his gate."

Ruby Bee choked on her sherry. After Harve
thumped her on the back and Lucy found her a paper
napkin, she said, "Raz made those circles?"

"All five of them," I said, then looked at Hayden
McMasterson. "You must be devastated. After all,
you've already spoken to your publicist about network coverage and a hefty book contract. Oh, and
don't let me forget the conference in Houston, where
you and Dr. Sageman were going to go into battle to
defend your hypotheses. He's beyond caring, but
you're still stuck with faked crop circles and some
embarrassing contacts, aren't you?"

He eyed me coolly. "It remains to be proven that
this ignorant hillbilly made the circles. Very often a

legitimate phenomenon is covered up with facile explanations and coerced admissions of guilt. Take the sightings in Gulf Breeze, for example. Despite the obvious geophysical correlation with the Bimini Road, people are quick to dismiss—"

Lucy reached across Ruby Bee to pick up Hayden's glass and pour the contents in his lap. She didn't say anything, but it did distract him.

I continued. "So Brian set it all in motion, then went back to California and waited for his choreographed shit to hit the fan. When it did, he made sure Sageman, McMasterson, and Cynthia Dodder learned of it. They reacted exactly as he'd planned, which was to come rushing here in hopes this was one truly awe-inspiring invasion of extraterrestrials."

"Or intraterrestrials," McMasterson inserted petulantly, still mopping his lap and flickering at Lucy.

"Brian also had a conversation with some local dignitaries. I don't have the details, but I'd surmise that he pointed out the infusion of tourists would have a positive impact on local trade. Said local dignitaries were willing to learn how to add a little pizzazz to the madness by releasing UFOs on Cotter's Ridge."

"Those orange lights?" Harve said.

"Most likely plastic garbage bags with candles taped in the opening," I said. "The heat caused the air to expand and rise, but when the oxygen was spent—poof."

"Poof," they all intoned obediently, their heads bobbling as if they were a row of dashboard hula girls.

"Poof," I said. "Let's return to Brian Quint. Why did he go to all this trouble to set up bogus incidents? If I were charitable, I'd suggest all of it was done for Arthur Sageman. His publisher was losing interest. His lectures were stale. He was out of abductees. How noble of his secretary to create an exciting new subject for books, lectures, television interviews, and even an episode on *Strange Stories*. Noble—and cheap, too."

Ruby Bee stared at me. "But he told Dr. McMasterson. They're in opposing camps. Why would Brian do him such a big favor?"

"Good question," I said. I waited for conjectures from the audience, but none were forthcoming. In the interim, I noticed that McMasterson was struggling not to slip off his stool. A shame. "All along I've heard how much money there is in ufology. I didn't believe it at first, but I looked into it. There're millions of dollars to be collected from a broad socioeconomic spectrum. Book sales are, if you'll excuse me, astronomical. Conferences charge hundreds of dollars for registration, and much of it ends up in the lecturers' pockets." I again focused on McMasterson. "How much does your foundation receive every year from donations and subscriptions to your journal?"

"Not that much," he said. "Couple of million maybe."

"And you're a nonprofit corporation?" I asked. "I suppose you pay yourself a salary out of the proceeds?"

"A minimal one."

"How about your wife? Does she take a salary? Do you have an allotment for living expenses? A car? Travel? Herbs?"

"We use the foundation's funds to cover our needs, which are simple. Insinuations to the contrary are a manifestation of negativity."

Ruby Bee leaned across the bar to shake my arm. "Are you aiming to delve into finances all day or to find Estelle?"

"We're getting there," I told her quietly, then resumed business. "Does everyone have the picture thus far? Brian Quint came to Maggody, told various people how to fake things, then made sure all the luminaries in the field showed up. I mentioned the charitable explanation, but it won't wash. I think Brian wanted Sageman and McMasterson to commit themselves to the validity of the circles and the UFO sightings. He wanted them to go on network television, dash off books, and make presentations at this conference in Houston. He wanted them to stake their professional reputations on their interpretations of these incidents. In general, he wanted them to crawl so far out on their respective limbs that there'd be no retreat—with the exception of splattering to the ground like ripe persimmons." I wadded up a napkin and dropped it on the bar.

This resulted in a lot of bewildered mutters and dark looks from everyone except McMasterson, who was paling by the minute. Gawd, this was fun.

Jules Channel was the first to pick up on McMasterson's discomfort. "Did they both fall for it?" he asked me.

"For the first few days. On Saturday afternoon Sageman made it known that he had scheduled a session with Dahlia Buchanon."

"That tormented child," Rosemary began, then stopped when I glowered at her.

I waited until she looked away. "Sagemen would be engaged for several hours. Brian was down at the creek across from Raz's field, which meant the motel room would be empty. All sorts of people saw this as a wonderful chance to sneak into his room and rummage through the computer files. Someone succeeded and was having a fine time when Sageman noticed the light and came storming across the parking lot to investigate."

"Who?" asked Ruby Bee.

There was so much electricity in the air that Las Vegas could have tapped in and lit every lightbulb on the Strip. Even Harve was so absorbed that he hadn't noticed his cigar butt had gone out. A couple of glasses were midway to mouths. No one so much as flinched when a car backfired out on the road.

"Hayden McMasterson," I said.

SIXTEEN

"That weenie?" Harve's sneer wouldn't win him any absentee votes from New Mexico.

"He lucked out," I said almost apologetically. "Jules and Lucy wanted access to the files, too, but McMasterson beat them to it. It didn't take much ingenuity or raw grit since his room key happened to work on the next door unit." I turned to Ruby Bee, who was not delighted with the drift of the discussion. "Is every last one of the locks keyed the same?"

"People are all the time running off with the keys. This way's a sight cheaper than calling a locksmith once a month, and it's not like someone has to worry about being burglarized or attacked."

"How about murdered?" I said. "That particular room is developing quite a track record. Next time you have it fumigated, you might think about having it exorcised at the same time."

Rosemary fluttered her hands. "Are you saying that all three of these people wanted to pry into Arthur's private files? Why?"

I positioned a bowl of pretzels between Jules and Lucy since they both looked wan and I didn't want anyone passing out on me. "I'll get back to these two later. I'm sure they were disappointed when they saw a light in Sageman's room, but there was nothing they could do except hang around and wait for another opportunity. With his nemesis occupied across the way, McMasterson got busy with the computer. I would hypothesize that he wanted to find out if there was anything his opponent had discovered about the crop circles and sightings that could be used at the conference to blow holes in the ITH argument. Sageman might have interviewed witnesses whom McMasterson missed or found some obscure correlation with previous incidents."

McMasterson toyed with his crystal, then curled his lip and said, "Arthur was unscrupulous. In several instances he hoarded pertinent data until he could publish them in a book with much fanfare. This was hardly conducive to fellowship within the movement. We are all seeking the ultimate truth rather than petty personal gain—"

"What about Estelle?" Ruby Bee growled at me.

"Let's move along," I said. "McMasterson knew how to access Sageman's files, and he was doing so when Sageman himself stormed into the room. The ensuing exchange couldn't have been pleasant, but for some curious reason Sageman returned to number two and resumed the session without even mentioning what had happened to Rosemary. Why didn't he? After all, she was one of his most ardent supporters. She would have condemned McMasterson's behavior. But he didn't say a word."

Rosemary thought for a moment. "No, and it is curious. His face was rosy, and I seemed to recall he was somewhat distracted as he eased Dahlia back into a deep level of hypnosis."

I took the tape recorder from behind the bar and placed it on the bar. "Ruby Bee graciously agreed to listen to the tapes for me. I heard most of the first one, but I never got to the second one. Was it interesting?"

Ruby Bee gave me a confused look. "There wasn't but five minutes on the second tape. Dahlia rambled on about how these silver men had her paralyzed on a table and were threatening to do something real nasty. She screeched, but they didn't pay her any mind and were closing in on her privates when Dr. Sageman stopped the machine. Then he started it again and told her to let the picture fade until it was gone, talked real gently about how she'd remember what she'd said but it wouldn't upset her, and told her to wake up. That was the end."

"That can't be right," protested Rosemary. "There should be approximately four hours of testimony, two on each cassette. I was present the entire time. There was only a brief interruption when Arthur went outside."

"I could play the second tape for you," I said, "but I doubt anyone else wants to hear it. You'll have to rely on what Ruby Bee told us, which is that the session was nowhere near four hours."

Harve gave Rosemary such a dark look that she pulled her head into her coat collar as if she were a turtle. "Somebody's lying," he said. "That's for sure."

I wandered down the bar until I was in front of McMasterson. "Let's talk about what you found. Sageman was quite proud that he was a computer illiterate, and he relied on Brian to transcribe his dictation and keep everything on disks. This meant that Brian could use the computer for his own private files, too. One of them was likely to be an account of his scheme to humiliate you and Sageman. The media loves nothing more than a juicy story of duplicity. Brian would have been the featured guest on the network talk shows, hawking a book that exposed the ufology's leading authorities as naive and pathetically gullible. For pity's sake, look who was fooling you and Sageman: a moonshiner with a third-grade education, a punk destined for the state pen, and the Maggody town council. Marjorie can beat any of them in a domino game."

McMasterson began to weep. Ruby Bee found him a dishrag and murmured at him until he regained control of his volatile tear ducts. "Brian's book not only would have destroyed the ETH and ITH foundations but would have undermined the public's confidence in the entire worldwide UFO movement. The skeptics would go wild with glee. Even our most dedicated believers would have dismissed any future incidents as more pranks. Without our meticulous investigations into phenomena, the government would be free to continue its conspiracy to hide the truth from all of us."

I wiggled my eyebrows at Jules to let him know I hadn't forgotten him, then turned back to McMasterson. "I'll bet Sageman was ready to punch you in the nose until you showed him what you'd discovered. Somewhere in the file Brian must have crowed about his ultimate caper, wherein he intended to make a total ass of Sageman. With any luck you might have been treated to the same indignity. Earlier that afternoon Brian arranged for Reggie to deliver the note to Sageman. At some point before nine he abandoned his post and drove to the low-water bridge, donned the silver suit and helmet, and waited for Sageman to come rushing into the clearing. Sageman was desperate for an encounter of the third kind. He was going to get one he'd never forget."

"It was all in the file," McMasterson said in a low voice. "Arthur was aghast at Brian's treachery. It was the closest I'd ever seen him to tears. We shared a moment of intense spiritual communion."

Ruby Bee tried to grab my arm again, but I edged out of reach. "What about Estelle?" she insisted. "The longer you carry on, the likelier she's in worse danger."

"No, she's not." I went to the window and pushed back the curtain. "Hey, the rain's stopped. I was planning to finish my story here, but I think a field trip is in order. We can all use a little fresh air, don't you think? Harve, will you help with the transportation?"

I made Ruby Bee ride with one of the deputies in order to avoid a discussion of Estelle's whereabouts. I was 99 percent sure where she was, but I had to let the scene unfold if I was to get a confession. There was not one percentage point in hell that Ruby Bee'd keep quiet and go along with me if she could go galloping to the rescue and have something to lord over Estelle to her dying day. Not my mother.

We assembled on the shoulder of County 102 and I resumed the narrative. "There was an imperfection in Brian's plan. He couldn't have predicted that the note would be read and acted on by Cynthia Dodder instead of Sageman. He concealed his car behind the garbage dump and went down the path to the creek."

I motioned for them to fall into step, and like an orderly garden club, they did. I held up my hand as we approached the clearing. "Let's have some playacting, just so everybody can follow along. Rosemary, you talked about this with Cynthia. You take her role, and I'll take Brian's. The rest of you just watch."

"You shouldn't wade across the creek," Ruby Bee said. "Your feet'll get wet and you're liable to catch pneumonia, honey."

I ignored this outburst of maternal concern. "Now I want all of you, including Rosemary, to turn around and close your eyes. No peeking, you hear?" I adjusted a prop I'd left nearby. "Here we go," I continued. "Cynthia stumbles into the clearing, stops when she sees the burn marks, and then looks up as a silver alien comes walking across the surface of the water." I waved from the middle of the creek, where I was teetering on a narrow plank. I'd been damn accomplished at such antics twenty years ago, but at the moment I was precariously close to landing on my butt in several inches of water.

Everybody assessed the scene. Harve finally broke the silence, saying, "Maybe Les should have looked a little harder at the garbage dump."

The accused (who did not suffer fools gladly) tapped his superior on the shoulder. "I listed every last item there, Harve. It wasn't like that board was still wet the next morning."

I completed my trip with only a minimum of water in my shoes. "To Brian's bewilderment, it was Cynthia who screamed and collapsed. He would have enjoyed embarrassing UFORIA along with everyone else, but I doubt he harbored any personal animosity toward her. All he could do was replace the plank and get out of the costume as quickly as he could. This was what he was doing when Sageman and McMasterson came down the path."

"But they didn't have the map," blurted Ruby Bee. "I had it in my apron pocket."

"Everything was in the file," I said. "They didn't need the map to know the location."

Rosemary was so agitated that her hands were a blur. "But I've already explained that Arthur never left the room again. I don't know what's wrong with the cassette, but the session ran four hours, and he couldn't have been here. Dr. McMasterson must have acted alone!"

McMasterson sat down in the wet weeds and slumped against a tree. He began to mumble under his breath, perhaps communicating with his subterranean chums about the necessity of raising bail in the near future. He didn't look capable of making any constructive contributions to my melodramatic presentation. Being pegged as a murderer has that effect on a lot of people.

"The logistics required two participants," I said to Rosemary, "and the two I mentioned had equally strong motives. Sageman needed to create an opportunity to sneak away to deal with Brian. He told McMasterson to wait, went back to number two, and put both you and Dahlia into a state of hypnosis so deep it was impenetrable. He'd hypnotized you so often that it was a snap, and Dahlia had already proven herself to be a cooperative subject. When he came back at eleven, he gave you a strong suggestion that the session had not been interrupted for more than a minute or two. What he couldn't do was fill the blank tape—or your notebook. That's why he had to take it."

Harve discreetly gestured at a deputy to station himself near McMasterson. "So they arrived and caught Brian in the middle of taking off the costume. That doesn't . . ." He shrugged.

I bent down and tweaked McMasterson's ponytail.

"Brian wouldn't agree to back off, would he? He was still going to ridicule your mindless acceptance of the crop circles and the sightings."

"Arthur was the one who would suffer the most," McMasterson said dully. "Brian went on and on about discrepancies in the older files, how Arthur had distorted findings to suit his premises, how contradictory testimony had been rewritten or ignored, how unprofessional he'd been with mentally unstable subjects. Arthur stood here in the middle of the clearing, getting stiffer and stiffer, his eyes blazing, his anger so intense that his aura was crimson. Brian was laughing when Arthur suddenly banged him on the head with the helmet and knocked him cold."

"But he would regain consciousness and remain a threat," I said, still tweaking the ponytail to keep his attention. "So the two of you came up with a brilliant way to silence Brian and at the same time enhance the soon-to-be-legendary events at Boone Creek. You carried Brian back to the rental car, attached a hose to the tailpipe, and asphyxiated him, then brought him back and arranged his body in the center of the circle he'd carefully made earlier. It was as if he'd drawn his own coffin."

McMasterson grimaced. "Arthur mentioned that it was a nice touch."

"What about the hose and tape?" asked Harve.

"Sageman couldn't be seen at the SuperSaver, so McMasterson must have gone. I don't think it would be too tough to find a checker who remembers him."

Harve looked down at the sandals. "Probably not."

I released the ponytail and stood up. "After they packed up Brian's suit, Arthur drove the rental car back to the Esso station, with McMasterson following in his car. There was no time to dispose of the costume and other incriminating evidence, so they left all of it in the trunk to deal with when they had a chance. The chance failed to materialize when Sageman inadvertently left the car key in Rosemary and Cynthia's room. McMasterson didn't know that, so he was searching for it last night when I was playing hostess."

"I was hoping to find my notebook," Rosemary contributed. "I was a tiny bit suspicious when Arthur insisted on taking it with him. He often used my little sketches in his books, you know, and it was customary for me to refine them before giving him my notebook."

Harve stationed a second deputy behind McMasterson, but it was merely a routine gesture. "I have a question or two. Why did Sageman hang on to the tapes when he knew they'd incriminate him? He had Rosemary here bumfuzzled about the session. McMasterson sure wasn't gonna talk about it, and neither was Reggie Pellitory. Even if we opened the trunk of the rental car and found the suit, there was a good chance we might never prove for sure who put it there."

"He needed the tapes for a new book," I said. "He was so desperate to regain eminence in the field that he was willing to risk it—especially after I ordered him not to have any more sessions with Dahlia. Yesterday morning he could have gone back to the rental car and used a crowbar on the trunk. If he had, the evidence would be buried in the woods and we'd never make a case. Instead, he went to the airport for an interview with a television producer. His behavior was obsessive, but not remarkable within this particular community. As far as I can tell, most of them are sincere in their beliefs. They buy books, send donations, and flock to conferences to gaze in awe at drawings of silver men with almond eyes. They accept a photograph of a bedroom window as proof of an abduction. Any evidence to the contrary is documentation of this vast, murky government conspiracy. No scraps from a crash? The government agents stole them. Enhancement of a photograph indicates a light is an airplane? The government agents doctored the negative. The more I read, the more a certain word kept popping up in the back of my mind."

"Paranoia," Ruby Bee said, then stalked over to Jules Channel and put her hands on her hips. "Well? Are you gonna tell everybody about the top secret underground laboratory in the desert and how Arthur Sageman had proof that aliens were gonna enslave my grandchildren and make 'em work in mines on Mars?"

He retreated. "I don't think this is the time to go into that."

"You fooled Estelle and me into trying to help you sneak into Arthur's room. Was he the secret agent, or are you? Did you kill him to keep him from telling what he knew on television?"

Jules didn't notice when he backed into a waist-high patch of poison ivy, and no one felt obliged to mention it. "I'm a reporter. It's my job to ferret out the facts and share them with the public."

"You're not a reporter, at least not for that tabloid in Florida," Ruby Bee went on. She was stealing my thunder, but I wasn't about to stop her (except from stepping into the poison ivy, which a deputy did). "The tabloids don't send reporters out to the places where things happen. The *Weekly Examiner* wouldn't even send one photographer to take a picture of a Chevrolet eaten by a dinosaur!"

This had a profound effect on everybody. Harve nervously examined the gravy stains on his tie. The deputies were bug-eyed. Lucy's face was tighter than the bark on the oak tree beside her. Rosemary was beyond fluttering. Even McMasterson had raised his head to frown. I was doing everything I could not to giggle, but I wasn't having complete success.

"A dinosaur ate your car?" said Jules. "What kind?"

"I already told you—a Chevrolet. Now just tell us who you are, Mr. Jules Channel!"

"I'm a government agent."

"So you did murder Arthur Sageman," she said, then realized she was in close proximity to a homicidal maniac and took refuge behind Harve. "Get out your gun," she whispered in Harve's ear. "Arrest him."

"He may be a government agent," I said, "but they come in more varieties than there are Buchanons in Stump County. Which bureau do you work for?"

"The IRS," he said sulkily.

I gave everyone a moment to let that sink in, then said, "And you're after the ETH Foundation with all its millions in donations and tax-free profits from the sale of books and related paraphernalia. The thought of missing out on your fair share bugs the hell out of you all, doesn't it? You just can't bear the thought of Sageman living in luxury without chipping in to ease the national debt."

Jules seemed to sense he wasn't the most popular person in the clearing. "All of you pay taxes. Why should these nonprofit groups get away with using the revenue for the personal advantage of the employees?"

"That doesn't give you the right to kill him," said Ruby Bee, standing on her tiptoes to glare over Harve's shoulder.

"I didn't kill him. I was trying to copy the disks with the financial information that fails to show up on his tax returns. I'd be amazed if he reports half the donations. His so-called legitimate expenses are as bogus as his UFO investigations. Every time he leaves his house, our agents go in and sift through his books and files, but we never find what we need to put him in a cell with Jim Bakker."

Ruby Bee wasn't convinced. "What about all your stories in the *Weekly Examiner*? Your name was right there on the story about how Hitler was a woman."

"Jules Channel is a nice man in Lantana, Florida, who never sets foot out of his office. We have an arrangement in which I use his name and credentials to gain access to the UFO investigators. I send him related stories, which he runs under his by-line. His other stories are entirely his own doing. In all honesty, I thought the Hitler-transvestite story was his best. One of these days I'll take a vacation and buy him a drink."

I was a little disgruntled by his identity, having pegged him as a private eye—and having fudged on a tax return or two in the past. "We'll run your name through your home office, but I believe that you didn't shoot Sageman."

Ruby Bee emerged, although she didn't look as if she were going to be offering Jules Channel (or whatever his name was) any lemon icebox pie anytime soon. "Then who did?" she asked.

I wasn't real surprised when I turned around and saw a gun pointed at me. I wasn't real happy about it, mind you, but it's one of the risks of the profession.

SEVENTEEN

◆

"Is Lucy Fernclift your real name," I asked, "or are you pulling the same crap as this clown?"

"I thought it was ingenious. If I'd ever dreamed the IRS would do this sort of thing, I'd come up with another way to ingratiate myself with the ufology group. An undercover taxman? Shit, this is embarrassing." She started to slap her hand to her forehead, then realized she'd knock herself silly and managed a self-deprecatory laugh. It was heartening to know she actually had a sense of humor—somewhere (mine was way downstream).

Harve and the deputies were shifting nervously. Les's hand hovered near his holster, and he appeared to be entertaining a fantasy of a medal from the mayor, a promotion from Harve, and a press conference of his very own. I imagined a bullet in my gut.

I positioned myself in the middle of the burn marks, where I was between him and his target. "You need to put down the gun, Lucy. There are too many witnesses and too many fingerprints. You're not very good at this, which speaks well of your character. I'll try to help you."

"Help me what?" she demanded.

"Help you get away." I shot an enigmatic look at Harve, trusting him to decipher it, and then said, "Your car's up there on County One-oh-two. Nobody'll stop you from getting in it and driving away—so long as you swear here and now that Estelle's okay."

"Of course she's okay." Lucy let the gun wobble in each of our directions, then aimed it at me with a steadiness I found disconcerting. "She was skulking around the parking lot when I came out of Sageman's room. He was the one who deserved to be stopped. He was forcing that foolish girl to remember things that never happened."

"But they did," Rosemary said. She might have intended to elaborate, but on the basis of Lucy's reaction, she may have well have seen her life flash before her eyes. Fluttering good-bye, she moved behind a tree.

Lucy continued to speak to me as if we were alone. "Would he ever stop to consider what would happen to the girl after he turned in his manuscript? Would he worry how she was going to handle the notoriety when she became the fashionable freak in the UFO sideshow? No, he was going to sit back, smile, autograph books, show slides, and lecture with great pomposity while he publicly humiliated her with the intimate details of her rape. Even if she committed suicide, he'd keep smiling as long as the royalty checks rolled in. I tried to reason with him, but he told me to go away so he could make notes for his next best-seller." Trembling, she lowered the gun, but not her fierce gaze. "What could I do? You tell me. I'm listening."

I murmured to Harve to control his deputies, then joined her at the edge of the clearing. "Get your affairs in order. Your brother's file contains his personal history. Since you didn't embark on a life of crime as a mere child, you'll be easy to trace through utility bills, credit cards, employment records, and so on. What I suggest you do is drive home and find a good ol' boy lawyer who understands the concept of family loyalty. He should have two first names, wear pinstriped suits, and play golf with the prosecutor and poker with the judge."

"Now that you mention it, John Earl January settled my granddaddy's estate last year after his own daddy was found dead in a whorehouse. He's running for the state court of appeals, but he might find time to hear me out."

"Go give him a call. Nobody's going to stop you, as long as you're telling the truth about Estelle. Let me make it clear that if she's not okay, I'll turn in my badge and come after you in a fashion the Fugitive never even had nightmares about."

"She's probably chewed off the duct tape and broken out of the closet by now. The last time I took the tape off her mouth to give her food, she commented loud and long on the greasiness of the chili dog and the lack of catsup for the onion rings, then offered to style my hair." Lucy pushed back her bangs and gave me a timid smile. "What do you think about my widow's peak? Does it make me look sexier?"

I was trying to decide as she trotted up the trail toward the road, and I made everybody else stand there and debate the question until I heard a car engine come to life. Sageman had been her victim, sure. She'd walked into his room, argued with him, and killed him. In the law's view, he was unarmed. In mine, he was as dangerous as a pit bull. He hadn't ripped any flesh off anyone, but he'd left souls ravaged. Psyches are fragile. There's a fine line between helping someone dredge up repressed memories and creating false ones. In some cases, people get to be the subjects of best-selling books; in others, they destroy their families and themselves.

The state police would come down on me for allowing her to escape, albeit temporarily. The irony was that I'd have to admit I was protecting Dahlia (née O'Neill) Buchanon, presuming I found her. The implications were downright terrifying.

Kevin snuggled his face into his beloved's breasts, luxuriating in their warmth, and said, "You were never absent from our bed. I love you too much to mistake your velvety thighs for a limp pillow. Never once have I reached for you and come up empty-handed." He went on to describe some things he'd done when he hadn't come up empty-handed; it was about the most romantic thing Dahlia'd ever heard, even on *Donahue*.

She wiped away a tear as she tried to get more comfortable. There was no gettin' around the dilemma; they were stuck as long as Bigfoot prowled the woods outside. Her one glimpse of him had been more than enough to send her fleeing into the outhouse, which, for the record, was one of her more regular refuges. Kevin's abrupt arrival had liked to stop her heart, but once she figured out who it was, she'd dragged him onto her lap and kissed the sweat offen his brow (there'd been a lot).

Bigfoot could have left. On the other hand, he could be right outside the door, his fists curled, his mouth salivating, his mind filled with perverted ideas. And it weren't all that unpleasant where they were, now that the rain'd quit dripping on 'em. They'd gotten used to the smell and the dim light that filtered through the knotholes, and it was kinda homey snuggling together in their little love nest.

Kevin forced himself to stop nibbling her nipples and lift his face. "You said you had proof. Whaddya mean?"

"I bought one of those home pregnancy kits," Dahlia said, blushing like a bride. "You pee on a strip of paper and wait to see what color it turns. It turned blue."

"We're having a boy?" Kevin came near falling on the floor as images flooded his mind: hunting, fishing, scaling fish, gutting squirrels, man-to-man talks about the birds and the bees. A boy, he sang to himself, lost in the image of a little Kevin Fitzgerald Buchanon, Jr.

"It just meant I'm pregnant," Dahlia said, although images were no slower to flood her mind: pink foam hair rollers, pinafores and patent leather shoes, ruffly curtains, hair bows, soap operas, woman-to-woman talks about how to please a husband. A girl, she sang to herself as she cradled Kevin in her arms and leaned back.

It wasn't long before both of them forgot all about what evil lurked beyond the outhouse door.

Putting the metal to the pedal, Brother Verber sped past the Pot o' Gold Mobile Home Park and squealed around the corner onto the highway without even looking to see what was coming. Paper cups and old church bulletins flew out the window, but he didn't pay any mind. His face was red, and sweat was coursing down his face till it liked to blind him. His breathing was so shallow he was close to passing out. Sprawled across the backseat, Sister Barbara already had.

"Get outta the way, you sumbitch!" he bellowed at a figure hesitating out in front of the barbershop.

The inadvertent profanity jarred him out of his frenzy, and he braked momentarily to add, "And God bless you, Brother Perkins."

He passed two or three more cars, then turned into the parking lot in front of the PD and slammed on the brakes. Arly's car was nowhere to be seen, but he could at least use her telephone to call for medical help and her radio to alert the sheriff. He jumped out of the car, squeezed by a white van, and hurried around to the other side to open the back door. Sister Barbara had slid to the floor sometime during the ride, and it took some tugging and struggling to get her limp body back on the seat.

"You're safe now," he comforted her between gasps. "I rescued you and you're safe."

"Rescued her from what?" asked a woman by the van.

Brother Verber scooted Sister Barbara's legs together and tried to figure out the best way to gather her up so he could carry her into the PD. "It was awful," he said without glancing over his shoulder. "Saintly Sister Buchanon was in terrible trouble. Look for yourself how her clothes're all muddy and her hair's tangled with leaves and twigs. Her bare feet are cold as a banker's heart." He bent way forward, wiggled his arm under her waist, and attempted to hoist her up. He wasn't sure, but he thought he heard something pop in his back. Easing her back down, he studied the situation in hopes of a better idea.

"What happened to her?"

"She was taken hostage by one of Satan's underlings. The ordeal was so horrifying that she's gone into shock." Brother Verber bent her knees and tried to turn her around so he could get a grip on her shoulders. "Speak to me, Sister Barbara," he pleaded as he rethought the idea, having gotten her jammed against the front seat. She groaned obligingly.

He finally got her knees free, raced around to the other side, and opened that door. Offering a silent prayer of apology, he slid his arms under hers and entwined his hands over her bosom. He'd got her halfway out when the pesky woman interrupted him for the third time.

"And who are you?" she asked in a smarmy voice.

"Brother Willard Verber, pastor of the Voice of the Almighty Lord Assembly Hall. This is Barbara Ann Buchanon Buchanon, the mayor's wife." All the while he was talking, he was pulling Sister Barbara's body along the seat. "And president of the Missionary Society for three years running," he added as he straightened up and hung on to her for dear life, having not suspected how heavy she was.

"Can you tell us exactly what happened that has left this woman unconscious? Who was her assailant? How long did the ordeal last? Were you the only one to rescue her, or are others on their way here right now?"

Brother Verber caught his breath and turned around to tell the woman to mind her own business. The last thing he expected was to find himself staring into a television camera. And the woman—why, she was the reporter who'd been up at Raz's shack when the crop circles appeared.

"Was she sexually assaulted?" she asked.

"I don't know for sure," he said, confused. "She said he'd grabbed her and took her to his cave. It was all squalid and wet. When the moon came out, she could make out bones scattered on the floor. He laid her on a smelly blanket and hunkered down to watch her all night. This morning he disappeared into the woods, even though it was pouring rain. At first she was too scared to move a muscle, but after a while, when he didn't come back, she crept out of the cave and stumbled down the ridge." He smiled modestly, wishing he had a free hand to smooth down his hair instead of having them clamped on Sister Barbara's honeydews. "I found her and carried her the rest of the way to my car."

The woman frowned, although not enough to wrinkle her forehead. Behind her, the camera whirred steadily. "Who did this too unspeakably vile thing to Barbara Ann Buchanon Buchanon, the wife of the major of Maggody and one of its leading citizens?"

"Bigfoot," said Brother Verber, surprised he hadn't already said as much. He was going to launch into a more precise description of his heroic rescue when an elbow poked him in his belly with so much force that the air whooshed out of his lungs.

"You fool!" snapped saintly Sister Barbara.

Earl Buchanon stood at his bedroom window, tugging at the waistband of his boxers and frowning. What in hell's name was Eilene doing out there in the field in the middle of the night? Sure, it was warm, but that didn't explain what she was doing just standing out there in the alfalfa, her face lifted like she was a kid catching snowflakes on her tongue.

He thought real hard about going out there to order her to stop her foolishness and come back to bed. There was something about her expression that made him uneasy, though.

He reminded himself of the Rotary club prayer

breakfast at seven and the appointment at the bank afterward. Refinancing the acreage along the creek had to be a sight more important than his wife's craziness out there in the moonlight. Hell, he was secretary of Rotary this year; the meeting couldn't get under way till he read the minutes. He climbed back in bed, pulled a pillow over his head, and within a minute was sound asleep.

I put down my fork and sighed contentedly. "There's something magical about your lemon icebox pie. It's the only conceivable reason for anyone to travel across the galaxy to come to Maggody." I was laying it on thick, but there was one last piece in the pan.

"I use real lemons," Estelle said from her stool at the end of the bar.

"And I don't, Mrs. Fannie Flagg?" Ruby Bee went into the kitchen.

"Then why were you buying bottled lemon juice at the SuperSaver last week?" Estelle said, although not loudly enough to be heard over the racket from the jukebox or, more significantly, through the kitchen doors. "I'm still feeling a little peaked," she said to me. "I've never been bulky like your mother, and I have a very delicate digestive system. Those chili dogs gave me terrible heartburn, not to mention gas. There I was, my hands and ankles taped together, tape over my mouth so I could hardly breathe, having to kick the door when I needed to use the bathroom, and—"

"We've heard this story a million times," Ruby Bee said as she came back through the door and took a plate of ham and beans to a customer at the far end. "We've heard it so many times I can recite it in my sleep. Lucy Fernclift didn't hurt you any more than she had to while she tried to figure out what to do. She could have gotten in her car and upped and left town. You'd have been a skeleton before Arly found you."

"Wait a minute," I protested. "I had to confirm Lucy's true identity before I confronted her. She did have a gun, you know."

"I knew that all along," Ruby Bee said, then clapped her hand over her mouth and gave Estelle the wide-eyed look of a frog confronting a gig.

"You did?" I said, wishing I had one. I reached for my fork, but it was snatched away at the last second.

Estelle arched her eyebrows. "We just happened to see it when we cleaned the rooms the other morning. I was going to tell you, but I didn't have a chance because I was kidnapped and locked in a closet and subjected to atrocities. It may have slipped Ruby Bee's mind."

"I was distracted by the murders and reports of Bigfoot," she said as she discovered a whole new reason to go back in the kitchen, leaving me to glare at the swinging doors. She returned to drop an order pad in the drawer beneath the cash register, then came back to her customary station by the beer taps and said, "Did you ever find Cynthia's purse?"

"It was in the trunk," I said, "and covered with McMasterson's and Sageman's fingerprints. I took it to her at the hospital last week. She wasn't nearly as thrilled as the ladies in billing."

"She got her Indians wrong," Estelle announced.

"Her Indians?" I said. I could see from Ruby Bee's expression that she wasn't doing any better than I was. "In the hospital?"

"In her past life. She told us she was an Apache

warrior who scalped Custer, but I looked it up in my encyclopedia. It was the Sioux what scalped Custer."

"Oh," I said, but only because something was expected of me.

Ruby Bee was more willing to pursue it. "What about her being a Viking with a red beard?"

Estelle patted her own indisputably red hair. "Only if she could buy Clairol back then."

I decided to change the subject before they started explaining whatever they were discussing. "Rosemary called this morning to tell me she was sending me an autographed copy of *Rosemary T: The Extrinsic Paradox*. She said all of Sageman's books went out of stock within hours after the story broke. None of the bookstores in Little Rock can order a copy anymore."

"I hope Dahlia's not disappointed," said Ruby Bee.

I knocked on the edge of the bar (walnut). "She and Kevin are being real quiet these days. I don't thick Eilene believed their story about going camping, and neither do I, but the last thing I want to hear is a detailed explanation for their three-day absence."

"There's been some talk," said Estelle, then gave Ruby Bee one of their significant looks that supposedly conveyed all kinds of subtle messages. They were about as subtle as an avalanche in the Swiss Alps, but I busied myself with my beer.

Ruby Bee took my glass from my hand and refilled it without any editorials—for a change. "I heard Mrs. Jim Bob's likely to lose the election at the Missionary Society. How long has she been president, Estelle? Two years, or has it been three?"

After all these years they'd perfected their routine.

"I don't rightly recall," countered Estelle. "Didn't Brother Verber tell that television reporter it was three?"

"He might have," she said. "Was that before or after he described how she was taken prisoner by Bigfoot hisself?"

"After, I seem to think."

They looked at me. I shrugged and said, "Diesel Buchanon's not bothering anybody. Squirrels and rabbits are not endangered species, and he promised me he'd stay out of the Lambertinos' backyard. When we have a hard freeze in the fall, he'll come down off the ridge. Maybe Mrs. Jim Bob will invite him over for Sunday dinner."

We debated the possibility until I realized it was almost time to follow the school bus to the county line. I slipped off the stool and started for the door, warmed by the knowledge I'd be protecting little Buchanons so they could grow up and become just like Uncle Diesel.

"Hold your horses," said Ruby Bee. "Estelle and me was talking about all the things that happened after the crop circle first showed up in Raz's field. Now, you already told us how Raz made the circle and how Jim Bob and the town council made the orange lights. You never said what happened across the creek from Raz's that first night."

Now that her boyfriend was serving time for slaughter of several thousand dollars' worth of livestock, Darla Jean McIlhaney was sweeping the PD on a daily basis and picking wildflowers to brighten up the decor. I shrugged and said, "Reggie Pellitory set off a cherry bomb and waved a flashlight. Anything else was nothing more than collective hysteria.

You have seen the same airplane fly over every night, haven't you?"

"Maybe," Ruby Bee conceded. "Wasn't there something else we meant to ask about, Estelle?"

She set down her sherry. "I can't rightly recall. Maybe it'll come to us when Arly gets back from her vacation. Doncha want to give her the present we picked out?"

"Present?" I said curiously as I went back to the bar. "You didn't need to buy me a present just because I'm taking off for a week."

"I just hope you don't lose your job because of it," Ruby Bee said as she ducked behind the bar.

I glanced down at my badge. "Someone else is going to apply for this job? I don't think so."

Ruby Bee reappeared with a bottle of calamine lotion. "Reckon you'll find a use for this down in Lantana, Florida."

"I don't have—" I stopped and took the bottle from her hand. "Reckon I might," I said, then walked across the dance floor and out into the bright lights of Maggody (pop. 755), a little town in the Ozarks where nothing ever happens.

HERE'S A
PREVIEW OF

<u>MIRACLES</u> <u>IN</u> <u>MAGGODY</u>,

COMING SOON
FROM
DUTTON.

The so-called extraterrestrials who'd visited Maggody a few months ago had found no sign of intelligent life, and I doubted anyone else could, either. Maggody's tucked up in the northwest corner of Arkansas, but it's not some picturesque little town with storybook houses, quaint cafés, and carefree, college-bound children flying kites in a field of wildflowers. Maggody is more a hodgepodge of rusty mobile homes, uninspired tract houses, shacks, a dirty barber shop and a dirtier pool hall, and snotty children playing serial killer in an illegal dump.

There may be more cars and trucks set on concrete blocks than cruising the roads. There certainly are more Buchanons; they're strewn across the county like rabbits. As a rule, rabbits are smarter than Buchanons, with damn few notable exceptions. You can spot a Buchanon a mile away by his or her yellowish eyes, simian forehead, and thick-lipped, repugnant sneer. Most of them are related to each other in more ways than one. Major Jim Bob Buchanon's my least favorite, with his wife Barbara Ann Buchanon Buchanon (aka Mrs. Jim Bob) running a real close second.

It's hard to explain why I, Ariel Hanks, had come limping back home to this oasis of poverty and incest. The primary catalyst was the collapse of a disastrous marriage to a hotshot Manhattan advertising executive. It had taken me a while to realize his office was the only one in the agency with a sofa that made into a bed. The divorce had been far from amiable; it was the one time he'd really gone out of his way to screw me. Now it was taking me a while to convince myself that my head was on my shoulders instead of in a place where the sun don't shine—as we say in Maggody, being partial to euphemisms.

I was entertaining all these gloomy thoughts as I drove past the town limits sign (pop. 755), past a peculiar metal structure known as The Voice of the Almighty Lord Assembly Hall, past a lot of storefronts with boarded-up windows, and into the gravel lot in front of the Maggody Police Department. When I first accepted the job as Chief of Police, I considered putting out a sign reserving the prime parking spot. However, it didn't take long—maybe twenty minutes—to realize that the citizens weren't exactly fighting for the privilege of parking by the door. I'd twiddled my thumbs for seventeen days before someone came in to report a stolen lawn ornament (a concrete garden gnome, I seem to recollect).

The pace had picked up, though. Tourists driving through on their way to the crowded country music theaters and go-cart tracks of Branson, Missouri, would never suspect the bizarre happenings that put everyone in a tizzy and me in bed with a pillow over my head. There'd been kidnappings, murdered movie stars, booby-trapped marijuana patches, feminist rebellions, a downright psychotic period when Maggody had been the hometown of a famous country singer, and fairly recently, the most absurd string of incidents imaginable involving crop circles, aliens, and dueling tabloid reporters. And let's not forget the Bigfoot sightings.

Somehow or other, we all kept muddling along. My mother, the infamous proprietor of Ruby Bee's Bar & Grill as well as maven of the grapevine, might go so far as to switch the daily blue plate specials or serve popcorn instead of pretzels at happy hour, but only when she's feeling risqué. Most of the time she sticks to the traditions, one of which is to make pointed remarks about my lack of promising beaus and my biological clock, which as far as I can tell is still ticking away at thirty-four. She's more enamored of the idea of grandchildren than I am of a icy cold beer on a sultry August afternoon.

It being a sultry August afternoon, I wasn't all that thrilled as I dutifully went into the PD, glanced through the mail that had accumulated in my two-week absence, and debated calling the sheriff's office to notify the dispatcher that I was back. I finally decided against it, since there was a real danger that Sheriff Harve Dorfer might actually have something that would interfere with my immediate objective. He seems to believe I'm the only officer in the county capable of writing up a really juicy accident report or intervening in a domestic dispute out on some remote dirt road. He may be right. A goodly number of his deputies are Buchanons; I can eat an ice cream cone without anything dribbling down my chin.

I wasn't in the mood for anything but that beer I mentioned earlier, and maybe a grilled cheese sandwich to tide me over until supper time. I made sure my bun was firmly affixed to the back of my head, applied a layer of lipstick, took my badge from a desk drawer and stuck it on my T-shirt, and walked down the road to Ruby Bee's.

There were more pickup trucks and cars in the lot than had graced the PD parking lot in the last three years. I squinted at Jim Bob's SuperSaver Buy 4 Less across the road. Heat was shimmering on the asphalt, but business was far from booming. There were a few people trudging in and out of the Suds of Fun launderette (also part of the Jim Bob Buchanon financial empire), and the old coots were nodding on the bench in front of the barbershop. Roy Stiver was sitting in a rocking chair by the door of his antiques store, playing the redneck for a couple of tourists ogling a pie safe. My amazingly inefficient efficiency apartment is above the store; at some point down the line I was going to have to drag my suitcases upstairs and start shaking sand out of my unmentionables. The sand was likely to enhance the decor.

No one appeared to be committing any crimes, so I continued inside the bar and paused to allow my eyes to adjust to the dim light before ambling across the dance floor. The jukebox was blaring some nasal lament of lost love, and the booths were filled with familiar (but not necessarily attractive) faces. Estelle Oppers, Ruby Bee's best friend and co-maven of the grapevine, was perched on her stool at the end of the bar. She's tall and as scrawny as a free-range chicken. The only thing different about her was her hairstyle; most of the time she piled her fire-engine-red hair into a daunting beehive, but today it shot out like a frizzy explosion.

"So you're back," she said as I selected a stool far enough away from her to give me a chance to take cover should her hair begin to flicker. Her tone was accusatory, but this was not extraordinary. She and Ruby Bee are pretty much always convinced I'm doing something wrong—like not subscribing to *Bride* magazine.

"Looks like it." I picked up a menu on the off chance it might be a chicken-fried steak day and Ruby Bee had leftovers in the kitchen. "What happened to your hair?"

She sniffed haughtily. "If you must know, I have been experimenting with a new product. What would the clientele of Estelle's Hair Fantasies think if I tried it on them and all their hair fell out?"

"Is all your hair going to fall out?"

The kitchen door opened and Ruby Bee came out, wiping her hands on a dishtowel. "Might be a blessing if it did, Estelle. It looks like you were roosting on a utility pole in an electrical storm." She turned her gaze on me. "Well, are you gonna sit there and insult Estelle, or are you gonna tell us about your vacation down in Florida?"

Decisions, decisions. I put down the menu and said, "May I have a beer, please?"

Ruby Bee is often mistaken for a grandmotherly sort because of her chubby cheeks, stocky body, and starchy apron, but she's more akin to a stevedore in drag. At the moment, her eyes were snapping below several layers of undulating pink eyeshadow, and her expression was sour enough to curdle milk as she banged down a mug of beer in front of me.

"At least you remembered to say 'please,' " she said. "Sometimes you act like you were raised in a barn. Last month Eula Lemoy told me you walked right past her in the produce section and didn't so much as ask about her arthritis. She's been feeling real poorly."

Estelle opted to butt in. "She told me she can't do any needlework on account of her knuckles swelling up like gnarls on a branch. When I happened to mention it to Elsie McMay while I was giving her a perm, she had the nerve to ask me if I thought Eula would be entering a quilt in the county fair this year! How's that for Christian charity?"

"I ain't surprised," Ruby Bee said as she filled a pitcher from the tap and took it to a bunch of good ol' boys in a corner booth. When she returned, she positioned herself in front of me, crossed her arms, and said, "So?"

"Is Eula entering a quilt?" I said, pretending to misunderstand her simply to amuse myself. Maggody's not a place where you find yourself rolling on the floor all that often.

"What about your vacation with that man who pretended to be a tabloid reporter just so he could snoop around town? Is he coming to visit any time soon? Did you stop spitting out smart remarks long enough for him to get a word in edgewise?"

Estelle gazed slyly at me over the rim of her glass of sherry. "You didn't find out he was married, did you?"

"Don't be absurd!" snapped Ruby Bee. "Arly wouldn't have gone off like that with a married man—not after the awful time she had with that philanthropist of an ex-husband."

If sperm counted, he'd have been right up there with Carnegie and Mellon. I took a swallow of beer, steeled myself for the inevitable counterattack, and said, "Jules and I had a perfectly nice time. We had dinner with his friend from the tabloid, spent a lot of time on the beach, drove through the Everglades one day, and bought each other incredibly tacky souvenirs. When we were ready to go our separate ways at the airport, there was some discussion of seeing each other again. But he lives in Washington, D.C., and works for the IRS, which is kind of spooky. One night while he was asleep, I started wondering if he was dreaming about widows in bankruptcy court and bond daddies in federal prisons."

"Just exactly what were you doing in *his* motel room, missy?" said Ruby Bee. Bear in mind she owns the Flamingo Motel out behind the bar, and although she doesn't rent rooms by the hour, she herself will admit there are rarely any cars parked in front of the units at sunrise.

Estelle waggled a finger at me. "Men don't respect girls who take a trip to Memphis with every man they meet—particularly on the first date. You might keep that in mind if you intend to catch yourself a husband in the next month of Sundays."

"Oh, I will," I said as I finished my beer. Instead of trying to wheedle a grilled cheese sandwich out of Ruby Bee, who was huffing and puffing, I slipped off the stool. "See y'all later. I need to unpack and run a few loads at the launderette."

"That doesn't mean you ought to go running off to Washington, D.C.," Ruby Bee began. "You don't know anything about this Jules fellow, except for what he told you. He didn't have any reluctance when it came to lying to me about how there was a government conspiracy to keep folks from finding out the truth about flying saucers." She was going to elaborate—at length, no doubt—when the door banged open and all three hundred pounds of Maggody's most recent bride, Dahlia (née O'Neill) Buchanon, thundered into the room. Her more typical bovine expression had been replaced with wide-eyed agitation, and her hands were flapping. Underneath her voluminous tent dress, every-thing quivered.

"You got to come see!" she shrieked.

"Now, Dahlia," Ruby Bee said soothingly, "you're in no condition to get all worked up like this. Why doncha sit down right here and have a nice glass of skim milk?"

Dahlia flapped harder, although her chances of be-coming airborne were poor. "It's the most unbeliev-able thing I've ever laid eyes on! Y'all come see for yourselves!"

A few dedicated beer drinkers stayed where they were, but everybody else followed her out to the parking lot. For the first time in ages, she was right. Driving up the road at a decorous rate were, in or-der: a gold Cadillac, a massive motorcycle driven by a figure clad in black leather, a recreational vehicle only slightly smaller than a tennis court, a white Mercedes, a bus with darkly tinted windows, and four trucks the size of moving vans. The bus, trucks, and RV were emblazoned with the logo HOPE IS HERE in swirly gold and silver letters.

"It's Malachi Hope," Estelle breathed over my shoulder. "Smackdab here in Maggody!"

"Who?" I asked as the last truck rolled by and the customers drifted back inside to discuss what they'd seen.

Dahlia's jaw dropped, squashing two or three of her chins. "You don't know? Malachi Hope is this really famous preacher who used to be on television on one of those cable stations. He had this show where he healed blind people and made cripples get right out of their wheelchairs and walk across the stage. Kevvie and I used to watch him every Sunday night, but then his show went off the air and we took to watching reruns of 'Gunsmoke.' Why do you think Marshal Dillon never married Miss Kitty, Arly?"

I ignored her question, which was distressingly earnest, and frowned at Ruby Bee and Estelle. "Do you know anything about this?"

Ruby Bee gave me an innocent smile. "I may have heard some rumors, but I didn't want to bother you when you have all this laundry to do. You might even feel obliged to go run a speed trap out by the remains of Purtle's Esso station so you can get your salary this month."

"Just tell me—okay?"

"I'll tell you, Arly," said Dahlia. "Malachi Hope's gonna have a revival out at the big pasture that belongs to Burdock Grapper. It starts on Sunday and will last for a whole week! He's gonna heal everybody and save all the sinners in Stump County. Then he's gonna build this humongous theme park and thousands of people will—"

"Theme park?" I said, addressing Ruby Bee and Estelle. "On Bur's property? What's she talking about?"

Ruby Bee wiggled her eyebrows at Estelle, who snagged Dahlia's arm and propelled her inside. She paused to collect her thoughts, then said, "What I heard is he aims to lease a thousand acres with an option to buy if he works out his financing."

I stared at her. "Does Bur have that much property?"

"No, but next to the Grapper place is a two-hundred-acre tract that Jim Bob bought from Bimbo Buchanon's widow when she had to go to the old folks' home. Beyond that is the land that belongs to Lottie Estes's second cousin Wharton. All together there'd be in the range of a thousand acres, give or take."

"What's he going to do with it?"

"Build something called 'The City of Hope.' It'll be this amusement park, with a church, rides, waterslides, restaurants, a campground, and I don't know what all. It's the most foolish thing I've heard since Perkin's eldest took that correspondence course in tap dancing and made everybody in town come to the recital, but Estelle keeps insisting this preacher's nigh unto a saint and we shouldn't be questioning his motives."

"Which are?" I said encouragingly.

"Did you ever see him on television?"

"I don't watch televangelists."

"Don't go thinking I do either, Miss Masterpiece Theater," she said, giving me an extensive view of her flared nostrils, "but a while back Estelle made me do it one night. This Malachi Hope was the smarmiest man I've ever seen, and I've seen a lot in my day. He was so oily I don't know why he didn't slip right off his stage and go flying into the laps of all those pitiful people in wheelchairs. After he got everybody all fired up, his wife floated down from the ceiling in a billow of smoke. She was dressed up like an angel and sang gospel songs. If she hasn't been to Memphis so many times she has a key to the city, then my name isn't Rubella Belinda Hanks!"

If you think I was getting all this, then you're sorely overestimating me. "This televangelist is going to build a thousand-acre religious amusement park in Maggody?"

"I said no such thing."

"Then what did you say?" I asked blankly.

"Burdock Grapper's property starts on the far side

of the low-water bridge, and Jim Bob's and Wharton's are beyond that. It's all within spittin' distance, but not inside the town limits. I heard over at the launderette that Mr. Malachi Hope's people made real sure about that."

I wrinkled my nose as the last exhaust fumes wafted over us. "Did he?" I murmured under my breath.

"You want something to eat?" asked Ruby Bee.

"No, but I'll see you long about suppertime. I think I'm going to look into this Malachi Hope business. It beats doing laundry."

"You never were much for doing laundry," she said as she went inside.

I seldom fool my mother.

Mrs. Jim Bob and Brother Verber stood in front of the Assembly Hall, watching the last Hope Is Here truck turn the corner and roll down County 102 toward the low-water bridge.

"I don't have a good feeling about this," she said as she brushed the dust off her navy blue skirt, then straightened up to give him a beady look. "What do you think?"

He thought she was as fetching as a little sparrow, with her yellow-flecked eyes and thin lips pursed into what sort of resembled a beak and her undeniably shapely calves and trim ankles. He didn't think that was what she wanted to hear, though. Sometimes— or even most of the time—it was hard to figure out what she *did* want to hear, but he always obliged her as best he could. "About this Malachi Hope fellow? Is that what you mean?"

"I wasn't asking if it was hot enough for you,

Brother Verber. Do you know anything about him and his plans?"

"Just what I heard at the potluck," he admitted as he pulled out a handkerchief to mop his forehead. "He's looking into buying land out past the bridge so he can build some ridiculous park. I saw a flyer over at the barbershop about a tent revival next week. Do you reckon I should call off the Sunday evening service and the Wednesday evening prayer meeting so folks can go?"

"You are not thinking this through," Mrs. Jim Bob said, her impatience increasingly hard to miss. "Cancelling a couple of services for the revival is one thing, but consider what'll happen if Malachi Hope goes through with this project. Where do you imagine most everybody in town will go on Sundays—to the Assembly Hall to hear Lottie Estes fumble through hymns on a piano, or to a big glitzy church where they can wander around afterwards, riding the Ferris wheel and eating cotton candy?"

Brother Verber sank down on the steps of the porch, his fat face all puckered up as he mulled over what she'd said. Lottie Estes got most of the notes right, but she was liable to lose her place in the refrain and they'd have to start all over. The Assembly Hall was hot in the summer, drafty in the fall, and colder than a witch's tit 'long about January. In the spring, most folks brought umbrellas. He himself always looked forward to the potluck suppers after the Sunday evening services, but the same green-bean casseroles and gelatin salads showed up just about every week, and he'd heard some tart remarks lately. There wasn't near enough in the coffers for a cotton candy machine, much less carnival rides.

Sighing, he looked up at Mrs. Jim Bob. "I reckon

it's gonna be the end of the Voice of the Almighty Lord Assembly Hall, Sister Barbara. There ain't no way to compete."

"Once he gets it built, you'll be lucky to fill the front pew," she said without sympathy, "but this Hope fellow doesn't own so much as a square inch of land—yet. I don't know about Bur Grapper and Wharton Estes, but Jim Bob got a long letter a while back. Jim Bob happened to be off in Hot Springs at one of those municipal league meetings, so I took it upon myself to open the letter just in case it was important and I needed to call him."

"You are so saintly," Brother Verber said, shaking his head in admiration. "I would never have thought of that."

"Well, I did. The letter was from a man named Thomas Fratelleon, who claimed to be Malachi Hope's business manager. It was all a lot of complicated jargon about the southeast quarter of the northwest quarter, but as far as I could make out, he was asking if Jim Bob would sell that parcel for a hundred dollars an acre."

"Generous offer, I suppose. It's nothing but scrub and rock out that way, and the only thing it's good for is chickweed. After ol' Mrs. Wockermann ran off to Mexico with Merle Hardcock, her nephew sold that pasture beside her house for more like fifty an acre."

Sometimes Mrs. Jim Bob wondered if he was exactly the right person to be the spiritual leader of the congregation. However, it was a thought unworthy of a pious Christian, and everybody knew she was the most pious Christian in town and maybe the entire county.

Brother Verber shivered like a wet dog. "Like I

said," he continued in the sonorous voice he used for funerals and the till-death-us-do-part moment in wedding vows, "there's no way to compete with a cotton candy machine. If I lose my congregation, I won't be able to take a modest percent of the offering to support myself. I might ought to write the seminary out in Las Vegas and see if they know of a vacant pulpit someplace else. It breaks my heart to think about having to leave my cozy little rectory over there under the sycamore trees." He was so choked up he had to clear his throat like a bullfrog. "And you, Sister Barbara. You are such an inspiration to us all, what with your soul as pure as the Lord's rain and—"

"Malachi Hope can be stopped," she interrupted, since he wasn't saying anything she didn't already know. "If you'd been paying attention, you'd have realized the significance of what I just said. He doesn't own any of the parcels as of now, and even if Bur and Wharton agree to sell theirs, Jim Bob's two hundred acres are in the middle of them."

"Jim Bob wouldn't turn down a hundred dollars an acre, would he? That'd add up to . . ." He tried to do the computation in his head, then finally gave up and said, "A right tidy sum of money."

"Twenty thousand dollars."

Brother Verber whistled through his teeth. "Nothing to turn up your nose at."

"It is if what's at stake is the salvation of the community. Jim Bob is the mayor of Maggody, and his first concern should be the spiritual well-being of his constituents. I watched some of Malachi Hope's television shows. He preached about how Jesus wants everybody to have themselves a good time in the here and now. From the way he carried on, you'd

think Jesus was a camp counselor. I don't recollect
him saying one word about eternal damnation. He
had celebrities on his 'Hour of Hope' who talked
about how they used to be miserable sinners, but as
soon as they dedicated their lives to the Lord, they
got rich and famous. He even had Matt Montana on
his show one time. He sang 'You're a Detour on the
Highway to Heaven,' and half the folks in the audience were bawling by the time it was over."

"I'll bet they emptied their pockets when the
plates were passed," Brother Verber said, getting
misty as he imagined the scene. "I wonder if I could
get—"

"Jim Bob has a duty to this community, and he is
not going to stand aside and allow this charlatan and
his hussy to lure everybody away from the Missionary Society after all I did to win a third term as president. I'll have a word with him this evening. If I
can't persuade him, you may have to throw in some
words about Satan and the root of all evil."

"You think it'll work?"

Her expression was so fierce he cringed. "It will
work, Brother Verber."

Burdock Grapper watched the trucks and buses
rolling up the dirt road next to his house, then took
a beer out of the refrigerator and sat back down on
the recliner. He was sixty-three, which made him
nearly twenty years older than his wife, Norma Kay.
He was also two inches shorter than she was. His
narrow nose was more crooked than his teeth, which
had been aching so much he was thinking about having 'em yanked. He had a full head of brown hair
tinged with gray; he dropped by the barbershop every six weeks or so for a trim, but mostly to hear the

latest gossip. Not that he'd hear what gnawed at him night and day—the identity of the sumbitch Norma Kay was having an affair with. If and when he found out, the sumbitch and Norma Kay would both be real sorry.

"You're late," he said as she came into the living room. "It's almost suppertime. Where were you?"

"At school. Where else would I be—over at Raz Buchanon's house gossiping with his hog?" Norma Kay went into the kitchen and took a pound of hamburger meat from the freezer. "I asked you this morning to defrost this, Bur. Is it too much trouble to get off your butt for one minute and help out? All you've done since the day you retired is watch those stupid soap operas and drink beer. One of these days you're going have a heart attack and die, and I won't even notice until you start to stink worse than you do already."

"Watch your mouth," he said, finishing the beer. He crumpled the can and tossed it on the floor with the others. "Why were you at school so late?"

"The schedule's a real mess. We were supposed to play Hasty the week after Thanksgiving, but the coach canceled because her best players have to go to a choir competition down in Clarksville. She knows we'll whip their asses if they don't have that six-foot-tall center." She stuck the meat in the refrigerator and pulled out the remains of the previous evening's casserole. She did so with a smug smile, since Bur hated leftovers more than he did soap and water. "I was on the phone all day trying to line up another team. We might be able to play Emmet, but then I have to figure out how to get us there since the boys are still playing Hasty. Cory's not about to let us take the bus."

"Talking to Cory, huh?"

She came to the doorway and glared at him. "Cory and I have to talk to each other because we have to transport both of our teams to the out-of-town games and we only have the one bus. For pity's sake, Bur, you were the basketball coach for thirty-three years. Did you ever tell your players to take a cab?"

Bur shrugged. "So you needed to talk about the bus. How's he doing as head coach while Amos is laid up over at the nursing home in Farberville?"

"I don't know. He just today started off-season training. Some of the first string are on vacation, but there's a new junior with promise, and the Mac-Namara boy must have grown two inches over the summer. He's going make a good point guard."

Bur aimed the clicker at the television set, having lost interest in basketball right after the buzzer went off to end the final game of his career. He'd never liked his players; the only pleasure he'd derived from coaching was being able to make their lives hell during practices and games.

Norma Kay returned to the kitchen to stick the casserole in the oven and fix herself a glass of iced tea. She never touched beer on account of her figure, which was holding up pretty good except for a broadening of her rump. She used a variety of expensive creams on her face, and took pains to color her hair at the first sign of a dark root. Estelle Oppers was always giving her snooty looks, but Norma Kay was proud of its bright yellow color and the perky little flip like she wore when she was a starter on the Coffeyville varsity team twenty-five years ago. Nobody except parents had ever come to the games, girls' athletics being a joke back then, but the team always played as if the bleachers were packed and a championship was at stake.

Thinking about that was enough to keep her entertained as she sat down at the kitchen table and waited for the casserole to burn.